Praise for *The One*:

'A life-affirming love story full of hope and heart'
Katie Marsh, author of *Unbreak Your Heart*

'Heartbreaking, heartwarming, uplifting – I loved
it' **Holly Miller, bestselling author of**
The Sight Of You

'A beautiful, poignant tale of family, friendship,
loss and love' **Milly Johnson,** *Sunday Times*
bestselling author

'A tender story of love, loss, healing and hope'
Laura Kemp, author of *Under a Starry Sky*

'Alternately heartbreaking and heartwarming. I
loved it' **Nicola Gill, author of *We Are Family***

More Praise for Claire Frost:

'A wonderful read!' **Sophie Cousens, author of**
Just Haven't Met You Yet

'Refreshing, brilliantly – written and highly
addictive!' **Helly Acton, author of *The Couple***

'If you're looking for a story to make you shed
a few tears and cheer, this is the one!' **Miranda
Dickinson,** *Sunday Times* **bestselling author**

Claire Frost grew up in Manchester, the middle of three sisters. She always wanted to do a job that involved writing, so after studying Classics at Bristol University she started working in magazines. For the last twelve years she's been at the *Sun on Sunday*'s *Fabulous* magazine, where she is Assistant Editor and also responsible for the title's book reviews. She can mostly be found at her desk buried under a teetering TBR pile. You can follow her on Twitter: @FabFrosty, and Instagram: @therealfabfrosty.

Also by Claire Frost:

Living My Best Life
Married at First Swipe

First published in Great Britain by Simon & Schuster UK Ltd, 2022

1 3 5 7 9 10 8 6 4 2

Simon & Schuster UK Ltd
1st Floor
222 Gray's Inn Road
London WC1X 8HB

Simon & Schuster Australia, Sydney
Simon & Schuster India, New Delhi

www.simonandschuster.co.uk
www.simonandschuster.com.au
www.simonandschuster.co.in

A CIP catalogue record for this book
is available from the British Library

Paperback ISBN: 978-1-4711-9387-3
eBook ISBN: 978-1-4711-9388-0

Typeset in the UK by M Rules
Printed and bound in Great Britain by
CPI Group (UK) Ltd, Croydon, CR0 4YY

claire frost

the
one

**SIMON &
SCHUSTER**

London · New York · Sydney · Toronto · New Delhi

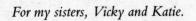

For my sisters, Vicky and Katie.

Chapter One

'And then I told him that I loved him. We both sat there grinning at each other and it was just one of those moments where you feel drunk even when you're not, you know? It was like we were the only people left in the world.'

'I can't believe you've used the "L" word already!' Em cried, the corners of her eyes crinkling in delight. 'You've only known each other a few weeks!'

'Well, he said it first,' Lottie replied, taking a large gulp of red wine from her glass and letting its fruity tartness roll round her mouth. 'And we've known each other almost three months, actually!'

'And when you know, you know,' Em said dreamily. 'And Annie and I did say he was a keeper after your first date, didn't we? Oh, Lots, I'm so happy for you.'

'But we haven't met him yet,' Annie said with a frown. 'I may have agreed he *sounded* like the real deal after you gushed about him, but, Lottie, you can't go around telling random men you love them when you haven't even introduced them

1

to your sisters. It's not on, and I'm putting my foot down. You either invite Leo to pub club next week or I'll camp outside your place and ambush him on the doorstep.'

Lottie rolled her eyes and reached for the comfort blanket of her wine glass again. Her older sister always thought she knew best.

'You really do need to be careful, though, Lottie,' Annie continued. 'I mean it. We all remember what happened with holier-than-thou Elliot—'

'I think what Annie's saying is we both care about you and don't want to see you get hurt, that's all,' Em broke in, reaching across the table to give the top of Lottie's arm a squeeze. 'But we're only human – of course we want to meet this amazing man we've heard so much about! *Please* say you'll bring him to pub club next Wednesday,' she implored, clapping her hands in excitement.

The three sisters had been meeting in the Rope and Anchor in the centre of Oxford every Wednesday night for years. They'd picked that particular pub because it was round the corner from Annie's work at a scientific institute, as well as an easy cycle from both Lottie's job and her flat on the not-quite-as-nice side of town. It was still a forty-minute drive from Em's fresh-out-of-an-interiors-mag home in the Cotswolds, but she had always insisted she didn't mind at all.

Now, Annie visibly made an effort to soften the worry lines etched across her forehead and smiled at her sisters. She stroked her sensible brown bob, a hairstyle she had sported for the last twenty years. 'I'll even try to be on time for once,' she said, breaking into a laugh so genuine Lottie instantly forgave her sister her bossiness. She knew Annie had been under a lot of pressure recently, both at work and at home, so it swelled Lottie's heart to see her laughing.

'OK, OK, I'll ask him! If I'd known that all it takes is the promise of meeting my new man to get you to arrive somewhere on time, I'd have introduced you to every guy who'd so much as DMed me in the last five years,' Lottie said. 'Although, to be fair, I'm not sure any of us need to meet the men I've had pictures from on Instagram.'

'On that rather sordid note,' Annie said, wrinkling her noise and joining up her freckles, 'I'll get us some more drinks. The usual?'

'Of course!' Lottie said, as Em replied, 'Yes, please.'

'Annie means well, you know,' Em said as they watched their sister head towards the bar. 'I think she's just desperate to get to know this person who's obviously had such an effect on you. We all met Charlie within weeks of their first date, didn't we?'

'I know,' Lottie said with a sigh, and then added naughtily, 'How much do you bet Annie set up a spreadsheet and plotted the exact dates when she thought she and Charlie ought to be reaching certain relationship stages, like meeting the sisters?'

'Lottie!' Em chided, but couldn't help giggling.

Lottie laughed. 'Sorry, I shouldn't take the mick. Also, in my defence, Leo was supposed to come to that Sunday lunch round yours a few weeks ago, but that migraine really floored him.'

'I know, bless him. My two are exhausting enough when you're rattling with vitamins, but if you're feeling under the weather then they can be way too much.'

'How are my gorgeous nephews?' Lottie asked, more than happy to move the conversation on. But she didn't get to hear an answer before their older sister appeared back at the table with drinks and snacks – and opinions.

'When will you hear whether you got Alex into St Swithin's?' Annie asked. Lottie grabbed greedily at the packets of crisps under her arm, tearing one open as her sister leaned over the table to deposit their drinks.

'Not for another few weeks. But if there isn't space there, the village primary is really sweet, so it's not a problem,' Em said serenely, pushing her long, blonde hair back off her face.

'But it's nowhere near as prestigious as St Swithin's. Plus, once Alex is in there, Dante will be a dead cert, and it will make such a difference when it comes to secondary school and university,' Annie said forcefully.

Lottie blinked a few times and laughed through a mouthful of cheese and onion crumbs. 'You do know Dante is only two, don't you, Annie?'

Em smiled easily but Annie remained adamant. 'It's never too early to get them on the right path. Why wouldn't you and Luca want to give them every opportunity you can? They're smart boys, and the right school will only make them smarter.'

4

Lottie could see that her older sister was about to launch into another of her diatribes, and so she forced herself not to reach for another handful of crisps and instead replied, 'You're probably right, Annie. Anyway, did you manage to move things around so you can go to that wedding in the Dordogne?'

Em shot Lottie a small smile of thanks and turned to Annie. 'Oh, it's such a lovely part of the world down there, what a beautiful place to have a wedding.'

'Yes, I booked our flights at the weekend.' She sighed. 'Though I still can't believe Alistair and Janey have given everyone such little notice about the wedding. We were going to start our final cycle of IVF at the beginning of July, but I think we'll put it back to September now we're going to France. Charlie can't understand why we don't just get on with it now, but I want to make sure we're following the rules to the letter and giving ourselves every chance of making it work.'

'Oh, Annie, sweetheart, that's hard, but it does sound like the best idea,' Em said immediately. 'And I'm sure Charlie does understand – he's just disappointed, as are you. But you know we'll all be here for you every step of the way.'

'Of course we will,' Lottie agreed, impotently wishing she had her little sister's knack of knowing exactly what to say and when to say it.

'I know,' Annie replied, taking a shaky sip of her drink then giving them a small smile. 'Thank you.'

There was a beat of silence while they all inwardly

acknowledged that this IVF attempt was probably Annie's last chance to carry a baby herself, and that it was just as likely to fail as the previous four cycles. But Em broke the suddenly sombre mood by smiling at Lottie and saying, 'So, Lots, now we know we're going to meet him soon, what else do we need to know about Leo? Ooh, Lots and Leo has definitely got a ring to it – how have I never noticed that before?'

Lottie giggled. 'We sound like a posh clothing brand, don't we?' She glanced up at Annie who managed a smile. 'I really hope you both like him. He's so make-your-heart-beat-faster gorgeous, and he has this ability to make you feel like you're the only person he wants to talk to.'

'You sound so smitten!' Annie laughed.

'I'm not sure I've ever heard anyone actually use the word "smitten" before,' Lottie said with a laugh, then straightened her shoulders a little. 'But yes, I really am. I think I've properly fallen for him.' She paused before adding, 'I even told him about Elliot.'

Both of her sisters turned their bodies fully towards her, their eyes wide.

'What did he say?' Em asked, a little cautiously.

'He was just kind and thoughtful. He said it wasn't a reflection on me – it was all on Elliot. And he promised *he* would never do that to me.'

'Well, you would be pretty unlucky for that to happen twice. Anyway, when we meet him next week, I'll make sure I grill him on his philosophical beliefs.'

'Annie! Swear to me right here and now you won't do

that!' Lottie cried. Her voice was laced with laughter, but she couldn't help feeling a little anxious. Over the years, she had taught herself to laugh along with Annie and the rest of the family about the Elliot affair to some extent, and part of her knew her sister was only teasing, but the other part knew that Elliot had left scars etched into her heart that could never be removed. Leo was the first man she'd ever told why her one long-term, maybe-this-is-for-keeps relationship had ended, and although his reaction had been everything she could have ever wished from him, that didn't mean she wanted her sisters bringing it up the first time they met him.

'She's only joking, aren't you, Annie?' Em stepped in quickly. 'Anyway, I want to see more pictures. It's rude to keep his "make-your-heart-beat-faster" face from us!'

'Seeing as you asked so nicely.' Lottie smiled, picking up her phone from the table where it had been lying face down on a beer mat. She frowned when she saw she had three missed calls from an unknown number, and just as she opened her photo app, her phone began to vibrate in her hand.

'Let me just see who this is,' she said, waving her mobile at her sisters and pushing her chair back. 'It's probably someone trying to sell me something. Give me a sec.'

Annie and Em nodded and shooed her away to take the call, and as she swiped her finger across the screen and raised the phone to her ear, she saw Em turn back to their older sister, rub her arm and quietly say something to her.

Five minutes later, even though the person on the other

end of the phone had long since hung up, Lottie was still standing in exactly the same spot near the door, her mobile clutched in her hand.

'Lots? Are you OK? We thought we'd make a move,' Em said as she and Annie appeared with quizzical looks and arms laden with coats and bags. 'Lottie?'

'He's gone,' were the only words Lottie could form.

Annie frowned. 'Who's gone? Gone where?'

'He's gone.'

'Lottie, sweetheart, what's happened?' Em asked, gently pushing her sister's arms into her jacket and leading her outside.

As a blast of cold evening air hit them, Lottie stared at her sisters. 'Leo. He's dead. He's gone.'

Chapter Two

Before

Every year Lottie dreaded the task of choosing a present for Annie's birthday. Em, of course, had the knack of finding something personal and heartfelt that only served to highlight Lottie's own shortcomings in the gift department. And while it was never Em's intention to show her up, it always made Lottie feel weirdly cross with her. Which then made her feel like both the worst younger sister in the world for being so terrible at buying presents, and the worst older sister in the world for feeling annoyed that Em was so much better at it than her. Just another curse of being the middle sister, Lottie mused three days before Annie's birthday, as she trudged through the slushy remnants of the previous day's snowstorm into the centre of Oxford, her shoulders up close to her ears.

She still had absolutely no idea what to buy her sister – and she had precisely forty-five minutes left of her lunch break to find something. It had only been three weeks since Christmas, and while Annie had emailed her exactly what festive gifts both she and Charlie wanted at the start of November (complete with shop-to-buy links), the sisters had an unwritten rule that birthdays were the occasions that *really* mattered and that presents should always be a surprise. They were expected to be thoughtful and inventive – and as a biting wind whipped around her body, almost knocking her over, Lottie couldn't think of a single idea that would be classed as either.

She let out a sigh of relief as she reached the warmth of the covered shopping centre, massaging feeling back into her frozen fingers. Of course, she'd managed to lose one of the misshapen mittens she'd spent much of December knitting. The idea had been to save time and money by knitting presents for her family instead of buying them. But it had taken her so long to finish the first attempt – a pair of bright pink woollen monstrosities – that she'd run out of time and had been forced to panic-buy gifts for everyone, except Annie and Charlie, of course, who she'd already sorted; she'd never been more thankful to her sister for her 'What To Buy Us For Christmas' email.

Lottie wandered into shops aimlessly, desperately hoping to set eyes on the perfect present for her sister. Her fingers were at least starting to look less blue and she was now able to feel the tips of them, so, standing in the thoroughfare of the shopping centre, she fished her phone out of her pocket and quickly typed out a *PLEASE HELP!* message to Em.

She stared at the screen for a few seconds, but she could see her sister hadn't read her message – unsurprising when she was probably trying to marshal Dante and Alex while they scampered around in their wellies attempting to build a snowman out of slush. Looking around in the hope a new shop called Perfect Presents for Annie might have sprung up in front of her, Lottie's eye was snagged by two men walking towards her deep in conversation. Or rather her eye was caught by one of the two men in particular – the one who was tall but not too tall and had light brown mussed-up but not too mussed-up hair and just a hint of a beard, and eyes that looked startlingly blue even from several metres away, as if he must be wearing coloured contact lenses like actors did in movies. As they strode past her, Lottie couldn't help staring. In fact, she was still staring at their backs several seconds later when she was brought back to her senses by the tutting and sighing of a woman trying to manoeuvre a double pram around her but refusing to actually say 'excuse me'. Lottie gave the woman a smile she didn't deserve, and continued her search for the seemingly non-existent perfect gift.

As she stood in John Lewis wondering how anyone could countenance spending fifty pounds – fifty pounds! – on a scented candle, her phone buzzed in her pocket and she forlornly pulled it out to find that Em had replied.

Hey, Lots, I'm sure Annie will adore whatever you buy her! But I know she was saying the other day she's been reading the Wallander series of books, so you could get her one of those – maybe one of the later ones so she definitely won't have read it yet? Or M&S has some gorgeous cashmere-mix jumpers at the moment – there's a deep red one that would really suit her. Does that help? If not, let me know and I'll see what else I can think of. E x

Lottie thanked God profusely for bestowing her little sister upon her, then sent Em a message thanking her even more profusely, before glancing at the time on her phone screen and calculating that, even if she legged it to M&S's womens-wear department, paid in double-quick time and jogged to the office, she would still be late back from her lunch break. So, she thumbed out a quick plea to her friend Rachel to make up some excuse if Reg, their eagle-eyed boss, spotted she was away from her desk for longer than an hour, and then made her way to the store, breathlessly walking past the Colin the Caterpillar cakes that, try as she might, she couldn't stop herself from gazing longingly at.

Her stomach rumbled and, realising that she could kill two birds with one stone, she paused to grab a posh ready meal and a chocolate mousse from the chiller cabinets, then turned towards the escalator in search of deep-red-coloured cashmere-mix jumpers in Annie's size.

Before she'd taken two steps, the side of her handbag snagged on the edge of the cabinet. Lottie wobbled, righted herself, and then dropped her chocolate mousse. Thankful it hadn't spattered the floor of the supermarket with unappe-tising brown sludge, she quickly reached down to retrieve it, only to feel her head come into contact with a hard object as she stood upright again.

The hard object turned out to be a man's chin. And the chin turned out to belong to the blue-eyed man with the perfectly mussed-up hair who she'd spotted across the shopping centre a few minutes before. Her hand rushed to her head.

'Oh gosh, I'm so sorry!' The sound that came out of his mouth was posher than Lottie had expected, as if he was trying someone else's voice on for size, and she continued to rub her head and gawp unattractively.

'Is your head OK, are you hurt? I'm so sorry, I was just trying to help you pick up your shopping. I didn't mean to ...' The man ran his hand through his hair in agitation, immediately ruining his carefully created style. But, some-how, it suited him better, Lottie thought – it made him look dishevelled and sexy.

An involuntary shiver ran through her and, realising her mouth was still hanging open in the manner of a panting dog, she quickly shut it, though she continued to rub her head in a dazed fashion. It had been a long time since her stomach had flipped like this in response to a member of the opposite sex and she hoped she wasn't drooling.

'I'm fine, I'm fine, don't worry!' she blurted into the silence. 'I'm such an idiot, not looking where I'm going!'

'Are you sure? Your head looks a bit red where it hit my chin.'

She immediately stopped clawing at her forehead,

smoothed down her mousey hair and pushed her hands into the pockets of her coat.

'No, really, I'm fine! Thanks, though. I was just on my way to the clothes section to buy a cashmere jumper. Well, cashmere mix – we're in M&S not Selfridges, after all. My little sister said to get the deep-red shade because it will suit our older sister's colouring – I'm not the best at presents. Anyway, sorry,' she stammered, inwardly pleading with herself to stop talking. 'You're going to think I've got concussion or something, and I only banged my head a bit so I definitely haven't, and I'm not sure you can get concussion from hitting your head on someone's chin, can you?'

Ten seconds too late, she came to an abrupt stop, her cheeks pinking up to match the red mark she'd created on her head. The man's eyes crinkled, and he grinned at her.

'I've never heard of anyone getting concussion from another person's chin, that is true.' He laughed. 'But then I've never heard of a pretty woman running into a man's Desperate Dan chin in the middle of M&S before, so who knows?'

She grinned back at him, thinking, *He called me pretty!*

'But in all seriousness, I hope your head is OK,' he said. 'Have you got someone at home who can check on you later – isn't that what you're supposed to do with head injuries?'

'No, there's no one at home to check on me,' she said, with what she hoped was a coy smile. 'Well, other than Ginger.'

An expression that could have been disappointment – or maybe she just hoped it was – swept over his face. 'Ginger?'

She grinned. 'Yep. He's a right peeping tom, always sidling his way into my flat when he thinks I'm not looking. Though I'm not sure a skinny, flea-bitten cat that isn't actually my cat is going to be much use if I'm struck down with concussion.'

His face lit up. 'In that case I'd better take your number so I can check up on you – you can't be too careful with head injuries, you know!'

'Are you a doctor?' She smirked, took his phone from his outstretched hand and keyed in her number, adding the word 'Headcase' in the 'contact name' field.

'No, I'm—'

'Mate, there you are. Are you coming?' A taller, darker man came up behind him, his face clouded, lines etched into his features.

'I'm coming, Ross, don't worry,' the man replied easily, grinning at Lottie as he read what she'd written in his phone. 'Hope your sister likes her deep-red cashmere-mix jumper.' He winked and followed his friend, before glancing back to her. 'I'm Leo, by the way. Text you later, Headcase.'

Chapter Three

Lottie was barely aware of being bundled into Em's car, and Annie going to find her bike, and it wasn't until she was clutching a cup of strong tea on Annie's sofa, with her sisters bookending her for support, that her brain finally began to acknowledge what was going on.

'How can he be gone?' she asked disbelievingly. 'I only saw him on Sunday. And I spoke to him on FaceTime last night. He was fine. I don't understand.'

Em rubbed her back. 'I know, Lots, it's crazy, completely crazy.'

'He was only thirty-four,' Lottie said.

'That's no age at all. Poor Leo.'

'He was the same age as me,' Annie said quietly. 'I just can't imagine ...' There was silence for a moment. 'What did his cousin say, Lottie?'

'He said it was something to do with his heart, but they don't know any details as yet,' Lottie answered robotically. Since Ross's phone call an hour ago, she'd felt like she was observing everything from several metres away. But seeing tears prick her sister's eyes triggered a stab of emotion in her own stomach, and suddenly her throat tightened and huge, uncontrollable sobs began to pour out of her mouth. She felt her mug being gently prised out of her grip and then she was cocooned in her sisters' arms, while they stroked her hair and held her tight, the three of them rocking softly as one.

She had no idea how long they stayed like that. But eventually when her throat was raw and there were no more tears to fall, a great weariness stole across her, punctuated only by her body's involuntary shudders as the rip tide within her started to ebb. 'I'd better go home – and you'd better get back to the boys, Em,' she snuffled.

'You're staying here tonight,' Annie said gruffly, grabbing them all tissues from the box on the coffee table. 'Charlie's making up the spare bed now.'

Lottie hadn't even noticed Charlie was there. She nodded, too exhausted to argue, and the lure of sleep too great.

'And I'll call in sick for you tomorrow, drop the boys at nursery and come here to collect you. You can then stay with us for a few days,' Em said.

'But—'

'No buts, Lottie,' Annie said firmly. She glanced up as Charlie appeared in the doorway.

'The bed is made and I've put a hot-water bottle in there and left you a pair of Annie's pyjamas,' he said quietly. 'I'm so sorry about Leo, Lottie.'

'Th-thanks, Charlie.' Lottie's eyes stung, and she allowed

herself to be led upstairs by her sisters, who made sure she was tucked up with the hot-water bottle. They each gave her one last kiss before closing the door softly behind them. Lottie felt the room swim and the world seemed to blur around the edges until, seconds later, her mind and body completely exhausted, she welcomed the oblivion-grey blanket of sleep.

The sun poked through the middle of the curtains and shone into Lottie's eyes. She squinted and pulled the duvet over her head, which immediately began to bang with the kind of headache she already knew would linger all day. And then she remembered. Leo was dead. It didn't matter if her headache turned into the migraine from hell and she lay hidden under the covers for twenty-four hours – nothing would change what Ross had told her the previous night. She pushed away the duvet and stared up at the blank, white ceiling above her, her brain replaying what he'd said on a loop. But no matter how many times she heard the words, it still didn't feel real. She closed her eyes to try to shut it all out, but Ross's soft Scottish tones still wormed their way in.

I'm so sorry, Lottie, Leo didn't make it. He died.

Feeling nausea rise into her throat, Lottie heaved herself out of bed and into the bathroom, where she promptly threw up. For a few seconds, she felt that whole-body relief that follows expelling everything from your stomach. But that relief was quickly chased away by a shaking in her hands and legs that forced her to curl into a foetal ball as she rested her cheek on the cold, tiled floor. The house was filled with a stony silence that meant Annie and Charlie had already left for work, and Lottie didn't know how long she lay in the freezing air of the bathroom before she managed to summon the strength to get up again.

She shuffled back into Annie's spare room, pulled her jumper from last night over her head and collapsed back under the duvet. She noticed a mug of tea on her bedside table, which her sister must have left her earlier, and she cupped the barely warm mug in her hands and held it against her chest. She tried to clear her mind and think of nothing at all, but the more she attempted to fall into the black hole in her brain, the more she felt herself spiral into fear and nausea. What had Leo felt at the end? Who had been with him? Had he asked for her? Or his mum? Had he known he was dying?

There was a tap on the bedroom door. 'Lottie?'

She made an indistinct sound and within a couple of seconds, she felt Em's arm across her shoulders, steadying her rocking body.

'Hey, Lots, I came over as quickly as I could after dropping the kids off. And I've spoken to Reg and told him you're not well and will likely be off work all week. He says to take whatever time you need and get better soon.'

Even in her fuggy state, Lottie was surprised at Reg's empathy. Normally her boss didn't have time for any illness other than his own. 'Did you tell him about Leo d— about Leo?' she stumbled.

'No, sweetheart. I thought you could decide a bit further down the line what you wanted to tell him. I just said that you were really unwell and I'm looking after you. And, yes, I may have put on a bit of a girly, flirty voice, but it seemed to do the trick, and if you don't tell Annie, I definitely won't!'

Lottie managed to raise a half-smile and clutched her sister's hand. 'Thanks, Em. I definitely owe you one.'

'Don't be silly, Lots, and I meant what I told Reg – I'm going to look after you for the next few days. So if you go and have a shower, I'll make you a piece of toast and then we can get a few bits from your house before I drive you over to mine. If you're feeling up to it, you can come with me to pick the boys up at lunchtime, and I thought we could go to the park and let them run off some energy.'

Lottie blinked heavily a few times, but took the towel her sister held out to her and allowed herself to be gently pushed towards the bathroom again. While she stood under the torrent of water and then wearily stepped into her clothes, she thought about how authoritative both of her sisters were in their different ways. Annie tended to boss people into submission, while Em's calm and reassuring manner meant people generally did what she asked without argument. It was a pity Lottie herself didn't have such authority. She often felt like her sisters listened but didn't actually *hear* her, while Reg at work seemed to purposely speak over her whenever she suggested ways to modernize the definitions in their online dictionary. Her best friend in the office, Rachel, did listen to her, but mainly when it came to Lottie's dating stories, and, more recently, stories about her perfect weekends with Leo. But there wouldn't be any more of those stories now. Her shoulders slumped and she sat down heavily on the bed.

Lottie saw that Rachel had WhatsApped to ask if she was okay – apparently Reg had somehow taken Em's phone call and run with it all the way to Lottie being on death's door with 'women's problems'. She knew she should reply, but it had taken all her strength just to dry herself after her shower and to pull on the clothes she'd worn to the pub the previous evening. She could hardly believe that it had only been a few hours since she'd been sitting there drinking a glass of wine, boasting about how handsome and funny her boyfriend was and how much her sisters were going to love him. She felt like she'd aged ten years. Despite hours of sleep, she was exhausted. She could barely lift her arms to put on her jumper and couldn't even contemplate her thumbs working enough to type out a message to Rachel.

Em appeared in the bedroom again and led her downstairs, all the time telling her, in a soft, reassuring voice, that she was going to look after her. She presented Lottie with a hot cup of tea and a piece of toast and jam. Lottie felt her throat close up, but realising that Em was going to stand firm until she ate something, she choked down a couple of mouthfuls.

The day passed in a blur and although Lottie was there physically, she was happy to let Em's and the boys' conversations wash over her. Usually, there was nothing she loved more than an afternoon in the spring sunshine surrounded by her adorable four-year-old and two-year-old nephews, who wanted Auntie Lottie to play rockets, be a human climbing frame or read the same book about superhero potatoes to them over and over again. But today, although the boys' laughter flowed and their boundless energy was no less boundless, Lottie felt like she was sleepwalking, as though only half of her was in the garden with them. For the first time ever, Alex and Dante grew bored of her reading about evil vegetables before she did, the familiar feel of the words bringing her comfort, even if they made little sense. When the boys climbed out of her lap and ran off to amuse themselves, daring each other to jump off the low brick wall at one end of the huge lawn, she continued to sit on the grass and stare at the book in front of her, her brain continuing to replay her phone call with Ross on an endless loop.

'Auntie Lottie, why do you look sad?' a little voice asked curiously. Alex had come up behind her and put his small hand on her shoulder. 'Are you worried about Supertato? Because he catches the pea in a jelly and everyone cheers,' he added earnestly. 'And then in a different one, all the superveggies help him and they get all the peas back in the freezer. So you don't need to be sad. But Mummy says you are allowed to be sad sometimes when something bad happens. Has something bad happened?'

His face creased with worry, and Lottie quickly plastered on a smile and ruffled his hair. 'You're right, Alex, I shouldn't worry about Supertato. He's well able to look after himself. But thank you for coming to check on me. You're a very kind little boy. Look there's Mummy – I'm thinking she might have a snack for you if you ask her nicely.'

'Wooooo!' he yelled and ran towards his mother.

'Lots, it's Ross on the phone for you,' Em called gently as she scooped up her son. 'I heard your phone ringing so I answered it for you.' Lottie pulled herself up, her heart thumping. Her sister walked towards her and handed her the phone, squeezing her shoulder before calling, 'Who wants to help me choose what we have for tea?' and ushering both boys into the house.

'H-hello?' Lottie said into the phone. Her voice sounded gravelly, and as if it belonged to someone else.

'Lottie? It's Ross. How are you doing?'

'I'm OK, thanks. How are you?' she replied like an automaton. She knew she should try to inject at least some warmth into her tone, but even the effort of stringing words into a sentence felt too much.

'We're ... well, you know,' Ross said quietly. 'Mum and I have come down to Oxfordshire and we're helping Leo's parents with the practical stuff as much as we can. It's good to feel like I'm being useful, I guess. Your sister said she's looking after you?'

'Yes. My sisters are both being brilliant.'

'Good, that's so great to hear. I'd hate to think of you on your own.' He cleared his throat and paused, and whereas normally Lottie would rush to fill the silence, she found she had absolutely no idea what to say and no strength to search her brain for an appropriate reply. After a couple of seconds he carried on. 'I was just calling to say that we're organising the funeral, but it will be a good few days until we have a proper date because the coroner has ordered a post-mortem.'

Ross's voice shook, and Lottie felt her mouth go dry. Thankfully, he rushed on and she didn't have to reply. 'And that probably won't happen until early next week now and then we have to wait for the results, and it's only after we've got those that we can properly set a date for the service. But I'll try to give you a call before then and I can make sure I text you all the details when it's sorted.'

'Oh, right, OK,' Lottie said. She stretched her shaking hand out to grip on to the climbing frame behind her. The word 'post-mortem' echoed through her head and her brain was filled with images of all the gory patholo-gist dramas she'd binge-watched on Netflix. The thought had never entered her head before that an autopsy could actually happen to someone she knew, someone she cared about. The glass of orange squash she'd chugged down a few minutes before swirled dangerously in her stomach as she tried to push away the mental pictures. She opened her mouth, then slammed it shut again as her throat filled with acid.

She was about to try again when Ross started speaking, this time more quickly than before. 'Lottie, I know you and Leo hadn't been together long, but it was clear how strongly he felt about you, and if you're ever not doing okay or you just want to talk about things – or about Leo – then give me a call, day or night, and I'll be here.'

'Thanks, I will,' she said, immediately knowing she defi-nitely wouldn't. 'Bye, Ross, take care,' she managed.

She moved the phone away from her ear to press the End

Call button, and heard a tinny voice say, 'And you, Lottie,' before she cut him off.

She shoved her phone into her pocket and gulped in the fresh air of the garden until the acid had burned its way back down her windpipe. When she walked inside the house, she found the boys chomping happily on slices of cucumber and carrot dipped in houmous, watching the iPad while Em calmly cooked some pasta on the Aga.

'They're doing a post-mortem,' Lottie said tightly in reply to her sister's questioning look. 'Ross said the funeral won't be for a while yet.'

'Then you should take the whole of next week off work and not go back till you're ready,' Em said immediately, closing the space between them and giving her a hug in one quick movement. 'You can hang out here for as long as you like. The kids will be in seventh heaven now they've found out you put on *much* better superhero vegetable voices than me and Luca.'

Lottie smiled briefly at her nephews, who were oblivious to the conversation, thanks to the brightly coloured cartoon characters on the screen in front of them. 'I don't know if I'm going to go yet.'

Her sister's brow creased. 'To the funeral? But you must, Lots! I know it will be hard, but it will help you process it all, it really will. And you'll get to meet all of Leo's friends and family and be able to talk about him with people who knew him too.'

'But that's the problem, isn't it? I didn't meet any of his

friends or family, other than Ross, and that wasn't … Well, it wasn't exactly a success. Probably no one outside of his parents and Ross even know I exist.' Lottie could feel her heart pounding in her chest.

'Lots, sweetheart, sit down,' Em said, gently pushing her onto the bar stool in front of the kitchen island. 'I'm sorry, I shouldn't have said you *must* go to the funeral – it's obviously completely up to you. If you don't want to go, that's totally fine. But the important thing is that you loved Leo, and that's all that matters,' she said softly. 'You may not have known him his whole life, but in the last three months you found out how funny and kind and handsome he was – and how he made you feel. I've never seen you so … passionate as when you talked about him to me and Annie. They're the important things to remember. And maybe sharing your memories with his friends and family, especially his parents, will help bring them some comfort too.'

'When did you get so wise, little sis?' Lottie managed a smile, dashing her hands across her eyes as she tried in vain to stop yet more tears falling.

'I'm most definitely a long way from wise. All I can do is be here for you and tell you what I think.' Em blinked back her own tears, and they gave each other watery smiles. 'You have to make up your own mind about going to the funeral, and whatever you decide, I will support you. Take some time to think about it, Lots – not for me, but for yourself.'

Chapter Four

Before

Leo had kept his word and texted Lottie to check she wasn't concussed the evening after they'd bumped into each other. She'd had a bit of a headache, but that had been more to do with her boss, Reg, who, despite Rachel's attempts to distract him, had actually tapped his watch and raised his massive monobrow when Lottie had made it back to the office ten minutes after her lunchbreak officially finished. He'd then proceeded to lecture her for the best part of the afternoon about the importance of timekeeping, thus taking up far more time than her slightly longer lunch break had. But Leo's messages had brought a smile to her face – even when he'd suggested a curry that Saturday night.

Dates had never been Lottie's thing. Rachel was always demanding she set up a profile on yet another supposedly amazing new app, and Lottie would sometimes agree to a quick afternoon coffee with a match Rachel declared was definitely going to be 'The One', but only really because it seemed to make her friend happy. She'd usually find a good enough reason not to progress to date two. She'd even tried telling Rachel she didn't need a man to complete her because, like Beyoncé, she was an 'Independent Woman', but Rachel had just replied by singing Beyoncé's 'Crazy in Love' at her until Lottie'd had no choice but to laugh and join in. But while it was most definitely true she didn't *need* a man in her life, she still found herself gazing in on her sisters' perfect marriages with an envy so green she was surprised it didn't create a glow-in-the-dark hue around her. It was only in her bleakest, wide-awake-in-the-middle-of-the-night-staring-at-the-ceiling moments that she was able to admit to herself that she was scared. Scared of being so hurt she found herself back in that dark place she'd had to work so hard to escape from just a few years before; scared that she didn't have the emotional skills to have a proper, grown-up relationship like the perfect ones she saw all around her; scared that maybe she just wasn't any other person's 'The One'. So she found it easier all round not to 'do' dates.

Which was why no one was more surprised than Lottie when, just a few days later, she found herself walking into a curry house to meet Leo. He was already sitting at the table when she arrived and they performed an awkward dance while neither of them could quite decide how to greet each other, which ended in a weird one-armed hug and lip-closer-to-her-ear-than-cheek kiss.

She wasn't quite sure what had made her agree to have dinner with him, except that his messages had made her properly laugh for the first time in a long while. Even so, she'd then spent most of her Saturday coming up with more and more ridiculous excuses that she could use to back out at the last minute. But eventually she'd run out of time and had pulled on some clothes, slapped on as much foundation and mascara as she could and run to the bus stop before she could overthink it any more.

The first five minutes had been excruciating as she stumbled over her words and searched the recesses of her brain for anything wittier than 'Poppadoms are just giant crisps really, aren't they?' and 'Gosh this beer is so cold!' Finally, she'd pretended to be engrossed in choosing her curry just to stop herself talking – even though she'd already studied the menu in detail on the internet and had settled on chicken tikka masala with a side of Peshwari naan. But then Leo had started telling a crazy, long-winded story about how he'd once found himself having to pretend to be a highly skilled chef in a restaurant in India, and Lottie had found herself shaking with proper laughter.

As delicately as possible, she scooped a blob of jam-like mango chutney and a pile of lime pickle onto a poppadom and then into her mouth. As she chewed, she became acutely aware that the back of her throat seemed to be growing hotter than the sun and, as she struggled to swallow the sticky, spicy mixture, she flapped her hand in front of her face in a vain attempt to cool herself down.

'Lottie, are you OK?' Leo stopped mid-flow and looked at her with concern. 'Your face has gone a bit ... pink.'

'Just ... hot!' she managed to get out. 'Lime pickle!'

Without missing a beat, he handed her his glass of mango lassi. 'Here, have some of this. It'll help, I promise. Commiserations on your rookie poppadom error,' he said, with a kind smile, which dampened her embarrassment slightly. 'Now, while you're drinking your body weight in lassi, I will stop boring you senseless about my early-twenties travels around India, and instead bore you with a monologue about me now, so that when you do finally feel less hot, I can then ask you a load of questions about you and you can't deflect any of them back on me.'

It might have been at that point that Lottie fell a little bit in love with Leo. As she tried to play firefighter on the blaze of chilli inside her mouth, she was touched by his thoughtfulness; he was giving her time to pull herself together while not making her feel like too much of an idiot for shoving the equivalent of ten Scotch bonnets down her throat. It did more to show her what type of man he was than any number of bouquets or showy, romantic gestures could have done.

'So, what can I tell you about me?' he continued. 'Well, I play the guitar, badly, love listening to definitely-not-cool music loudly, and often find myself watching a TV show all the way to the end even when I'm really not enjoying it because I can't be arsed to have to look through Netflix again to find something I'll actually like. Oh, yes, and I'm quite often to be found in this very curry house drinking bottles of overpriced Singha beer and eating chicken jalfrezi. But never touching the legendarily lethal lime pickle. Sorry, I probably should have warned you about that. And I also hasten to add that, while I do spend quite a lot of time in here, it's not normally with a beautiful woman. Or even a beautiful man. Just my mates, who I had to threaten to force-feed lime pickle in order to stop them "bumping into" me in here tonight and checking you out. This chin has bumped into enough people this week, I think!'

Lottie looked up just as he finished talking and their eyes met. She filed away the 'beautiful woman' comment for later, but was powerless to stop her heart thumping and stomach fluttering. She looked away and risked a nervous laugh. Finding that her throat didn't immediately catch fire in protest, she replied, 'Thanks for the heads-up. At least if I see a bunch of guys come in, unable to take their eyes off me, I'll know why.'

'I'm not sure they'd be that subtle. They'd definitely feel it was their duty to pull up a chair and awkwardly turn our dinner into a free-for-all.'

'Was the guy you were out shopping with the other day one of your mates?' Lottie asked, regretting her dumb question the second she'd asked it – he was hardly likely to be shopping with a man he had never met before.

'Kind of. Ross is my cousin – although he's more like a brother, I guess. He was down here for the week and he thought it would be a good idea if I increased the range of my wardrobe a little. But, if I'm honest, I wasn't massively in the mood, so cracking your head with my Desperate Dan chin was the highlight of my afternoon.'

Lottie smiled. 'Hmm, you must have been *very* desperate for your shopping trip to end if you resorted to picking people's items off the floor and cracking them round the head.'

'Well, Ross had apparently decided he was the British one off *Queer Eye* and that I was in need of a Fab Five make-over – without any of the actual Fab Five and in fact just a very Scottish, opinionated, and actually not that stylish guy. So, yes, things were getting desperate.'

'I'm definitely getting a good insight into your Netflix viewing habits this evening,' Lottie grinned. 'Although, you didn't do a bad job of pretending you were 1990s Hugh Grant the other day.'

'Wait, what?' Leo put down his fork. 'You can't just lob that insult into conversation and hope to get away with it!'

'Lots of men would be flattered to be told they resemble a posh, floppy-haired iconic actor millions of women fancy – or at least fancied.'

'Except said actor was then arrested for publicly engaging in a sex act with a prostitute, if I remember rightly. And, anyway, I am not posh – that was my *concerned* voice.'

'Maybe it was the whole meet-cute thing that suddenly made you think you were in some nineties romcom?' Lottie laughed.

'A meet-what?' Leo's eyes sparkled mischievously.

'A meet-cute. Like in romantic movies,' she mumbled, now a little embarrassed.

'Ah, I see. You mean that moment when the geeky boy falls off his skateboard and into the path of the gorgeous, universally loved pretty girl and it's the start of the romance of the year?' Leo grinned. 'In that case, does that mean me GBHing you in the middle of M&S was the start of something beautiful between us?'

Lottie blushed and held her beer to her lips, her mind suddenly empty of any witty retorts, and all she managed was a smile that she hoped was shy and coy, but was more likely to look oddly manic. He was definitely flirting with her. Wasn't he? It was so long since she'd been on a date with someone she actually liked that she barely remembered what it felt like.

'So did your sister like her deep-red, cashmere-mix jumper?' Leo asked.

'No, I mean, I'm not sure yet,' she stumbled. She was pleasantly surprised that he'd remembered the details of what she'd been buying. 'I'm giving it to her tomorrow at her birthday lunch.'

'That sounds fun. Is it the kind of birthday lunch that starts at lunchtime and then turns into an all-day drinking session? Are you going to wake up on Monday morning wishing you'd had the foresight to book the day off work?'

Lottie giggled. 'Possibly, yes. Especially since my parents have flown over for the occasion and my mum will spend the afternoon gushing about my sisters and their husbands and sending me pitying looks. Then she'll tell me she's worried about me and ask when I'm going to get a new job.'

'What's wrong with your old job?'

'My mother thinks that working for an *online* dictionary is a waste of my lexicographical skills. It's the *Oxford English Dictionary* or nothing for her.'

'You're a lexicographer? Like Su—'

'Yes, like Susie Dent.' Lottie rolled her eyes and Leo laughed. 'But, as my family love to tease me, I am very much a cut-price version of Susie Dent and very definitely not as good at solving *Countdown* Conundrums.'

'A cut-price version of Susie Dent is better than 1990s Hugh Grant any day,' Leo grinned. 'Susie D wins Top Trumps hands down.'

'Although Hugh Grant is about a hundred times richer than Susie D – and about a million times richer than cut-price Susie D, but I appreciate your support.' They grinned at each other, and as her whole body seemed to heat up, Lottie found herself no longer caring whether her smile was coy or completely manic. 'What do you do? When you're not impersonating Hugh Grant circa 1995, I mean?'

'My lookalike work has dried up of late so I've gone back to being a project manager for an engineering firm.'

'Like in *The Apprentice*? Did you get everyone to vote for you to be PM?'

'No, not nearly as interesting as *The Apprentice*, I'm afraid, although I work with just as many people with their heads stuck up their own arses. Thankfully, there are some normal people there, too. It's not changing the world, but I don't hate it and it's what my parents call a "good" job, so they're happy. Which means I'm happy.' He smiled a little thinly. 'And, thankfully, as an only child, my parents don't have anyone else to compare me against.'

'God, I can't imagine that. My parents now live in Spain

so we don't see each other that much, but my sisters are such a big part of my life. We're all pretty different – they both have their lives sorted, for one thing! – but we're super close.'

'I wish I'd had brothers and sisters,' Leo said. 'I was lucky that I grew up with Ross, though. Our mums are sisters and they're really close too.'

'Where did you grow up?' Lottie asked, finding herself genuinely interested in what he had to say.

'Scotland – Ross still lives up there now.'

'So you're Scottish? No way! You don't have an accent at all.'

'I moved down here with my parents years ago and even they've lost their accents a bit. They're still proudly Scottish, though, so they'd hate me saying that. I never really think about it until I go back up there, or Ross comes down here, and I remember that's how I used to speak too.'

'Oh, yes, now you mention it, he did sound very *och aye da noo!*' Lottie said in an embarrassingly terrible accent. Leo burst out laughing, and Lottie cringed, wondering if the lime pickle had done something to her brain.

'Please never try out your accent on him if you ever meet him again.' He sipped his beer before adding, 'On second thoughts, actually, you absolutely should try that accent in front of him, but only if I can watch!'

'OK, refrain from any *och aye da nooing* if I ever meet your cousin properly, noted.'

He smiled and then his face became more serious. 'You should meet him. I think you'd really like him. Everyone who meets him does. He's just one of those people, you know? In all honesty, I don't know where I'd be without Ross. My whole life would be so different.'

Leo's eyes shone and Lottie felt for him. She barely knew this man, but as she listened to him speak and looked into his bright-blue eyes, a strange part of her felt like she'd known him for ever. She held his gaze and instinctively reached across the table to take his hand.

'He sounds amazing. It seems we're both lucky to have brilliant people in our lives. Annie and Em have helped me through the toughest times in my life too. I know they'll always be there to hold me up, and that is something really special.'

'Exactly,' he said. For several seconds, neither of them said anything but they held each other's gazes. To Lottie, it felt both intense and also strangely familiar, and instead of backing away, or trying to fill the silence, as she normally would, she found herself just content to sit there in the moment.

Then their waiter bustled over to ask if they wanted any more drinks. Lottie pulled her hand away and they continued to chat and laugh as before. But she found herself stealing glances at Leo as she ate, and her heart seemed to bang in her chest that bit harder.

A little later, full of curry and enough beer to wash all but a faint tingle of lime pickle from her throat, they stepped out onto the bustling Oxford streets. Whereas inside the restaurant Lottie had felt they were in their own little bubble, now the real world rushed in and she suddenly felt awkward and unsure of herself. But Leo continued to chat easily as they walked towards her bus stop, and she forced herself to relax, giggling at the story he was telling about trying on some jeans that had taken the term 'skinny' to a whole new level.

There was a gaggle of people gathered around the bus shelter, so they stood a few metres down the road, a little apart from the crowds. There were a couple of seconds of silence between them, and Lottie couldn't help but imagine Leo's bum squeezed into a pair of very tight jeans. Her cheeks flamed again, and she was thankful they weren't standing directly underneath a streetlamp.

She cleared her throat at the same time as Leo said, 'I had a great time tonight.'

She grinned up at him, very glad he couldn't read her mind. 'Me too.'

'Maybe we could, you know . . .' He swallowed, and Lottie's heart banged so hard in her chest it was in danger of bursting through her coat. The silence lasted a beat too long, and she gently smiled at him.

'If you're asking if I'd like to do this again – go on another date, I mean – then, yes, I would.' She grinned as his face broke into an immediate, if still quite nervous, smile.

'That is exactly what I was asking,' he said quickly. 'God, you'd have thought after thirty-four years I wouldn't be quite so rubbish at this!'

'I think we're all rubbish at it,' Lottie said with a laugh. 'We're far too British.'

They grinned at each other and Lottie was struck again

by just how blue his eyes were. But before she could open her mouth to ask if he was wearing coloured contacts, he'd moved his lips towards hers and all thoughts dropped from her mind.

It wasn't until a few delicious minutes later that she opened her eyes and saw the pavement was almost deserted and realized that she'd missed her bus.

Chapter Five

Before

'We need to talk!' Rachel whispered urgently in Lottie's ear as they spilled out of the meeting room after one of Reg's random 'ideas huddles', as he liked to call them. Even though the team had an editorial meeting every single Monday, Reg still insisted on having yet more brainstorms whenever he chose and expected them all to come up with knock-out suggestions with just a few hours' notice. Normally, Lottie rolled her eyes with everyone else and felt relieved if she managed to produce a couple of just-about-passable suggestions, but that Thursday, she'd been on fire, and even Reg had been impressed with her ideas. So much so that he'd berated the rest of the team for not being up to scratch and she'd noticed a few of them shooting her aggrieved looks across the table. Now, she glanced at her friend and wondered whether it might have been more sensible to rein in her creativity a little and save some of her ideas for another time.

'Meet me in the kitchen in five,' Rachel instructed.

Lottie did as she was told. She pressed a button on the coffee machine and watched as a sludgy brown liquid – that the machine assured her was hot chocolate – slithered its way into her mug.

'Are you . . . *humming* to yourself?' Rachel said, appearing next to her and shaking Lottie out of her reverie.

'No, of course not!' she replied, grabbing her mug and taking a gulp of its thick, syrupy contents.

Rachel frowned at her. 'What has got into you today? You've had a strange grin on your face since you came in this morning, then you were sickeningly on it in the ideas huddle, and now you're humming into your hot chocolate. Come on, out with it!'

Lottie shrugged, but her mouth widened into a smile almost involuntarily. 'What? I don't know what you mean.'

'Oh my God, you've got that glint in your eye! Did you go on a secret Tinder date last night and finally get some? Tell me everything.'

'No!' Lottie laughed. 'I haven't been on a secret Tinder date and I didn't finally get some, and even if I had I would not be "telling you everything".'

'Did I just hear you say you'd been on a Tinder date, Lottie?' Guy – the third part of their office trio – barged into the kitchen. Guy had joined the company on the same day as Rachel, and although at first Lottie hadn't been sure about his outspokenness and love of a good gossip, gradually she'd been won over by his kindness, loyalty and the way he always laughed at her jokes, however lame they were. Over the last few years, the three of them had got drunk together countless times when going for a 'quick drink' after work on a Friday, and they'd bonded over hungover WhatsApp chats the following day.

'How come you're telling Rach about Mr Tinder and not me? Right, I want all the details. Come on, spill,' he said.

'There isn't a Mr Tinder, I promise,' she protested. Both Rachel and Guy raised their eyebrows and continued to look wholly unconvinced until she couldn't take their stares any longer. 'OK, OK! I wasn't lying, there really isn't a Mr Tinder. But I did go on a date at the weekend.'

'You told me you'd barely left the house all weekend!' Rachel said. 'Or are you telling me you didn't leave the house because you spent the whole time in bed with this man? Give us something, Lottie – I'm part of a boring married couple now, don't forget, so I need to live vicariously through your dating stories. No pressure.'

Lottie rolled her eyes good-naturedly. 'No, I didn't spend the whole time in bed with him. We went for a curry, I ate some spicy lime pickle and went red in the face, and then we had a bit of a kiss and went home to our respective houses.' Lottie felt her whole body heat up again at the memory of Leo's goodbye at the bus stop. She'd certainly not felt the cold on her journey home despite the near-freezing temperature. She glanced at her friends; Guy was grinning from ear to ear while Rachel looked about to burst.

'You kissed him? But you never kiss anybody!'

Lottie immediately went beetroot red. 'Shh! Lower your voice, woman, we're in the office. And I do kiss people. You make me sound like a bloody nun!'

'But you *never* kiss anyone on a first date!' Rachel said.

'And you *never* have a second date,' Guy chimed in, 'so that means you never—'

'Yes, all right, thank you, Guy,' Lottie cut in quickly, wishing she'd kept her mouth firmly shut about the whole thing. She'd told her sisters about Leo at pub club the night before, and while they'd managed to wrangle every last detail out of her and been very excited and happy for her, she was aware that she was currently standing in the middle of an open-plan kitchen and neither Rachel nor Guy were known for the quietness of their voices.

'So this "bit of a kiss" – it was good, I take it?' Rachel said, eyeing her beadily.

'A lady never tells,' Lottie replied primly, taking a sip of her hot chocolate. It was nice to see how excited her friends and family were for her, but it did also bring home quite how long it must have been since she'd gone on a second date with someone. She really wasn't a nun and there had been a few dalliances here and there, but nothing to write home about, and she'd always been careful not to give Rachel and Guy too much detail for fear it would only egg them both on.

Last time she'd been on a date – someone from Hinge who Rachel had badgered her into meeting – Lottie had managed to slink off home after just an hour, having spent the previous forty-five minutes wishing she was curled up on the sofa in her pyjamas stroking Ginger, the cat that wasn't her cat. She'd ended up having to embellish just how bad the date was to save herself from her friends' wrath. She knew they'd have said she gave up too easily. But after Elliot and everything that had happened with him, dating and relationships were just another part of being an adult that she seemed to be useless at.

'But the kiss was good enough to mean you're going on a second date?' Guy probed when it was clear they weren't going to wheedle any more information out of her.

'Yes. We're going to crazy golf this evening, actually. You know, that place where they serve those amazing cocktails?'

Rachel and Guy both burst out laughing, and Rachel managed to say between giggles, 'I'm guessing you haven't told this man – what is his name anyway?'

'Leo.'

'Well, I'm guessing you haven't told Leo about our company away day last year?'

'You guess correctly. What happened on that pitch and putt course stays on that pitch and putt course. And anyway, it's all indoors so the holes will be really short, and you just tap the ball rather than whack it, right?'

'Let's hope so, for Leo's sake!' Guy said, still shaking with laughter. 'Just remember to keep your hand on the club at all times, and whatever you do, don't let go mid-swing.'

'Thanks for the tip, Tiger Woods.' Lottie pulled a face at him, but his giggling was infectious and she started laughing too. 'Seriously, I don't know what happened that day. I'd been practising for weeks – I even got Charlie to take me out and show me how to swing properly and everything.' This only made Guy and Rachel laugh even harder and in the end Lottie rolled her eyes again and left them to it.

Later that day, Lottie came out of the ladies' with a face full of make-up to find that the office was deserted. Her phone lit up with *good luck* and *have fun* messages from not only Rachel and Guy but Em and Annie too. She was so nervous she wished she'd never mentioned Leo to any of them. The pressure of knowing how much they all wanted her to be happy made her shoulders slump and her chest tighten.

As she walked into the centre of Oxford and followed Google Maps down a side street behind the shopping centre, she found herself coming to a stop. If she turned around now, before Leo saw her, she could invent a crisis at work and cancel. At least then there was no way the evening could be a disaster, and she wouldn't disappoint her friends and family. But if she didn't go, they'd all be disappointed anyway and she'd feel like she'd let them down. She sighed and forced herself to keep walking, but the butterflies in her stomach wouldn't settle. This was exactly why she liked staying at home on the sofa in her pyjamas with only someone else's fluffy-haired cat-food-breath pet for company.

Turning the corner, she saw Leo shifting from foot to foot outside the bar.

'Lottie, you came!'

She took a breath; there was no going back now. 'Of course,

I'd never turn down a game of crazy golf on a Thursday evening!' She grinned brightly, hoping Leo couldn't tell how many doubts were whizzing around her brain.

He smiled, and Lottie thought he looked relieved. He hugged her hard and even the brush of his lips on her cheek made her stomach tingle, like she was a teenager. He let her go and grinned, leading her inside the venue. 'Just to let you know, I won't be going easy on you tonight,' he said.

'And I'm just going to say that my golf skills are actually legendary around these parts, so you'd better watch out.'

'Well, if they're as impressive as your lime-pickle-eating skills, then I'm going to need to be on my A game, that's for sure.' He looked around, locating the bar. 'I think it's mandatory at these places to have a lurid-coloured cocktail before we start. Shall we get our order in?'

Minutes later, Lottie clinked her bright green 'Fairway to Heaven' against Leo's glass and took a grateful swig. It was the sweetest, most moreish, and possibly most dangerous drink she'd ever tasted, but as the sugar and alcohol hit her veins, she sighed appreciatively. 'You didn't go for the "Slush Puttie", then?' she said with a nod at his pint of lager.

'I save my Slush-Puttie drinking for the weekend.'

'Ahh, is that what happens when you reach the grand old age of thirty-four? Thank God I have two whole years of Thursday-night Slush Putties ahead of me!' She grinned, and took another huge gulp of her drink. A few minutes later, she found herself draining the last of the sweet liquid. 'God, these are addictive! Shall I get us another one?'

'I'm all right for now, thanks.' He smiled and Lottie noticed he'd barely touched his drink yet. She knew she should probably slow down and wait until he'd finished his, too, but the confidence the hit of alcohol had given her was already ebbing away, and she knew she needed another.

She slid off her stool and made her way to the bar where the bartender somehow persuaded her to buy two Slush Putties so she could try out both flavours, and she returned with a fluorescent drink in each hand. 'I couldn't decide which one to get, so you'll have to break your rule and do some Thursday drinking with me,' she said.

'Life is tough sometimes,' he said with a grin. 'Shall we start our round? You bring the Slush Putties and I'll bring the actual putters.'

Lottie followed Leo a little unsteadily, then put her ball down on the first hole and handed him her cocktail. She gripped the club tightly and knocked the ball through the tunnel so it landed safely on the other side ready for her second shot.

Leo nodded. 'Not bad. I can see I have some competition here.'

They made their way round the course and Lottie managed to acquit herself pretty well, she thought, even if she did lose count of exactly how many shots it took to get past the annoying windmill on hole five.

At the mid-point, they ended up stuck behind a group who were struggling to navigate a particularly difficult-looking see-saw-like obstacle. Lottie and Leo stood waiting, sipping their drinks, which Leo had magically refilled when she'd slipped off to the loo. She forced herself to take bird-like pecks at her cocktail, her head already at that deliciously fuzzy-round-the-edges point. She looked up from her drink and caught Leo gazing at her. He averted his eyes, and Lottie's stomach fizzed. The alcohol bolstering her confidence, she asked, 'So how come you're single?'

'Because I hadn't met you until a week ago.' Lottie gulped and felt her heartbeat speed up, but then the corner of Leo's mouth started to tremble and he burst out laughing. Lottie blinked and then she too began to giggle, and both of them were quickly in hysterics. 'Jesus, I nearly spilt my beer everywhere,' he wheezed. 'I'm so sorry, that was the cheesiest thing I think I've ever said. Please believe me when I say I don't normally go round spurting cringey chat-up lines.'

Lottie made an effort to rein in her hysterics. 'Don't be embarrassed! I can't remember the last time anyone tried to chat me up in real life. Tinder creeps don't count, obviously.'

'Obviously.' He nodded. 'Are you on all the apps and things then?'

She raised her glass to her lips. 'I was, although I've deleted them now. I just find them exhausting. Without meaning to lump all men into one stereotypical box – and obviously excepting you from that box – the men on dating apps are pretty depressing. You're doing well if you can go more than three messages without them asking if you want to hook up round their place. The bar is set so low, you end up meeting people not because you actually think you might be attracted to them, but just because they haven't been a total dick, unlike the last seventy-five men you've matched with.' She took a breath, suddenly aware her voice felt a bit loud, then added more quietly, 'I'm sure if I could be bothered to put a bit more effort into dating apps I'd find more nice men, but it just all feels like such a lot of work, you know?'

Leo nodded. 'I do know, yes. So dating isn't really your thing then?'

She glanced up at him and found his eyes were fixed on her face. 'Not really,' she said. 'Though I'm not sure how else I'm going to find The One.' There was a pause and it felt to Lottie like the room around them fell completely silent. For a moment, all she could hear was the sound of her heart throbbing in her chest like the bassline at a gig. Leo laughed, and Lottie suddenly felt a bit sick. Why on earth had she just said that? 'Oh God, now I'm the one who's embarrassed!' she said, and forced out a laugh, before taking a large gulp of her cocktail. The blood rushed to her ears and into her cheeks, and someone pressed the Play button on the world again. 'What I mean is no, I'm not Bridget Jones, but one day I'd like to find someone to settle down with.' Leo smiled again, and Lottie reached for her drink. Casting around for something to say to fill the silence that seemed to have settled between them, she ploughed on with the first thing that came into her mind. 'I was reading an article on some website a few weeks ago and it was discussing what questions you should ask someone you're thinking about dating.'

'That sounds ominous!' Leo raised his eyebrows.

'Well, some of them *were* a bit, er, ominous, I guess – like, "When was your last STD test?" and "Do you have any debts?"'

'About a year ago and it was clear, and no, other than the whopping great mortgage I have on the house my parents generously helped me buy. How am I doing?' He grinned and Lottie felt herself relax a little, although that could also have been the third cocktail she'd now almost finished.

'Gold star so far!' She said. 'One of the less ominous questions was, "What qualities – good and bad – would previous partners say you have?"'

'Ooph, I think I prefer the ominous ones.' He laughed. Lottie fought the compunction to fill the silence and waited for him to answer. 'I guess they'd say my plus points are I'm a fairly good cook and pretty well house-trained. I love spending time outdoors, and I find trying new things really fun. I never have arguments with anyone or hold grudges, and I like to live in the moment and not worry too much about the past. Oh, and that I'm drop-dead handsome.'

Lottie giggled. 'Goes without saying.'

'And I'm modest, too, obviously.'

'Obviously. OK, so what would they say were your bad qualities, then?'

Leo scrunched up his eyes. 'Have you ever considered becoming a police detective? You'd have criminals confessing their crimes in no time with this kind of questioning! OK, I think they'd say my bad qualities are that I spend too long in the bathroom styling my hair – it's a total nightmare to get it to do what I want. It's a running joke in my family that I have a mane like a lion – as in Leo the lion.' Lottie laughed then raised her eyebrows to motion for him to carry on. 'What, is that not enough for you? What other sins should I confess to? Oh, yes, I insist on squeezing the toothpaste from the centre of the tube and not the end, I hate mushrooms – although I'm not sure that's a bad quality. I mean, they're actually a fungus and who wants to eat fungus? And if I can't find something within thirty seconds of looking for it, I tend to give up.'

'Ahh, you mean you do a *man look*? I am familiar with this phenomenon. It seems to afflict all members of the male species,' Lottie replied. 'But I suppose I will let you off since that's not really your fault.' As she drained her glass, she hoped she'd lightened the slightly serious turn she'd taken the conversation in, but she couldn't help worrying that Leo must be wondering what the hell he'd done asking her out tonight.

She felt his gaze on her and raised her eyes to meet his. Without breaking the eye contact between them, Leo gently took the glass out of her hand and placed it wordlessly on the table behind him. Then he tilted his head towards her and kissed her gently at first, and then with an increasing intensity that made Lottie feel dizzy and she pulled away.

'Sorry. I – I didn't want to stop,' she stuttered. 'I just feel a bit … like I need to sit down.'

'I've never actually made a woman go physically weak at the knees before,' Leo quipped, and she tried to smile, but her head suddenly felt foggy. Leo put his hand on her arm.

'Maybe let's go and get some fresh air – I know I could do with it.'

'But what about our round of glof, I mean golf?' she said, leaning into him and feeling her legs stagger slightly. 'I'm fine really.'

Leo steered her towards the door and said lightly, 'Well, I think you'll find that I was two shots ahead of you so I'm happy to declare victory and leave it at that.'

'I demand a rematch!' Lottie cried. Or that's what she said in her head anyway, though it felt like her mouth wasn't quite her own somehow.

'Absolutely, though maybe on a Saturday night when I have my Slush Puttie A game going.' He smiled. 'Shall we sit down here for a bit and I can call us an Uber?'

Lottie allowed him to steer her over to some steps and enjoyed the weight of the arm he placed behind her. Leo chatted quietly, although she was barely listening by that point, until he gently pushed her into a standing position and said, 'Our car is just over there. Do you think you can make it that far?'

'Of coursh! Are you inviting me home, Leo?' Lottie said in what she hoped was a seductive voice as he gently helped her into the car and climbed in himself. Before he could answer, she'd leaned her head against his shoulder and fallen fast asleep.

She was vaguely aware of getting out of the car, finding her keys in her bag and letting them both into her flat. She had a brief moment of panicked clarity when she remembered what a mess she'd left her bedroom in that morning, but by the time she'd kicked off her shoes, stumbled out of her dress and was lying on her bed, she found she no longer cared. She'd started to fall asleep when Ginger suddenly appeared next to her cheek and pawed at the duvet.

'Gerrof!' she said, pushing him away, then blinked as Leo walked into her room carrying a glass of water, which he set down on her bedside table. 'I'm talking to Ginger, who's a cat but not my cat and isn't allowed to sleep with me. I didn't mean you, Leo,' she began to explain.

'I'm not sure Ginger got that memo!' Leo smiled and glanced at where Ginger was now happily curled up on the bed. 'Let's pull that duvet up over you. There you go,' he said, smoothing out the bedspread on top of her.

'Will you stay with me, Leo?' Lottie said woozily, her body already pulling her towards sleep.

'Of course. I'll stay until I'm sure you're safely asleep, don't worry.'

'Thanksh. Night, Leo.'

He leaned over and placed a gentle kiss on her lips. 'Night, Lottie.'

Chapter Six

As grateful as Lottie was for both Em and Annie's company and support, after four days of being asked how she was feeling – when, if she was honest, she had absolutely no idea beyond the word *numb* – the need to go home was overwhelming.

Lottie knew her little sister only had her best interests at heart, but there was a limit to how much smothering she could take. And Annie wasn't much better. She'd taken to calling Lottie at seven o'clock each evening when she knew Em would be deep in the bath and bedtime routine, so Lottie would likely be on her own. Annie was usually multitasking, finishing off some experiment analysis or in the supermarket buying dinner, but she always managed to tell Lottie exactly what she thought she should be doing and feeling. Again, Lottie knew Annie was only doing it because she cared, but the constant barrage of attention from her sisters had just become too much. So, the next day, she told Em that she needed to go home tomorrow and have some space to herself.

The only way Em would let her go was if Lottie promised to answer a FaceTime call from either her or Annie every morning and every evening. Lottie rolled her eyes but grudgingly agreed – anything to be able to escape the sympathetic looks directed at her seemingly 24/7.

The next day, before Lottie could leave, Em insisted that she stay for lunch, so she could make sure Lottie had eaten at least two proper meals that day. So it was already afternoon by the time Lottie and Em opened the door of her flat and were met by a musty odour of damp laundry and rotting food. Em immediately set about opening the windows and cleaning the kitchen, while Dante padded around after her, picking up random pieces of detritus from the floor and trying to put them in his mouth. Lottie found she was too exhausted to feel even the slightest embarrassment about the state of her flat, and instead of helping her sister, she sank onto the sofa.

When she'd left her flat on Wednesday morning to go to work, and then on to pub club, it had been just a very normal day. She'd been excited to tell her sisters about the perfect night she'd spent with Leo, for once having a successful relationship to talk to them about. But just five days later, it felt like all that had happened in another lifetime. That was 'before'; this was 'after'. She was hit by the sudden realisation that there was no turning back the clock, no returning to the 'before'. Her breath caught in her chest and her hands started to shake.

'I've put some clean sheets on your bed and put a wash on for you,' Em's soft voice said, and Lottie looked up to find her sister crouched in front of her, Dante on her hip. 'Oh, Lots, I feel awful leaving you here on your own. Why don't you come back to ours for just a few more days?' she coaxed.

'I – I'm fine,' Lottie replied quickly, but she was unable to stop her voice from shaking. 'Really, I am. Thanks, Em.'

Her sister looked less than convinced, but made an obvious effort to keep the worry from her face. 'Of course. It's up to you, sweetheart, but don't forget I'm always just a call away and I can be here in forty minutes to pick you up.' She gave her another searching look before finally giving in. 'Dante, say goodbye to Auntie Lottie and give her a big kiss.'

Her sister placed her nephew on her lap and he proceeded to give her a kiss that mostly involved sucking her nose extremely wetly, before Em gave her a proper kiss on the cheek and held her tightly. 'I love you, Lottie. Me and Annie are here for you whenever you need us, I promise,' she said fiercely.

The front door had barely shut behind them before Lottie gave in to the tide of emotion raging through her. Waves of torrential sadness rose up over her until she was so far beneath the surface she was sure she would never be able to emerge again. Time didn't matter to her, but her body could only take so much before it fought back and her survival instinct kicked in, pushing her back to the surface, when all she wanted to do was sink lower and lower. Slowly, her sobs began to fade and the tsunami of tears and shuddering began to ease, until she was left, hollowed out like a shell washed up on a deserted beach.

She curled into the foetal position on her sofa and closed her eyes in the hope sleep might creep over her aching limbs. But despite feeling tired on a level she'd never known before, her mind refused to rest. She'd hoped that finally, openly, submitting to her grief, might be cathartic. But, however natural the process felt, it hadn't left her feeling refreshed like crying at a weepy movie always did. Her body might not have been capable of producing any more tears right then, but the sadness continued to gnaw at her heart. It hit her again: there was now only the 'after'.

Time passed, not by days turning into nights, and not with the eat, sleep, work, repeat cycle, but instead punctuated by her sisters' daily routine of calls. When they FaceTimed her, Lottie would answer, say the right things for just long enough and convincingly enough that they didn't insist on coming round right that minute, before ending the call and resuming her position on the sofa. She went hours, maybe even days, without eating, and then greedily stuffed an Uber Eats delivery down her throat and spent the next few hours wanting to throw it all back up again.

And the same went for sleep. She'd lie on the sofa staring at the blackness outside the window until the sun rose and lit up the world and all the plants and animals and people in it. But it was their world, not hers. Her world had shrunk to just her living room. She didn't need to wash when the only person she saw was a food delivery man every few days. She had her phone and all its handy filters when she did need to communicate with their world. She couldn't see why she'd ever need to leave the comfort of her own world again.

It was Ross who eventually bridged the chasm between her bubble and the real world outside her flat. Early Friday afternoon, Lottie's phone rang, piercing the silence of the living room. She immediately jabbed the Decline button without even looking at the caller and heaved herself up on the sofa, her heart thumping. Realising she must have knocked her phone off its usual silent mode when it slipped from her hand and onto the floor when she fell asleep after her morning call from Em, she quickly put it back on silent and checked her missed calls. There was a long list of names in red, including Rachel and Guy and even her mum, none of whose calls she'd returned, but at the top of the log was Ross's name. Her head span and she reached for the glass of water on the table beside her, not caring how long it had sat there, then jumped as her phone began to vibrate in her hand.

'He—Hello?' she said, her tongue feeling like cotton wool and her voice sticking in her throat. She took another sip of water.

'Lottie, is that you? How are you doing?'

'Yes.' She swallowed. 'Hi, Ross. I'm fine, how are you? And L—Leo's parents?'

'We're doing OK, thank you. It's been a strange week, as you can imagine, trying to organise the funeral when we didn't know when we'd be able to hold it, as we had to wait for a post-mortem because it was so unexpected and Leo was so young. That hasn't been easy. But that's what I'm calling about actually.'

'What did it say? The post-mortem, I mean?' Lottie tried to force her brain into action and string words together into proper sentences.

'We got the results this morning and it confirmed what we suspected: a sudden cardiac arrest. He had something called Long QT syndrome, which can cause an irregular heartbeat that sometimes sorts itself out and returns to normal, but sometimes it doesn't, and it sadly means the person's heart stops.'

'And . . . and Leo's heart just stopped then?' she said, tears already running down her cheeks.

'Yes, we think so,' Ross said gently. 'They said he wouldn't have felt any pain and wouldn't have known what was happening. He was literally alive one minute and not the next.'

'Did he know that he had—' Lottie heard his voice break and a sob thrust its way out of her own mouth too. 'S–sorry,' she said. 'I just can't get my head around it still.'

'Me too,' he said quietly. She heard him swallow hard. 'I seem to have spent the last week doing nothing but cry. At least I've had the funeral to organise, though, which is helping a bit, I think. We're having it next Friday at midday at the Oxfordshire Natural Burial site, and then the wake will be at the Pheasant pub just in the next village. I'll text you with the links so you have them.'

'OK, thank you, that would be really helpful.' There was silence for a second before she quickly added, 'Thanks for sorting all of that, and please send my love to Leo's parents.'

'I will, and I know they'll appreciate it, thanks Lottie. I'll see you next Friday, but do just message me if you need anything before then, or you just, erm, you know, well, I'm here.'

'See you then. Bye Ross.'

Lottie ended the call and threw her phone onto the table like it was a hot potato, then immediately picked it up again and googled 'Long QT syndrome'. Within seconds, she'd discovered it was a genetic condition that, as Ross had said, caused irregular heartbeats that can result in fainting, seizures, and in some patients, death. It seemed lots of people didn't even know they had it until they experienced symptoms, which presumably was what had happened with Leo – if he'd known about it, he'd definitely have told her. As she checked site after site, she read every word she could find about the condition, but even with all the medical information, she kept coming back to what Ross had said: he was alive one minute and not the next. She couldn't get her head around it. She was sitting on her sofa on a Friday afternoon feeling as dead inside as she could ever remember feeling, but her limbs were all functioning, she was still breathing the air around her and her heart was still beating. Despite how she was feeling, she was very much alive. And Leo wasn't.

That night, she slept fitfully. Come 5 a.m., when she realized she'd been lying wide awake on the sofa listening to Ginger scratching at her front door for the best part of an hour, she finally gave in. She opened the door and luxuriated in Ginger weaving in and out of her legs, purring like Lottie was his long-lost owner. He pushed his head against her hand and made pathetic mewling noises that was clearly cat language for, 'No one has fed me for sooo long and I know you have some of those posh pouches of food in the cupboard.' Ginger was of course correct – Lottie had been meaning to stop feeding him, but she couldn't say no to his little face – and soon he was tucking into a plate of Furbaby Luxury Chunks in Gravy while Lottie's stomach heaved at the smell. Thankfully, the food disappeared into the cat's mouth within seconds, and after a cursory rub against her legs, he stalked back down the hall towards the front door, stepping over a heap of clothes in the process, and demanded to be let out, presumably so he could return to his actual owner and enjoy a second breakfast. Lottie sighed, did Ginger's bidding, then made a mammoth cafetiere of coffee and gazed at the mess of her life around her.

A little later, fuelled by caffeine and unable to listen to the cacophony of thoughts all vying for space in her head any longer, she found herself saying out loud to her empty home, 'Come on, get focused, Lottie. Busy is good. Let's sort this shit out!' like some motivational speaker on a bad Netflix show.

She launched into action and attacked her flat with a pace and fervour she usually reserved for packing for holiday an hour before she was due to leave. She cleaned every room from top to bottom, stuck the pile of dirty pyjamas she'd been living in all week into the washing machine and buffed, exfoliated and moisturised her whole body until she smelled like the headache-inducing atmosphere of a Lush store.

It was amazing what feeling clean could do, and for the first time in days she felt like she actually wanted to leave the house. She went for a coffee with Annie, where she nodded along to whatever her sister said. When she got home, she was so tired that all she wanted to do was collapse on the sofa and wallow in front of trashy TV, but she knew she needed something to occupy her thoughts, so she forced herself to instead bake a loaf of banana bread, began assembling a lasagne for dinner, then logged into her work email account and read all four hundred of the messages waiting for her in her inbox.

When she'd told her sisters she was planning on returning to work on Monday, they had both asked her if it wasn't maybe a little too soon. They'd suggested she take the week off and only go back after the funeral, but Lottie had assured them that she'd rather be in the office working than at home with her own thoughts. Both Em and Annie just seemed so relieved to see her up and about again that, thankfully, they didn't argue. Lottie was so exhausted, she was in bed by 8 p.m. and instantly fell asleep.

Come Monday morning, she was the first to arrive at the office, having woken at her apparently new normal time of 4 a.m. As she sat down at her desk and drank in the familiar surroundings, it felt like she'd been away for a year, not just over a week. So much had changed in that time in Lottie's life, yet so much had stayed the same here, and for once she was pleased to read the familiar 'Reg's Earl Grey: do NOT use' label on the Tupperware next to the large box of Tesco Value teabags the rest of the staff had to make do with.

As she sipped her drink and waited for her computer to finish its various updates, Lottie realized that she had kept herself so occupied over the weekend, she hadn't stopped to come up with a proper plan about what she was going to say to Reg – and more importantly Rachel and Guy – about why she'd been off for so long. Reg was unlikely to ask for a doctor's note for the 'women's problems' story that he seemed to have misunderstood from Em, since that would mean he'd have to ask Lottie an actual question about her health and he was far too squeamish for that. But neither did she want to lie to him if he did ask her directly.

When it came to Rachel, however, perhaps a lie was preferable. Lottie wasn't sure she was ready for Rachel's reaction when she found out the truth. And although Guy was a complete sweetheart, she knew he would feel awkward and wouldn't have a clue what to say to her.

Equally, Lottie wasn't sure if she could deal with having to explain why she wasn't seeing Leo any more. It would inevitably come up in conversation, since Rachel loved nothing more than discussing Lottie's love life, and the word discreet just wasn't in her vocabulary, despite her working at a dictionary.

'Lottieeeeeeeee! You're back!' came a shriek a few minutes later as Rachel pushed the door open. 'You're here early.

How are you feeling? I can't believe you had some kind of operation *down there* and Reg knew about it and I didn't. I felt like a right chump when he mentioned it at the morning meeting. Did it hurt? Are you still in pain?'

'Lovely to see you, too, Rachel.' Lottie smiled, giving her friend a quick hug and taking a moment to bask in the company of someone who didn't yet know what had happened and wasn't fixing her with a kind but pitying expression. 'And if there was anyone in Oxford Reg hadn't talked to about my lady parts, then they certainly know about them now!'

'Give over, there's no one else here, and the window is only half open. So what did you have done? Are you sworn off sex for weeks now? What does Leo think?'

Lottie winced and steadied herself against her desk. 'Shall we grab a quick coffee before the meeting and catch up?' she said, snatching up her coat and heading for the door before Rachel could reply. Hoping that Rachel's reaction would be dimmed in a public place, she pulled her into the Starbucks a few doors down from the office. But as the reality of what she needed to tell her friend struck her anew, she swapped the seats they'd originally chosen for a booth right at the back of the shop.

'So, how *are* you?' Rachel asked as they sipped their lattes. She tore into her croissant and looked at Lottie expectantly.

'I'm ... well, I've not been the best.' Lottie fiddled with the lid of her coffee, the smell suddenly turning her stomach. 'Something happened. I didn't have an operation down there, or anywhere else.' She cleared her throat. 'I, erm, I ... Leo died.' She saw her friend move her hand up to her mouth in horror. Lottie swallowed and hurried on, wanting to get it over with. 'It was his heart. He had a genetic condition only no one knew he had it, and his heart just stopped beating out of nowhere.' No matter how many times she said it, either to herself or even out loud, nothing about the words felt real to her.

'Shit, Lottie, that's fucking terrible.' Rachel gawped at her. 'I'm so sorry, and there was me going on about you not telling me you were going to be off work. Oh God, I'm such a dick. Christ, Lottie. How are you feeling? Did you go to the funeral?'

'It's on Friday. They had to wait because they had to do a post-mortem, which apparently they always do when someone young dies unexpectedly with no obvious cause.' Lottie knew she sounded like she was reciting facts she'd learned for an exam, but it still felt as if it had happened to a different man called Leo, someone she didn't know, didn't love.

'Right. Why didn't you tell me, Lottie? If you'd messaged or called, I could have ... I don't know, I could have been there for you at least.'

'Sorry, it just all felt a bit much. And I stayed at Em's most of the time.'

'Good, I'm glad your sisters were with you. God, it's so much to take in, isn't it? No wonder you weren't replying to my messages.'

Lottie grimaced and nodded, glad to have at least got the conversation out of the way, but she was at a complete loss about what to say next. She knew she should ask Rachel how she was and how things had been in the office over the last week, but when she couldn't even begin to make sense of what was going on in her own life, other people's lives seemed completely alien and unimportant.

She glanced at her phone. 'It's after nine o'clock, we'd better be getting back,' she said as brightly as she could. 'Reg will be tapping his watch as we speak.' She smiled weakly and Rachel squeezed her hand.

'Why don't you stay here and finish your coffee. Have something to eat – have my croissant, please – and I'll tell him you'll be in after the morning meeting?' Lottie went to argue, but seeing her friend's determined face, she nodded meekly.

'And, look, Lottie, do you want me to tell people at work the truth – or rather, a version of the truth: that you've had a bereavement and are still a bit upset and would rather not talk about it?'

'Th-thanks, Rach. Although I suppose I'd better speak to Reg myself, and tell Guy properly.'

'No, leave Reg to me,' she said firmly. 'I'll speak to him and say you're upset and that will stop him coming near you for weeks – you know he can't deal with any kind of emotion whatsoever. And don't worry, I can tell Guy as well, that's fine.'

Rachel gave her a hug and ordered her to get some fresh air before she came back to the office. Lottie sighed. It was barely half past nine and she felt completely shattered.

Later that day, once everyone had smiled at her in the

corridor and quietly said it was good to have her back, she'd never felt more grateful to Rachel. And she'd found the normality of wading through emails and Google Docs and listening to the light chatter of her colleagues in the office comforting. She was just shutting down her computer and congratulating herself on getting through the day when a shadow appeared at her elbow.

'Hey, Lottie,' Guy said.

'Hey, Guy,' she replied with a small smile. 'How are you? Sorry, I've barely seen you today. I meant to come over and say hi.' She did feel guilty; he was definitely too good a friend to hear what had happened from Rachel instead of from her herself.

He grinned at her, but his smile was quick to disappear. 'Rachel told me about Leo. I'm so sorry. It's just so shit.'

'Thanks, and yeah, it is pretty shit.' She raised the corners of her mouth. 'I'll be fine. Might need to give our Friday nights a miss for a bit, though.'

'Of course. But we'll miss you.' Then he said all in a rush, 'And I know it doesn't feel like it at the moment, and there's obviously never a good time for it to happen, but at least it happened less than three months into the relationship and not three years. At least you hadn't had a chance to fall in love with him.'

Guy hugged her and gave her a kiss on the cheek and said he'd WhatsApp her later. But Lottie barely heard him. Her head filled with white noise and the tears she'd been holding back all day finally broke through her defences.

Chapter Seven

Before

Lottie wasn't sure she'd ever been quite as embarrassed in her whole life as she was when she woke up the morning after the golf incident, with a headache so intense it felt like she was wearing a vice clipped to her temples.

Her memories of the previous evening were fuzzy, but she remembered Leo helping her out of her dress while she'd treated him to a monologue about how she thought it was totally fine for men to wear pyjamas in bed as long as they weren't weird Wee Willie Winkie striped ones. She had no idea if Leo had agreed or not and she was very glad she couldn't remember his expression as she'd chattered on.

Now, she heaved herself upright, tutting at the ginger furball that had clearly already spent all night kneading his dirty paws into her expensive John Lewis duvet cover, but not having the strength to turf him off. Trying to ignore the drumming inside her head, she reached for her phone.

There were a couple of messages from Leo asking how she was feeling, but her head swam as she tried to compose a reply, so instead she pressed the Call button.

'Morning, how are you doing?' came Leo's warm voice after just two rings.

'Yeah, I'm good!' she replied brightly, just as another wave of nausea hit her. 'Actually, that's not true. I'm feeling a bit rough,' she confessed. 'And maybe a little embarrassed.'

'You have nothing to be embarrassed about,' Leo said immediately.

'Hmm, well you're not the one who drank God knows how many cocktails and then proceeded to witter on about cats and pyjamas to the date she was trying to impress.'

'I happen to like chatting about cats and pyjamas, especially to cute women who are kind enough to allow me to win at crazy golf.'

'Yes, I definitely *let* you win!'

Leo laughed and Lottie relaxed a fraction before she took a deep breath. 'Th-thank you, though, Leo. For taking me home and looking after me, I mean. And sorry for ruining the evening.'

'You didn't ruin the evening. I had a great time, Lottie. And I liked looking after you.' There was a pause, and despite her hangover, Lottie felt the butterflies start up in her stomach. 'I was going to suggest we maybe go to the cinema at the weekend?' he added, and the fluttering intensified.

'I'd like that,' she replied. Then smiled. 'My only stipulation is that it doesn't star Jennifer Aniston.'

'Wait, I thought you said the other night you wanted to be best friends with Jen?'

'I do, but that doesn't mean I have to like the movies she's in.'

'Because that makes sense, obviously!' He laughed then added. 'I'll have a look what's on and text you some options, how's that?'

'Sounds perfect!' Lottie beamed.

They said goodbye, and riding high from their chat, Lottie immediately emailed Reg a story about a water leak, asking if she could work from home. Of course, as soon as Rachel heard she wasn't coming in, she assumed it was because Lottie had been up all night in bed with Leo, and sent her a string of messages asking for details. Lottie replied with a 'hangover from hell' text and left it at that. She spent the rest of the day eating as many carbs as possible and taking paracetamol at four-hourly intervals until she finally felt more human. When she allowed her mind to return to the previous night, she still died a little inside at the thought of her drunken ramblings, but the tenderness Leo had shown her made her feel warm and fuzzy.

They eventually settled on watching the new Batman movie that weekend, though neither of them were entirely sure of the plot afterwards, since they'd spent quite a lot of time focusing on each other, rather than the screen in front of them, giggling like teenagers in the back row.

Their cinema trip was then followed later that week by dinner at a fancy-pants restaurant (Leo's idea, and while the meal was gorgeous, Lottie was very glad when he announced he was going to pick up the tab), and although far less alcohol was consumed, Lottie could feel the connection between them grow and grow. For the first time in as long as she could remember, she felt something close to content. Of course, there was a corner of her brain that kept telling her she was only four dates into this – whatever *this* was – but the glass-half-full part kept saying it was four dates more than she'd had – or even wanted to have – with anyone for many years. She and Leo had taken to texting each other during the day, even sneaking in a few calls in their lunchbreaks when they had time.

Her obvious happiness seemed to have the magical effect of calming Rachel down completely, so now instead of interrogating her about every detail, she and Guy just looked at her with fond grins whenever she mentioned anything about Leo, which Lottie found slightly disconcerting. And her sisters were clearly revelling in it too, though Annie had already asked twice when Lottie was going to bring Leo round for dinner so everyone could meet him.

The following Saturday, it was Lottie's turn to come up with the perfect date activity. And it might only have been the very beginning of March, but after refreshing her weather app multiple times, it seemed the sun gods were smiling on her, and so she fired off a message to Leo suggesting an afternoon walk along the river.

When she spotted him already at their meeting point on the edge of Christ Church Meadow a few hours later, she couldn't help but laugh at the bulging rucksack at his feet. He kissed her hello, for slightly longer than was probably appropriate given the number of tourists weaving around them, and then stood back and grinned at her. Lottie could practically see the chemistry buzzing between them.

'What on earth have you got in that backpack?' she said. 'We're walking down the river not across the Sahara!'

Leo laughed. 'It doesn't hurt to be prepared for all weathers. Don't forget I grew up in Scotland, which isn't exactly known for its temperate climate.'

'Oh, yes, sorry, I forgot you're a pretend Oxfordian.'

'Oxfordian? You've been spending far too much time hobnobbing with the posh students round here.'

'Thankfully, there weren't too many poshos up in Manchester when I was at uni there, or not in the English department anyway. Although I did come back down south afterwards, and I shared a flat with Annie for a bit.'

'That must have been cool house sharing with your sister?'

'It was. Though Annie can definitely be pretty full on, especially to live with!' Lottie smiled but immediately wished she hadn't made her older sister sound so scary. They stopped to watch a family of swans swim past them down the river, the younger birds still grey, fluffy and very cute, their parents watchful and protective. Once the two of them had set off again, Lottie steeled herself to say as casually as she could, 'I'd love you to meet Annie and Em. We could maybe go out for dinner sometime?'

It was only when Leo answered, 'I'd really like that too,'

and squeezed her hand, that Lottie realized quite how important his reaction to her suggestion had been to her. But now she squeezed his hand back and grinned before he added, 'Do I need to be worried? You three are pretty tight – will they grill me about my intentions towards their sister?'

'It depends what your intentions actually are.' Lottie's smile widened even further when she saw the glint in his eye. He pulled her close to him and kissed her, causing several walkers and joggers behind them on the riverbank to tut. One even asked loudly why people couldn't just move to the side if they needed to stop. 'I'm pretty sure you'll be able to hold your own,' Lottie said once they'd reluctantly pulled apart and continued to meander their way along the path. 'But I'm equally sure they'll fall under your spell within minutes anyway.'

Leo smiled. 'Well, if they're even half as lovely as you, I know I'll like them.'

Lottie laughed and laced her fingers through his, enjoying the way they fitted together like the pieces of a jigsaw. She noticed a group of teenagers sitting on a bench in front of them who had clearly clocked Leo and were giggling and whispering to each other while shooting him admiring glances. But he barely seemed to notice. 'I bet you've always been able to easily win over your girlfriends' families in the past,' she said. She knew that angling to find out how many ex-girlfriends he'd built up over the years was probably ill-advised, and that she very likely didn't want to actually know the answer, but she couldn't stop herself prodding at the sides of the question just a little bit.

'I know your game, Lottie Brown,' he said. 'You won't catch me out that easily. Let's just say that I've had enough experience to know that *no* answer to the question "how many exes do you have?" is the right one. Anyway, who wants to talk about the past when there are much more interesting things to talk about?'

Lottie glanced at him curiously for a second, but he took the opportunity to pull her towards him again and her thoughts were carried off on the wind as she let her mouth melt into his. When they resumed their walk a few minutes later, she said, 'OK, let's not talk about the past. Let's talk about ... what countries have you never been to but really want to?'

'What, is this not enough for you?' Leo laughed, sticking his arm out and waving it towards the river and the greenery beyond it.

'I mean, I love Oxford, but God, I wish I was wandering through a pretty little Croatian fishing village on my way to a tiny restaurant only the locals know about. Just imagine watching the sunset while drinking a glass of wine and eating freshly caught calamari,' she replied dreamily.

'When you put it like that, I'm completely there with you. Or maybe we could be making our way through one of New Zealand's national parks, surrounded by lush green on all sides before launching ourselves off a huge zipline through the trees.'

'That also sounds pretty tempting,' Lottie agreed with a grin. 'As long as the sun is shining, and I'm not sat at my desk,

I'm generally happy. But you've made New Zealand sound amazing – can I go and book a flight now?'

'Only if I can come too,' he said and squeezed her hand. Lottie smiled up at him and a feeling of total contentment washed over her, until Leo broke into her thoughts. 'Is it me or has it got really dark all of a sudden? I hope it's not about to—'. But before he could finish his sentence, huge dollops of rain splashed onto Lottie's face and they both dived for the cover of the trees, along with every other person who'd previously been enjoying a leisurely walk down by the river.

'Oh my God, it's torrential!' she cried as the rain found its way through the branches and soaked every part of their bodies.

'Put this on,' Leo instructed, rooting around in his rucksack and handing her a waterproof. It was clearly made for a man almost twice as tall as Lottie and with arms double the length – a man very like Leo in fact – but Lottie gladly folded herself into it and pulled the hood up, despite struggling to see anything other than grey waterproof as it came so far over her eyes. 'You have no right to look that cute in an oversized utilitarian waterproof, you know,' Leo said into her ear, and Lottie couldn't help but giggle.

'What are you going to wear, though?' she said. 'Don't tell me you brought two oversized utilitarian waterproofs with you in that rucksack of yours?'

'Sadly not.' He shook his head ruefully. 'I think when the rain eases off a bit we might just have to make a run for it, and I'll try to dodge the raindrops as best I can.'

'You'll get soaked!' Lottie protested.

'A bit of water won't kill me. And we can probably hop on the number forty-three bus on the main road – it goes pretty much to the door of my house. Do you want to come back to mine and dry off there?' he added in a tone that Lottie thought was probably an attempt to be nonchalant, but ended up sounding rushed and embarrassed. A delightful chill ran down her spine that was nothing to do with the pelting rain.

She smiled. 'As long as you have radiators and towels then you're on.'

'I might even stretch to a hot toddy,' he replied.

Half an hour later, drenched but laughing, they jumped off the bus, and Leo led them the few hundred metres to his house. The rain was still biblical, and Leo's hair was plastered to his head, drops of water raining down his cheeks, but somehow the look suited him. Lottie was aware she looked more bedraggled than come-to-bed, but she was finding it difficult to concentrate on anything except the man in front of her, her heart pounding in her chest.

'Well, um, here's my humble abode,' he said, as he opened the front door and ushered her inside. 'Chuck your shoes on the mat there and let's get these wet clothes off. I mean ... Sorry, I didn't mean ...'

Lottie laughed and put a calming hand on his arm. 'I will if you will,' she said with a mischievous raise of her eyebrow.

She saw a whole gamut of emotions pass across Leo's face before he finally settled on raising an eyebrow to match hers, and the sexiest grin she'd ever seen spread across his face. He said nothing, but pulled his sopping top up over his head. Lottie's eyes widened as she took in his well-defined chest with just the right amount of hair. His eyes on hers the whole time, he slipped his trousers off and tossed them on the floor, his entire body now on display. Still neither of them said anything as he closed the gap between them and slowly pushed down her hood and kissed her hungrily on the lips. Then, without breaking eye contact with her, he unzipped her dripping jacket, leaving it in a pool on the floor, took her hand and led her upstairs.

'If I'd known how much oversized utilitarian waterproofs turned you on, I might have worn one before today,' Lottie murmured later when they were lying in bed, both in that delicious state between snoozing and wakefulness.

'Are you telling me you wanted to sleep with me before now? You should have said,' Leo teased her lazily.

'You were the one giving me PDAs in the middle of crazy-golf bars, I think you'll find,' she batted back.

'Is this where I make a lame joke about a hole in one?'

'Not if you want a repeat performance of earlier any time soon.'

'But you're not wearing a huge grey cagoule. I just don't know if that's going to work for me.' He grinned.

'Oh, and there was me about to try out the move that *Cosmopolitan* magazine promised would never fail to turn a man on . . .' she said mock-regretfully, throwing herself back against the pillow.

'I mean,' Leo stammered, 'I suppose you could give it a go just to see.'

'I suppose I could, yes.'

'I'm absolutely starving,' Leo announced quite a while later, getting up to fetch them both a glass of water. 'Fancy some wine and a takeaway?'

'Now you're talking!'

Full of chow mein and prawn toast, they lay curled up on the sofa together that evening, scrolling through Leo's somewhat eclectic Spotify playlists.

'Are you a secret Elton John fanatic?' Lottie said, heaving her food-laden body back up straight. 'I think you've got pretty much every song he's ever released on here.'

'Well, I wouldn't say fanatic, exactly . . . '

'I would! Look, you've even got those weird ones he did when he was high the whole time in the eighties.'

'It's mostly so my dad can listen to them, obviously.'

'Obviously,' she said with a grin. 'And it takes one to know one – a fanatic, I mean.' She stopped grinning and made her expression much more serious. 'Maybe it's a bit early on in our relationship for me to be telling you my deepest, darkest secrets, and I totally understand if you want to call a halt to proceedings right now – but I think you should know that I am a closet, or maybe not so closet, Elton John groupie.'

Lottie looked closely at Leo, whose expression remained impassive.

'How bad an affliction are we talking?' he asked gravely.

'I have all the weird albums from the eighties, despite not even being alive myself then. And, erm, I've also got all the greatest hits albums, even though they're all the same.'

'Including the live greatest hits albums from Madison Square Gardens that he released in 2000 and 2007?'

'Oh my God, you're an even bigger fan then me! I actually don't think I have those two. I'll have to download them immediately!'

His mouth twitched. 'Before I make my final diagnosis, dare I ask what your favourite song is? Something obscure I – or rather, my dad – has never heard of, I presume?'

Lottie looked a little sheepish. 'Actually it's very basic, I'm afraid. It's "Your Song".'

'*My* song?' Leo looked confused for a second, then his face split into a smile. 'Oh, I see. That's funny.'

'It's a *little bit* funny, you mean? Sorry, I couldn't resist.' She laughed and Leo rolled his eyes good-naturedly. 'Anyway, why is that funny? What's *your* favourite Elton song?'

'I do love "Your Song", but it's just too hard to pick only one as my favourite.'

'OK, let's do this properly. What Elton songs were on your Spotify Wrapped most played from last year?' Lottie tucked her legs under her on the sofa and faced her body towards him.

'Hmm, definitely "I Guess That's Why They Call it the Blues", probably "Rocket Man" and maybe "The One".'

'I can't remember how "The One" goes,' Lottie said, frowning.

'Call yourself an Elton fanatic?' he scoffed. 'It starts all piano-y with a load of swirly whooshing in the background.'

'No, it's not ringing a bell.' She shook her head and tried unsuccessfully not to laugh.

'It goes ...'

As Leo launched into what sounded suspiciously like a wail, Lottie didn't even try to stop her giggles. 'I thought you said you played the guitar! I assumed you must be vaguely musical, at least. You might be a Premier League Elton fanatic, but you've got a way to go before you can become an Elton impersonator.' Leo snorted and began shaking with laughter too. 'Ow stop, my stomach's trying to digest 3,541 calories of Chinese food – it can't cope with hysterics as well!' she gasped. 'We could just listen to the song, you know on that Spotify thing you like so much.'

Leo scrolled through his app. 'Right, here we go then.' Lottie lay back on the sofa as the opening notes began to play from the speakers. 'See, I told you it was all piano-y and there are the swooshing sounds.'

'Shh! I want to listen properly.'

They were both silent for a couple of minutes as the room filled with music and the song swelled to its crescendo.

'It's still a classic Elton masterpiece,' Leo sighed.

Lottie nodded. 'Yeah, as soon as he started singing, I recognised it after all. I think it's one of those amazing songs that gets a bit forgotten by most people.'

'We could make it "our song" like they do in teen movies,' Leo joked.

'It would be better if "Your Song" was our song, surely,' she replied, before they both started giggling. 'Stop, my stomach can't take any more laughing, I told you!'

'Fine,' Leo said when they'd calmed down again and he'd wrapped his arms around her. 'As neither of us appear to be "most people", let's say "The One" is our One.'

Lottie smiled in agreement then turned her face up to his and kissed him.

Chapter Eight

Before

It was five weeks after Lottie had inhaled lime pickle in the curry house, and those five weeks had felt both like five days and five years of talking, laughing, listening to Elton John, and the kind of kissing that stopped her brain from concentrating on anything other than the feel of Leo's lips on her own. The embarrassment of crazy golf felt like a lifetime ago now, and, while she definitely didn't feel the need to drink four lethal cocktails in the space of sixty minutes, she felt secure enough now to know that if she did, Leo would be there to look after her.

Guy had asked her the other day if she and Leo were officially girlfriend and boyfriend, and she had laughed at him and said they weren't in the school playground now. What she'd really wanted to say is that it felt weird putting an ordinary label on what she and Leo had – because that supposed that it was ordinary to feel this way after only five weeks, and she knew what they had was truly special.

Today, however, her stomach was flip-flopping with nerves. She was on her way to Leo's house, where Leo's cousin would be, too. It was the first time either of them had introduced a family member or friend into their bubble, and, to even things up, Lottie had played diary ping-pong with her sisters until they'd settled on a Sunday later that month, and she'd told Leo it had been decreed that he was coming to Annie's to meet not only her sisters, but also their husbands and kids.

She couldn't wait to show him off to Em and Annie, but she was also apprehensive – she wanted them to not just like him, but to love him (almost) as much as she did. She'd told herself so often it wasn't a competition, but Luca had universally won over the whole family almost as soon as Em had introduced him. And even Charlie – who Lottie still didn't really feel like she had a proper connection with as he seemed to inhabit such a different world of hedge funds and bonds – had impressed everyone with how clearly devoted he was to Annie, even if he had seemed a bit bland in other respects.

While she hated to admit it, Lottie sometimes caught not just her mum but even her sisters glancing at her in pity at big family parties when she turned up very much on her own. Maybe when Annie and Em met Leo, the family would finally see her as a proper grown-up with a relationship that was just as perfect as her sisters'.

The previous evening, Leo had been both excited and apprehensive about her meeting Ross, and while she completely understood how he was feeling, still a contrary part of her wanted him to have no doubts at all.

'Ross can be a difficult nut to crack sometimes,' Leo had explained as they'd FaceTimed each other from their respective beds. 'He's always been pretty protective of me and even more so recently ...' There'd been a slight pause and for a moment Lottie had wondered whether their connection had dropped, but then he'd carried on. 'Well, yeah, anyway, he can be a bit tough on the outside, but once you get to know him, he's one of the good ones, you know? He was like a proper brother to me growing up and I owe him a lot.' There was another slight pause, then he added, 'And of course I know all his secrets so he has to be nice to me!'

Lottie had laughed along, but she had lain in bed that night worrying how tough a nut Ross would prove to be. He hadn't seemed very friendly when she and Leo had bumped into each other in M&S, but he was related to Leo and he seemed pretty close to perfect to her, so surely his cousin couldn't be too awful, could he?

She'd woken up with dark circles so heavily weighing down her eyes that all the brightening, anti-wrinkle, glow-to-go serum in the world couldn't shift them. So she trowelled on primer, foundation, concealer, illuminator and bronzer, until her face felt satisfyingly unlike her own, and hoped her personality would be as sparkling as her complexion now felt. She hadn't told her sisters she was meeting

Ross today. She could have done with some of their love and support, but she'd known it would lead to the inevitable outrage that she was meeting Leo's family before they'd been introduced themselves.

Now, arriving at Leo's front door, she shook herself, plastered her best 'I'm a perfectly normal, smart, interesting, funny woman' smile on her face, and knocked.

Leo greeted her with a kiss that almost made her forget all of her worries, followed by an encouraging smile and a whisper of, 'He's going to love you.' Then, he propelled her into the lounge and thrust her in front of the man sitting on the sofa. 'Lottie, meet my cousin Ross. Ross, meet my girlfriend Lottie!'

There was an awkward moment when Lottie and Ross's greetings clashed in the air, but then Ross pushed himself up off the sofa and stuck out his hand. 'Pleased to meet you, Lottie,' he said stiffly.

'And you!' Lottie smiled, the weight of her make-up settling into the lines around her mouth. 'It's nice to meet you properly, and not in the middle of Marks and Spencer.'

'Hey, I thought that was *our* meet-cute!' Leo laughed. Seeing Ross's face barely move, Lottie felt nerves rise in her throat acidicly and she regretted the vat of coffee she'd gulped down that morning to help pep her up.

'Right,' Leo said, 'we thought we might grab lunch in town maybe?' He placed his hand gently on her waist. 'Are you hungry?'

'You know me, always hungry!' Lottie cringed at herself

and clamped her mouth shut to stop herself saying anything else horribly try-hard. She was far too aware of how vital it was that she and Ross not just got on, but really liked each other. Thankfully, Leo laughed heartily, though Ross continued to remain impassive, as if he wasn't really in the room with them.

Leo chatted happily as the three of them walked into the centre of Oxford and eventually settled on the Lion's Head for their pub lunch. Neither Lottie nor Ross said anything directly to each other, all of the conversation passing through Leo. But when Leo insisted he be the one to go to the bar and order their drinks and food, leaving just the two of them together, Lottie felt she had no alternative but to break the awkward silence. It certainly didn't look like Ross was going to take the initiative.

'So, Leo says you live in Scotland?' she tried. Then when all he did was nod, she added, 'Whereabouts are you from?'

'Outside Edinburgh. You wouldn't know it.'

'Right.' There was silence again. 'Do you like it up there?'

'Yes.'

'I've been up to Edinburgh a few times for the festival. It's a lovely city.'

'It is. Especially when all the tourists have gone home.'

Nausea began to swirl in Lottie's chest. She was gripped by a very English need to fill the gaping chasm between them, but she was fast running out of polite conversation in the face of his rude, monosyllabic responses. She played with the seam of her jeans and searched for something else to say. 'What do you like—'

'Look, Lottie—' Ross said.

They were both interrupted by Leo arriving back with their drinks. 'Food shouldn't be long, although apparently they've run out of "applewood smoked bacon" so you're getting common-or-garden bacon on your burger, Ross, I'm afraid.' He grinned. 'What have you two been gassing about? Hope you haven't been spilling all my secrets to my girlfriend, eh!'

Lottie was surprised by the hard look Leo gave his cousin, but then immediately wondered if she'd imagined it as he clapped him on the back and grinned again.

As she sipped her wine and felt the cool liquid hit her body, she tried to relax. Halfway down his pint, Ross seemed to loosen up a little, too, and the conversation began to flow more easily. Ross even laughed at a couple of her jokes, and he asked her what she'd thought about the film she and Leo had watched a few weeks before at the cinema. Their food arrived and they all hungrily got stuck in. Leo nicked a chip from Lottie's plate, and they both took the mick out of Ross when he added a blob of tomato ketchup to his roast dinner. When he went off to get another round of drinks, Leo immediately grabbed Lottie's hand and said, 'He really likes you! I knew he would – how could he not, obviously? But I know Ross, and he's definitely your fan.'

Lottie allowed herself to bask in the glow of passing the first test and getting a big tick from the closest person her boyfriend had to a brother. But it wasn't long before her smile started to slip. When Ross came back clutching their three drinks, Lottie could immediately sense a different vibe, from the set of his face to the way he turned his body away from her and solely towards his cousin. It was as if all the warmth that had built up over the last hour had been washed away and in its place the awkward frostiness had returned.

Leo himself didn't seem to notice, and he launched into a long story about a hilarious incident that had happened with some friends who Ross also seemed to know. Lottie tried hard to listen attentively and join in with their laughter – though she noticed Ross's smile never quite reached his eyes – but she found herself tuning out and instead tuning in to Ross's body language. It very clearly said that he'd rather be anywhere but at a pub table with his cousin and his cousin's girlfriend. Lottie racked her brain to think of anything she could have said to make his demeanour towards her change so suddenly, but the last thing she remembered saying before he left the table to go to the bar was that she'd like a medium-sized glass of wine. Leo had joked that she should just have a large one and be done with it, and she'd laughed and admitted she'd only said medium to be polite and a large glass of wine would be lovely, thank you. Surely Ross hadn't taken against her just because of that?

She was shaken out of her introspection when she felt Leo move beside her. 'Just nipping to the loo,' he said.

Lottie froze. She picked imaginary fluff off her jumper for a few seconds, willing herself to be strong and ask Ross why he was acting so strangely towards her. She shuffled her chair closer to the table and sat up straighter, opening her mouth to speak, but Ross beat her to it. And she quickly wished he hadn't.

'Look, Lottie, this thing you have with Leo, it can't go any further.'

'W-what do you mean?' she stuttered.

'I mean it can't go any further. Leo isn't in the right place for a relationship right now, and I don't want you getting any ideas.'

'Ideas?'

'Yes. That whatever you think the two of you have is serious or going anywhere. Because it isn't. It can't.'

Lottie stared at him. Her brain whirred with a million different responses before settling on, 'Oh.'

Another silence stretched between them. Lottie's eyes never met Ross's. She cleared her throat, chucked a huge mouthful of wine down it then took a deep breath. 'But why?' she asked.

Ross's face darkened. 'Because there are things about Leo he won't have told you. And it's best you don't know. You seem like a nice girl, but you just need to back off, OK? There is no relationship, this isn't going anywhere. I'm telling you for both your sakes. You need to leave Leo alone.'

Lottie's head snapped up at the intensity of his words and saw his eyes flash with an emotion she couldn't read. All she knew was it wasn't one she wanted to confront. She shrank into her seat.

She felt Leo's hand on her shoulder as he came back from the bathroom, and she turned and gave him a smile she knew was more of a grimace and hurried off to the loo herself. She sat in the cubicle, her heart racing, and felt her initial shock and fright turn to anger. How dare this man tell her what she should do? How dare he frame it as if he was doing it for her sake? Maybe he was just jealous his cousin seemed so happy with his new girlfriend because his own life was so sad and lonely up in 'somewhere near Edinburgh'. Whatever the reason, how the fuck dare he?

Lottie pulled up her jeans, washed her hands and strode out of the bathroom and back over to their table. She draped her arms around Leo's neck, and as he turned his head to meet hers, she gave him the kind of kiss that was definitely not meant for the eyes of the children on the table next to theirs. It was a while before either of them pulled away, put when she did, she immediately stared up at Ross, who was jabbing hard at his phone. 'I wish you were staying at mine tonight,' she breathed into Leo's ear.

'Jesus, me too,' he whispered, his hand snaking round her bum and drawing her in.

Lottie piled on the PDAs as the three of them left the pub and wandered on to the busy Oxford streets beyond, taking great pleasure in sneaking glances at Ross's stony face.

'I've just had a great idea,' Leo said, stroking his fingers against hers as they came to the crossroads where Lottie needed to head off, 'you should come with us to my parents' tomorrow, Lottie.' But before she could so much as open her mouth, Ross had moved between them.

'Mate, don't forget you promised your dad we'd go to that

airfield he's been going on about. Not sure Lottie will want to be dragged round that in this weather.'

Lottie went to argue that *of course* she wouldn't mind looking at old aeroplanes in the middle of nowhere on a cold Sunday afternoon, but Leo got there before her.

'Of course, I'd forgotten I'd promised Dad. Don't worry, Lots, I won't subject you to that.' He chuckled. 'Meeting the parents and making you look at planes would be the quickest way to end a relationship, I'm sure.'

Lottie half-expected Ross to suddenly backtrack and suggest she did come after all if it would spell the end of the 'thing' she had with Leo – *dickhead* – but he remained quiet.

After she'd said a *very* heartfelt goodbye to Leo and told Ross what a *pleasure* it had been to meet him, she spent the rest of the afternoon seething at just how rude, arrogant and downright presumptuous Ross had been. She couldn't decide if he had taken a dislike to her because of something she'd said – although she still couldn't fathom what – or if maybe he was jealous of his cousin. Or maybe he was just a horrible man who liked causing trouble. But then again she'd seen glimpses of a kind, self-deprecating, chatty guy while they were eating lunch. It didn't make sense.

Perhaps there *was* some genuine reason that she and Leo shouldn't be together? Though unless Leo was an undercover MI5 spy, she couldn't for the life of her think what that reason could be.

*

She was still both outraged and confused by the whole situation a few days later when Ross was safely on his way back up the trainline to Scotland.

'Ross is very different to you, isn't he?' she said one evening as she lay in bed with Leo's face in front of her on FaceTime.

'I guess.' Leo shrugged. 'We were thick as thieves growing up, though, and he's always been there for me, through ... through everything. I know he can sometimes be a bit intense, but he's such a kind-hearted, loyal guy.'

'Mmm,' Lottie replied non-committedly. She was more confused than ever about the way he'd behaved towards her. Part of her wanted to ask Leo for Ross's number and message him demanding an explanation. She couldn't get the look in his eyes when he'd told her to stay away from his cousin out of her head. There had been real anger in his stare, but also something else, something that felt to Lottie like fear. None of it made any sense, but it was also creating a barrier between her and Leo, for her at least. She took a deep breath and added as nonchalantly as she could, 'He said something to me about there being things I don't know about you. What do you think he meant?'

Lottie was surprised to see Leo's face darken and his lips curl at the edges. 'What? When did he say that?'

She tried to keep her tone light. 'Just when you went to the loo, I think.' She blinked and when she looked back at the screen, she wondered whether she'd imagined his furious expression, because he was smiling now.

93

'I'm sure he just meant that we haven't been together very long. Maybe he thought we don't know each other that well,' Leo said, and then added a little sheepishly, 'As I said, he can be a bit intense and he's always pretty protective of me. But he's so genuine. I just know you two will hit it off when you spend more time together.'

Lottie couldn't help but smile back at him. 'You're right, I probably just need to get to know him a bit better,' she said, determined not to let her first impression of Ross taint her perfect relationship with Leo. 'I can't wait for you to meet Em and Annie in a couple of weeks. And Alex and Dante are going to love having another person to give them endless piggybacks!'

Leo smiled. 'They sound very cute. I bet you're a great auntie.'

'Luckily, I know the way to their hearts – a secret stash of sweets and tickling them until they're almost sick. Although I don't think my little sister would appreciate knowing that.' She laughed. 'And the perks of being an auntie mean that I don't have to deal with the inevitable low after the sugar high when they play up and won't go to bed afterwards.' She swallowed. 'Do you think you'll ever want kids?' she asked. There was a pause, during which Lottie realized just how big a question it was to ask late at night over FaceTime, and she opened her mouth to apologise, but then stopped herself, realising that she desperately wanted to know the answer.

'I think so, yeah,' Leo replied eventually. 'I've not thought about it much until recently, but I guess everyone wants to leave behind some kind of legacy when they're gone, don't they? What about you?'

Her heart banged against her chest, and she gave herself a second before she answered. 'Yes, I think I do too,' she said.

'Good.' Leo smiled a little shyly, before laughing and adding, 'And one day when they're old enough and we're shopping in M&S we could totally embarrass them by casually telling them how we met in the dessert aisle!'

'If we were Instagram influencers, we'd already have done a deal and sorted a load of M&S-sponsored posts by now and got them to give us chocolate mousse for life,' Lottie joked, while her brain tried to process the fact Leo was casually referring to the children they might have together.

'Jesus, that would be the dream, wouldn't it?'

'If they threw in some of those delicious white chocolate bakery cookies they make, then, absolutely. So . . . ' Lottie took a breath. 'How many kids do you think you'll want?'

'Well,' Leo said, 'being an only child myself, I'd want *loads*!'

'When you say loads, what do you mean? Three, four?'

'At least five. If you're going to do it, you might as well do it properly.'

'Is that right? Not sure I fancy popping out five babies – can you imagine!'

Leo winked and said, 'I've heard it can be quite fun actually making them though!'

And they both grinned.

Chapter Nine

Before

It was one of those perfect early-spring days when the patches of sky finally outnumber the clouds. The river was cast in a blue haze and the daffodils proudly trumpeted their wares along the banks. Lottie allowed her bicycle to come to a standstill and turned her face upwards to feel that first heat of sun on her face. 'This is the life!'

Leo brought his bike to a stop beside her and laughed. 'You remind me of one of those daffodils, trying to drink in the sun. You haven't stopped smiling since we left the train station.'

'Well, I wasn't smiling so hard when we hit that massive stretch of mud before the path proper!' She grimaced. 'It's all right for you with your hired mountain bike with all its fancy gears and fat tyres, but poor Bertha here nearly sank.'

'I've never met a girl who actually has a name for her bike. You're so cute.' Leo said, shuffling over to give her a kiss on the nose.

'Mind you don't scratch Bertha with your massive wheel!' she warned, before giving him a proper kiss on the lips. 'Come on, we best get going if we're going to make it to the lock and have that drink you promised me and still get back to the station again before it gets dark.'

'Race you!' he shouted, pedalling off and switching to top gear before Lottie had barely had time to get back on her seat.

An hour later, they were sitting outside the pub at Sandford Lock, sipping delicate half-pints of lager, while they kept an eye on their bikes next to them and shivered a little when the sun hid itself behind the fluffy, white clouds.

'I love Saturdays when you have Monday off work. Isn't it the best knowing you won't have that Sunday-night feeling and that you still have two whole days of not working stretching ahead of you?' Lottie sighed happily. 'I'm really looking forward to dinner tonight,' she said, picturing the posh burger with mac-'n'-cheese-topped fries and fried gherkins that she'd already decided she was going to order that evening.

'Let me guess, you read the menu last night and made an exact mental note of everything you're going to order,' Leo said, shaking his head fondly. 'One of these days—' He was cut off by his phone vibrating on the table between them. He checked the screen. 'It's Ross. Do you mind if I get it? I'll be quick.'

Lottie nodded and smiled, though her stomach clenched uneasily at the mention of his cousin's name. 'Course.'

'Ross, mate, how you doing? Oh, yeah. Of course.'

Leo turned his body away from her. She couldn't hear Ross's side of the conversation, but she saw Leo's shoulders slump, and then he got up and walked into the car park behind them without even a glance back at her. Lottie shivered yet again and drank a large mouthful of her beer. It was typical that Ross would call in the middle of their perfect afternoon and steal Leo away. She drummed her fingers impatiently on the table. By the time she spotted Leo walking back across the car park, hunched over and his fingers jabbing at his phone, Lottie was shivering so much from the cold that her whole body felt on edge and uptight.

'Everything OK? You were gone for ever,' she said, more snappily than she'd meant to, the cold worming its way inside her head.

'Yes, fine, why wouldn't it be?' he replied, barely raising his head to look at her as he continued to thumb his phone screen. 'Can we go now, though?'

'I'm the one who's been sitting here on my own waiting for you!' she said. Before quickly adding, 'And you haven't had a chance to finish your drink.'

'I don't want it, don't worry. Right, let's get this over with.'

He busied himself putting his phone in his pocket, zipping up his jacket and picking up his bike from the grass verge. Lottie just stared at him. 'Are you sure you're OK?' she asked, more softly this time.

'I'm fine.' He gave her a brief smile before pushing off. Lottie quickly grabbed her own bike and scrambled to follow him. But, whereas on their way down to the lock they'd cycled beside each other down the path, now Leo positioned himself in front of her and accelerated away whenever she looked like she was going to catch up with him.

They reached the station in what seemed like no time. Lottie tried to make conversation standing on the platform as the minutes ticked slowly by, in the way time always does when you're waiting for a train, but Leo was almost mono-syllabic in his answers, so she gave up and let the quiet settle between them, punctuated only occasionally by the rush of high-speed trains hurtling through the station. She allowed the silence to stretch across the ten-minute train journey while she alternated between anger at Ross for poisoning her day with Leo, and worry that actually it was something she herself had done, though she had absolutely no idea what. Once they'd fed their tickets through the machines at Oxford station and Leo was all set to climb on his bike to ride it to the hire centre, Lottie couldn't help herself any longer.

'Leo, will you just tell me what's wrong?' she burst out. 'Is it something I said? Is Ross OK?'

Leo straightened up and turned towards her. 'Sorry, Lottie. I'm not feeling great, to be honest. I started feeling a bit weird earlier and I've got a right headache now. Can we put dinner on hold till tomorrow evening? We've got Monday off together anyway. I'll cycle back to the hire centre and drop the bike on my own, and you can just head home from here. It'll be easier for you, won't it?'

Lottie knew she wasn't doing a very good job of hiding her surprise, but Leo didn't seem to notice. He bent over, kissed her cheek and said softly, 'I'm sorry, I just know I won't be very good company this afternoon. I'll text you later though, OK?' Before she could reply he quickly cycled off through the taxi rank, narrowly missing a double-decker bus that was indicating to pull out. Lottie took a sharp gasp of air in and her heartbeat quickened, but even once she'd watched him safely navigate his way through the buses and taxis and out of her sight, her heart still banged in her chest.

Did he really have a headache? He'd definitely had a migraine the previous weekend when he was supposed to have been meeting Annie and Em. Lottie had built herself up for the momentous occasion all week, but he'd been so poorly when she went round to his place that she'd known immediately she was going to have to cancel. He hadn't seemed that ill today though, she mused. Maybe Ross had realized Leo was out with her and said something during their phone call to warn him off? Or had Lottie herself done something to annoy him? She just didn't know what to think, and it unnerved her. What she did know was that she didn't want to spend the rest of her Saturday going over and over everything she'd said that day, trying to figure out if that was the thing that had caused Leo to start acting so weirdly. She reached for her phone and tapped out a quick WhatsApp to her sisters asking if either of them were free later. Within seconds, she could see Annie was typing.

God, men can be such wimps when it comes to headaches. I swear if they had periods, too, the world of painkillers would be VERY different. Sorry, Lottie, we're going to that dinner at Charlie's boss's, remember? Although if you'd like to swap and go in my place, then be my guest, seriously!

Lottie winced on her sister's behalf, knowing even ambitious, career-driven Annie was never going to enjoy spending her Saturday night surrounded by boring work people discussing boring financial talk. Her phone lit up again as Em's message hit the chat.

Poor Leo, hope he's OK. Has he tried those sticks that you swipe across your forehead? They work wonders with the boys when I don't want to give them more Calpol. Or maybe he should see his doctor, as that's two in a week he's had, isn't it? I'd love to come round this evening but Alex is having his first sleepover and he's spent all day making a duvet tent in his bedroom. I can't imagine any of us are going to get any sleep tonight! Why don't you have a gorgeous evening in and pamper yourself then watch something amazingly trashy on Netflix, Lots? I just wish me and Annie could join you! Text us later, OK? Xx

Lottie smiled sadly and her stomach twisted. She loved both her sisters fiercely, but if she was completely truthful, she was jealous of Em and her gorgeous life in her perfect house with her beautiful children and handsome, adoring Luca. And she envied Annie with her complete self-belief that she could make anything happen if she only worked hard enough, plus her amazing career and hedge-fund-manager husband, even if he was a bit stuffy. And sometimes, despite how close the three of them were, and how they knew each other inside out, she couldn't help feeling they didn't understand her. She could spend any evening having a bath and watching Netflix on her own – in fact, before Leo, that's exactly what she'd done pretty much every Saturday night she wasn't with her sisters. But what she really wanted was to have what they had: a house and a family, and to stop being the odd one out.

She started her cycle back home and tried to give herself a pep talk, stopping off at the supermarket for a bottle of wine and a family-sized tub of tiramisu that would test her will power to the max. By the time she'd put her bike away, unpacked her shopping and had a shower, her phone screen was full of notifications from Leo.

I'm sorry I bailed on you this evening and I'm sure I'll feel better tomorrow, think I just need to chill this eve xx

Going to get into bed now and try to sleep it off. I really enjoyed cycling with you and Bertha in the sunshine – hopefully we can do it again soon. Xx

Hope you have a good evening and can't wait to see you tomorrow. Leo xx

Chapter Ten

Lottie supposed she was lucky that her only direct experience of funerals over the thirty-two years she'd been on the earth were her grandparents'. But having never been to a service for anyone under the age of seventy, let alone a man struck down in his prime – and even less so a man who fewer than three weeks before had told her he'd fallen in love with her – her brain was a jumble of emotions.

Rather than allow herself to focus on how she was feeling, she'd spent the last few days agonising over what to wear. Her grandparents' funerals had largely been head-to-toe black affairs, but her instinct was that a memorial for such a young man should be less gloomy and more colourful. But how colourful was colourful? Ross had messaged her a couple of times over the last week to ask how she was, and their exchanges had been pretty perfunctory, especially on her part, and she hadn't felt able to broach the dress code question. So she'd turned to her sisters for advice, and Em had rifled through her wardrobe and picked out a pretty navy blue dress studded with tiny yellow buttercups that fell just above her knee, which, paired with tights, felt respectable. Annie had agreed but said she should also wear her favourite yellow cardigan on top as a nod to the late-April sunshine and pointed out that if she took a handbag large enough, she could stuff it inside if all the other guests had gone for funereal black.

Her sisters assured her she looked both pretty and appropriate, but as soon as the taxi arrived and Em pressed a final packet of tissues into her hand, she immediately began to doubt not only her outfit, but also her decision to go to the funeral in the first place. As the car pulled up at the burial ground and the driver gruffly said he hoped the service went OK, she realized she didn't have much choice but to leave the comfort of the cab and join the people scattered in groups about the entrance.

As the taxi pulled away and she was left stranded between four or five large groups of strangers, a horrifying thought suddenly struck her. Not only did she not know anyone else at all, but she couldn't even be sure they were all gathered here for Leo – what if his friends and family were all waiting at a different entrance, or what if they'd already congregated inside the grounds? What if she was at the funeral of the completely wrong person?

She fiddled with her cardigan buttons and rearranged her handbag on her shoulder, which suddenly felt far too big and cumbersome for the occasion, and looked around her. There was a gentle buzz of low chatter and the clusters of people were all dressed smartly in an array of colours, except for a gathering of older-looking couples whose coats were darker and more sombre. All around them were trees and pretty clumps of crocuses and primroses, and the smell of freshly cut grass filled the air. If Lottie hadn't known better, she'd have thought she'd just walked into a particularly polite garden party. Just as she was contemplating whether she should take the excruciating walk over to the smallest, least-intimidating-looking group in front of her, she spotted Ross making his way out of the trees and into the clearing where they all stood. He clapped his hands lightly together and cleared his throat. Quiet immediately fell.

'Hi, everyone,' he called, his voice shaking a little. 'Would you like to come this way?'

Everyone started to murmur and move forward, and while Lottie immediately lost sight of Ross, she was able to hide herself among the mourners as they began to walk slowly as one. They rounded the corner and continued down a gravel path lined with saplings on both sides, set in a meadow dotted with pretty wild flowers in shades of pinks and blues.

A small party of people came into view at the front, and a few steps further on, Lottie saw it was headed up by four men carrying a long willow-coloured burden on their shoulders. Her breath immediately caught in her throat. It may have been topped with a cascade of anemones, tulips and forget-me-nots, but nothing could disguise the fact that it was a woven wicker-like casket. It hit her like a punch to the stom-ach. Leo's body was in that coffin. Nausea rose into Lottie's throat, her heart began to race and she felt sweat prickle her back despite the cooling April breeze. Her trembling legs somehow kept propelling her forward but her chest was so tight she couldn't get enough air into her lungs, however deeply she tried to breathe.

She'd had three whole weeks without him, but it was only now that she fully understood the reality. Leo was dead. He was never coming back. Her legs stopped moving, and she didn't even care about the people behind her stumbling then turning to glance at her curiously. She couldn't go on, but neither could she go back. But then she felt a soft tug on her arm and she was encircled by a group of darkly dressed, grey-haired men and women, one of whom slipped her arm through hers and said gently, 'It's been such a shock, hasn't it, hen? But it's important we all come to pay our respects. You'll feel better that you did, believe me.'

Lottie blinked and found herself nodding. She allowed herself to be led on down the path, though her eyes were fixed on the ground. The same calm voice kept up a gentle patter as they slowly continued their procession, with the rest of the group commenting in low voices, 'What a lovely idea,' and 'It's so peaceful here, isn't it?'

Gradually, Lottie managed to get her breathing under control, although the knot in her throat was still just as big. She squeezed her hands into fists in her pockets, digging her nails into her palms, and forced herself to look up. The procession grew quieter as the landscape changed to denser woodland, and a few hundred metres later, they came to a stop. The elderly lady gave her arm a gentle squeeze before unhooking her hand and giving her a sad smile. Lottie raised the corners of her mouth gratefully and tried to breathe in and out as slowly and deeply as she could.

The celebrant began to speak, but Lottie found she couldn't take in any of the words he was saying, so she just concentrated on the ebb and flow of his voice while keeping her breathing as even as possible. When he had finished, Ross stepped forward, and Lottie's heart began to thump in her chest again as she saw the paper in his hand tremble. He cleared his throat and started to talk in his distinctive Scottish lilt.

'Thank you all for coming today. I know how much it means to Eddie and Margaret, as well as me and Mum and Dad.' He swallowed and Lottie followed his glance to the four people standing just behind him to his right, who gave him watery smiles in return. 'And I also know how bummed Leo would be that he isn't able to have a drink and catch up with all his favourite people gathered here in one place.' There was a small chuckle of laughter and Ross smiled briefly before looking down at the pages in his hands. 'It's hard to believe he's been taken from us so soon and we're never going to see him again.' His voice broke and he squeezed his eyes shut for a moment. Lottie pulled the sleeve of her cardigan across her cheeks and looked at the ground, willing herself not to let out the howl that was building at the top of her throat. She glanced over at Leo's parents; his mum was dabbing at her face with a tissue while Leo's dad placed a protective arm across her shoulders.

After a pause, Ross began speaking again, his voice sounding stronger and less crinkled with every sentence. 'But while he can't be here in person, Leo can most definitely be here in spirit. And we can learn from his spirit. Just like so many of us, Leo wasn't perfect. He had some dark times in his life, but he also had more than his fair share of high points too. Margaret and Eddie have asked me to celebrate him today flaws and all, because that's what made him our Leo. Everyone who knew him loved him for and not in spite of his stubbornness, his ability to change the subject when he didn't want to answer something and his questionable taste in music – who can forget those two months in his teens when he listened to one Nine Inch Nails album and nothing else? Well, Margaret and Eddie certainly won't forget it – nor will their ears! And let's not even mention his secret Elton John obsession.' Lottie found herself smiling despite herself, and as the congregation laughed along with her, Ross seemed to grow in confidence. 'But we also loved him for all his many brilliant qualities: his loyalty, his fun-loving nature, his sense of humour, his determination to make the most of life, and his move away from heavy metal music, thank goodness. Leo was always close to his parents, sharing his dad's love of aeronautics and his mum's love of the great outdoors – which is one reason we're standing in this wood today, giving him the green send-off I know he'd appreciate.

'I was lucky enough to grow up with Leo in Scotland – before he and his parents moved down here and he promptly lost all hint of his Scottish accent, the traitor! And being only children, we were more like brothers than just cousins.' He paused and took a breath, and Lottie noticed him glance towards Leo's parents and smile warmly despite his sadness. 'In fact, we weren't *like* brothers, we *were* brothers. We did all our "firsts" together growing up – first day at school, first illicit drink, first kiss, and no I won't be going into details of either of those last two for both our sakes! So when he moved down here to Oxfordshire with Eddie and Margaret when we were seventeen, I think we were both a bit lost, for different reasons maybe, but lost all the same. Things weren't easy for either of us, but Leo showed courage and bravery as strong as his lion namesake. And now I couldn't be prouder of how far he had come and how many people he touched in some way. I couldn't be prouder to call him my brother.'

Lottie was unable to stop a huge sob escaping before she clapped a hand over her mouth, and a salty torrent of tears poured down her face. She felt a soft nudge on her arm and the man next to her handed her a tissue and nodded, briefly resting his hand on her arm. She took the tissue gratefully and tried to control her ragged breaths. She could hear Ross still speaking, but she only caught every fourth word or so about the reception and drinks afterwards.

She followed the rest of the procession back down the path on autopilot, glancing back to see Leo's close family standing round his graveside, and immediately wished she hadn't when she saw the casket being lowered.

'Would you like a lift to the reception, hen?' said a voice at her side. 'I noticed you came in a taxi, and Sue and Gordon have a spare seat in the car, so you're very welcome.'

Lottie nodded, managed to stutter out a thank you to the elderly lady, and gratefully slid into the backseat of a waiting Ford Mondeo. Sue introduced herself and her 'hubby' Gordon and appeared very happy to deliver a monologue as Gordon drove them slowly down a series of country lanes, sparing Lottie the need to even try to speak. Once they'd arrived at the picturesque pub where the 'after-party' – as Sue was determined to call it – was being held in a private room, Lottie immediately made her excuses and found the ladies'.

As she sat in the cubicle she suddenly felt bone-weary, as if someone had squeezed all the energy out of her. She checked her phone to see if there was the slightest possibility of an Uber turning up this far into Oxfordshire, and then quickly added the number of the taxi company Em had used to order her a cab earlier to her contacts, so she could book a car as soon as she was able to leave without looking impolite. She mindlessly scrolled news websites and her social media apps without reading a word, until she realised she'd been in the loo for almost half an hour. She hastily applied a swipe of powder and another layer of waterproof mascara and hoped there was some wine left.

She grabbed a glass from the table by the door and took a large gulp, before scanning the room and locating a lone seat at a table for two, the other chair having clearly been claimed by a larger group. She downed the rest of her wine, helped herself to another and slipped across the room. The table next to hers was just beginning to fill up with people balancing plates of food, and while she hadn't planned on eavesdropping, Lottie tuned in to their conversation as she sipped her drink.

'God, I need this. I'm starving!' said a slim woman with long, blonde hair and perfect make-up as she forked up what looked like a mound of plain lettuce. 'I couldn't eat any breakfast this morning, and I'm already feeling that gin and tonic.'

'Not like the old days when we'd think nothing of going to lectures straight from a night out,' smirked the well-groomed man next to her, raising his pint. 'Do you remember that amazing party we had in second year when Leo made us drink shots of something unspeakable and do that ridiculous game he'd played as a kid but only he knew the rules to? I was still wasted at nine the next morning and had to discuss bloody James Joyce at my seminar. That did not end well.' He chuckled.

'Oh God, yes! What was that game called? Something about a horse? And then he tried to make Ross teach us it next time he visited.' She sighed. 'Those were the *very* old days, Andy. I can't remember the last time I went to the pub of an evening, let alone stayed up all night partying!'

'Ahh the joys of kids, eh? I am very glad I'm not there yet.'

'I'm not sure you'll ever be there, Andy. You have to stop being a kid yourself first!'

'Ha ha, very funny.' The man named Andy lowered his voice. 'Have any of you spoken to Leo's parents yet? I had a quick chat with Ross earlier and he says they're doing OK, but who knows. And Ross certainly looked a shadow of his former self.'

'Can you imagine how they're feeling? I haven't seen Leo for a year or so and I was completely poleaxed by the news. I just can't get my head round it all,' the blonde said.

'Ross said that Leo's dad has the same heart condition that caused the cardiac arrest and now Eddie's got to take meds for it for the rest of his life. It's scary, isn't it? We're all the same age as poor Leo and we could drop down dead at any minute.'

Lottie accepted a top-up from a passing waiter and took another sip of her drink. Despite sitting in a room with tens of other people, she'd never felt quite so alone. It was her boyfriend's funeral, yet she knew just one other person there. Tears threatened again, but she pushed them away with a gulp of wine and angled her body so she could hear the table behind her instead.

'Do you remember Johnny's stag weekend at Thorpe Park? Leo's face when we made him go on that Saw ride – he was crapping himself!'

'Poor bloke! I swear I've never seen anyone look that scared on a rollercoaster. I actually thought he was going to be sick when he got off. It was always a joke between us that if he ever got married I'd have to make sure it was at Alton Towers.'

As the rest of the group laughed and shook their heads, Lottie swallowed. She'd had no idea that Leo hated rollercoasters or what drinking game he'd made his mates play at uni, and she was sure there were hundreds, if not thousands, of other tiny things she didn't know about him. But as she tipped yet more wine into her mouth, she knew it didn't matter. She and Leo had shared something unique, something completely different from the relationships he'd had with everyone else in this room. They'd *really* known each other.

She felt the alcohol gently blurring the edges of the room and realized she should try to eat something. She was reaching for a sandwich at the buffet table when she felt a hand on her shoulder and jumped.

'There you are, Lottie! I'm so glad you came.' Ross smiled warmly at her.

'R–Ross, hi. How are you? The service in the woodland was really beautiful, and your tribute to Leo was lovely.'

'Thank you, that means a lot.' He smiled a second time, and Lottie couldn't help comparing his caring expression with the look of outright hostility that had been on his face after their lunch in the pub. She shivered.

Ross held his arm out. 'Let me introduce you to some people. In fact, you must come and say hello to Eddie and Margaret. They really want to meet you.'

Glancing longingly at the buffet, but not feeling she could really refuse, Lottie put her plate down and followed Ross towards the part of the room where most of the older guests had gathered.

'Sorry to interrupt, but could I just borrow Margaret and

Eddie a wee second?' Ross said, flashing a charming smile at a small, wiry lady with a shock of white hair, who simpered at him in return and replied, 'Of course, hen, of course. I'll be off to spend a penny.'

'Lottie, this is Leo's mum and dad – and this is Leo's, erm . . .'

'Don't worry, I know exactly who you are,' Margaret said, smiling and grasping Lottie's hand in hers. 'Leo told us all about you and had promised we would get to meet you soon. I'm just so sad it's under these circumstances.' She shook her head and tears glinted in the corners of her eyes. Lottie immediately felt her own tears start to fall in sympathy, and for a moment, they both stood there, struggling to regain their composure. For the first time that day Lottie felt like she belonged with all the people mourning the man she loved, which only made it harder to stem the flow of her emotions.

Ross stepped in. 'Lottie was saying how much she liked the woodland and I was about to tell her about the tree plant-ing you and Eddie are planning.'

Margaret squeezed his arm. 'Oh, yes, thank you, Ross. The woodland site is a beautiful place, isn't it? Despite, well, why we were there. But there's something so right about being in an environment that's all about new shoots and growth, and we thought that was somewhere Leo would like to be, didn't we, Eddie?'

'We did, love.' Eddie's smile didn't reach his eyes, and Ross glanced at him quickly.

'Shall we find you a seat over there, Eddie? You must be

exhausted. I know I am. And I'll bring Mum and Dad over too – they'll be glad to take the weight off their feet.'

'Ross is such a good lad,' Margaret said as they watched him lead Eddie over to a table and settle him into a chair. 'He's always been the sort of boy who looks out for others, you know. He was a complete rock for Leo when all that awfulness happened, and he's been amazing organising all this.'

Lottie nodded politely. She wasn't sure what awfulness Margaret was referring too, but her brain was occupied with trying to match the Ross she'd heard so much about today with the sullen, unpleasant man she'd met a few weeks before. 'Ross mentioned you were thinking of planting a tree?' she gently prompted.

'Yes, that's right. The burial ground plant a tree every time someone new arrives – their words, not mine.' She grimaced. 'But we also thought we'd plant a fruit tree or a rose bush in our garden in a few months, and every time it flowers or bears fruit, it can remind us of all the happiness Leo brought to us all.'

Lottie smiled. 'That's a lovely idea.'

'It was Eddie's idea actually. He loves his gardening, and it's been such a tough time recently – what with his heart diagnosis and then finding out that Leo had the condition too, and then ... this happening just a few months later, I think it's going to be an important way for him to deal with things.'

Lottie nodded sympathetically, but inside, her mind was

whirring and trying to make sense of what Margaret had just said. *And then finding out Leo had the condition too . . .*

'You need to make sure you're looking after yourself too,' Lottie managed to reply.

'Oh, you're just as sweet as Leo said you were. He told us the whole story of how you met, and I told him off for not looking where he was going – silly boy!'

At that moment, Ross came hurrying over to insist Margaret join the others at the table and have something to eat.

'I'll be back in one sec, Lottie. What are you drinking? I'll get you a glass.'

Ross appeared a couple of minutes later with a large glass of red wine and a tumbler of water.

'Are you not drinking?' she asked. She had no idea how anyone could get through a funeral, let alone a funeral of someone close, without alcohol.

'I will later, once I've made sure everyone's got home OK. Have you had some food? I can get you a plate now if you want?'

'No, don't worry, I'll get some in minute,' Lottie assured him. 'I just wanted to ask you something about Leo.' She swallowed hard as Ross's brow creased a little, but knew she needed to vocalise the thoughts forming in her head. 'I know what you said to me on the phone about his heart. But Margaret just mentioned that Eddie was diagnosed with a heart condition months ago – and that they'd also found out Leo had it at the same time. But I thought Leo *didn't* know about the heart condition?' Ross looked downcast, and Lottie felt a pang of guilt for cornering him at his own cousin's funeral, but her need to know what had happened was too strong for her to stop now.

'It's a bit complicated.' He sighed. 'But essentially Eddie was having an MOT at his doctor's as he'd been feeling a bit faint on and off, and after doing lots of tests they told him he has Long QT syndrome. His specialist prescribed him some meds to help regulate his heartbeat and then said that Long QT is a hereditary condition, so Leo should be tested too. He was diagnosed with it a few weeks after Eddie.'

'So Leo did know? But he never told me.' she said. The full force of the realisation hit her like a thump to her stomach. 'Why didn't he tell me?'

'I think he was still only just starting to get his head around it himself. For weeks, he'd barely even talk to his dad about it, or me.'

'So you knew too?' Another thump to the stomach. But she found there was also something else rising inside her: anger.

'Look, Lottie, maybe now isn't the time,' Ross said, stepping back from her almost imperceptibly.

'You knew. But you chose not to tell me, and instead you were just absolutely horrible to me when we met. And then even when he died, you chose not to tell me the whole truth.' She was surprising even herself with the strength of her anger.

'It really wasn't my place to tell you. If Leo had wanted

to tell you, he could have,' Ross tried to gently reason with her. But Lottie was beyond listening to anything he had to say now.

'How dare you tell me what my boyfriend could or couldn't have said to me?' she shouted. Then, just as quickly as the anger had erupted, all the fight seemed to leave her body, and a wave of exhaustion washed over her. She knew she should apologise to Ross, as well as his parents, who must have overheard her words, but she didn't have it in her at that moment.

'I'd better go,' she muttered, hurriedly pulling out her phone and pressing the call button on the taxi company. 'Will you say goodbye to Margaret and Eddie for me?'

'Lottie, wait, let me explain—'

'Hi, yes, could I get a taxi please?'

And she walked out of the door.

Chapter Eleven

Before

'I can't believe it's taken eleven weeks for me to witness how weirdly you eat a burger!' Leo was grinning as he took Lottie's hand and they strolled out of the restaurant.

'It's not weird to use a knife and fork to eat your dinner,' Lottie protested. 'It's not like you just took me to McDonalds and I got out a cutlery set from my handbag and proceeded to eat a Big Mac with it. We were in a proper restaurant and I find it easier and less messy than using my hands. Maybe next time I'll order a big bowl of spaghetti carbonara and start sucking it straight out of the bowl. Is that what you want?'

'OK, OK, point made.' Leo laughed, holding up his hands in surrender.

They stopped at a pelican crossing and she gazed up at him, feeling like she needed to pinch herself for the six hundredth time that she was with such a gorgeous, kind and emotionally mature man. He really did seem to be the perfect partner for her. Maybe Rach was right and there was such a thing as The One for everybody, and maybe she had actually found hers. 'Anyway, you have your fair share of weird quirks, too,' she said now. 'Luckily I haven't found any deal breakers yet. What would be a deal breaker for you, do you think?'

'I think if a woman was a rubbish kisser, that might be grounds for breaking up,' Leo said, looking down at her with a grin.

'I hope you're not implying that *I'm* a rubbish kisser?' Lottie said, her eyebrows raised in mock outrage.

'I mean, I don't *think* you are, but it's always good to be sure . . .'

Their lips connected in a kiss that was just starting to get very interesting when the beeping of the crossing interrupted them.

'Maybe it's a good job the green man interrupted us,' Leo said. 'I was starting to get—'

Whatever Leo had been about to say was forgotten as a shiny black Golf, complete with booming bass and the unmistakeable smell of cannabis, almost knocked them flying. Leo grabbed Lottie and pulled her backwards onto the safety of the pavement. She could feel the boom boom of his heart along with her own.

'Fucking dickhead!' Leo shouted, although the car was long gone. 'Jesus, he nearly killed us!'

'Lucky you were there to save me,' Lottie said, a little shakily, though she could feel her heartbeat was starting to return to normal. 'Well, I think my deal breaker would be if my boyfriend drove like a crazy person in a souped-up car!' she joked.

Leo didn't respond, but his face seemed to darken. He removed his hand from hers and stuffed it into his coat pocket as they continued walking towards his house. Lottie looked at him, confused, but seeing the fiery look in his eyes and the grim set of his mouth, she decided not to push things, figuring the near-miss must have affected him more than she'd thought. Instead, she started babbling about how her burger had been one of the best she'd ever eaten, only beaten by the huge stack Luca had cooked last summer when they were having a barbecue. He'd insisted she have mozzarella, tomato and pesto with it, and it had been the best thing she'd ever eaten. As soon as the weather got warmer, Luca would be clamouring for Leo come over for a barbecue to try one for himself.

'Everyone was so disappointed when you couldn't make it to Annie's the other weekend,' she said. The unwelcome thought that he'd used a headache as an excuse twice now hit her again, before she shook it out of her mind. 'They're all so excited about finally meeting you. It's like you're royalty or something. It wouldn't surprise me if Luca came up with a whole new burger recipe just to impress you at the next barbecue, seriously! We have to get another date in the diary before my sisters turn up at your house demanding to meet you.'

She laughed and hooked her arm though his, and eventually she felt Leo's pace slacken a little and the stiffness in his body start to recede. She reached for his hand and slipped her fingers through his, and he smiled down at her. 'And I'm excited to meet them,' he said, visibly pulling himself together. 'Especially if it involves a barbecue!'

A few hours later, they were lying in Leo's bed and although her phone screen said it was after midnight, Lottie felt wide awake.

'Leo?'

'Yes?' came his slightly sleepy reply.

'I was just seeing if you were awake.'

'Hmm, well I am now!' He rolled over and smiled lazily at her.

She grinned then squirmed around in the bed until her head was lying on his chest. 'Tell me if I'm crushing you, won't you?'

'I don't know what you mean!' he pretend-wheezed and they both giggled. Then all Lottie could hear was the beat of Leo's heart, strong and constant.

'You know earlier when I was talking about deal breakers? Shall I tell you what my real deal breaker would be?' she said.

'As long as it's not a weakness for heavy metal bands of the eighties and nineties, because I might have a confession that will make my Elton John love seem positively normal.' He kissed the top of her head.

'Let's come back to the heavy metal admission in a moment.' Lottie took a breath. 'My deal breaker is – and let me explain before you think I'm totally mad – it's if my boyfriend wanted to become a priest.'

'What? That is not what I thought you were going to say.' He gently manoeuvred her head off his chest and sat up, plumping the pillow behind him, then turning on the bedside light to cast a soft glow across his face. 'Before we go any further, I can assure you I am not going to become a priest.'

'Good.' Lottie smiled briefly. She sat cross-legged on the mattress and pulled the duvet around her shoulders. 'It's just – and I've not told anyone about this for years, to be honest. But I want to tell you.' She took another deep breath. 'When I was twenty-five, I met Elliot. He was an editor at the small educational publisher where I worked and we hit it off. Within a year we'd rented a flat together, and within two years we were talking about marriage and kids and spending the rest of our lives together. A couple of years later he proposed.' She snuck a glance at Leo to see what his reaction was to the news she'd had such a serious relationship in the past, but he merely gave her a small smile and an encouraging nod, so she continued.

'But not long after that, I noticed he was becoming distant and didn't seem to want to spend time together, just me and him, and things went quiet in the, erm, bedroom.' Lottie felt her cheeks redden mentioning her sex life with another man while in Leo's bed, and she rushed on. 'Anyway, we didn't argue or anything – I hate confrontation as you know – but then one night when we were eating dinner in front of *Corrie*, he just turned to me and said, "I'm really sorry, Lottie, I never wanted to hurt you. I love you, but I can't do this any more. I'm becoming a priest. I've thought

about it for months and months and it's what I want to do."
And that was kind of it, the end of our five-year relationship.'
She breathed out, aware she'd been talking very fast. 'There
wasn't really any discussion, and he moved out the next day.
The following week he'd moved to the Midlands to begin
training to become a priest. He now lives near Stoke-on-
Trent and is known as Father Murphy.' She stopped speaking
and squeezed her eyes shut momentarily, before daring to
meet Leo's gaze.

'Wow. That's . . . crazy,' he said, his eyes wide. 'It's crazy
that it took him five years to come to that conclusion. Crazy
that he told you while watching flipping *Coronation Street*.
And crazy that he left you – kind, beautiful, amazing you –
to deal with the fallout on your own. How on earth did you
begin to process it all?'

Lottie blinked, then took his hand and threaded her
fingers through his so they were meshed together as one.
'Thank you,' she whispered. 'Thank you for not laughing at
me, and for understanding.'

'Of course I wouldn't laugh at you,' he said, pulling her to
him. 'It's one thing someone saying they don't love you any
more, but it's a whole other thing when they say they love
you but they love their religion more. It must have been so
unexpected.'

Lottie closed her eyes and thanked God, whether he was
fictional or as real as Elliot believed he was, that Leo had
come into her life. She leaned into his warm, safe body.
'It was definitely unexpected, yes, and for months it didn't

feel real,' she confessed. 'I was embarrassed, to be honest. I mean, who breaks up with their fiancé because he wants to dedicate his life to God? So I guess I decided the way to cope with it was to make a bit of a joke of it in the end, because that felt like the easiest way for other people to deal with it, too. So, yeah, sometimes even now my sisters tease me about it.'

'But underneath you were still hurting, I imagine?' Leo murmured into her hair.

'Yeah, I think I hid a lot of that hurt and sadness – and anger, actually – and it took me a long time to deal with it.' She sighed. 'And don't get me wrong, my sisters are never mean to me about it, and they do know that it affected me quite badly, but maybe even now they don't really know how much. I guess the whole thing has meant I haven't given some dates enough of a chance over the last few years. I've never been able to get over the thought that they were hiding something and had some big secret they weren't telling me, like Elliot did.'

'Not every man is like Elliot,' Leo said gently.

'I know, I know.' She forced a laugh. 'You'd better not be keeping any deep, dark secrets from me! You're not secretly a spy are you?'

'What? I am the last person MI5 – or is it 6, I'm never sure of the difference? – anyway, I am the last person they would recruit. I'm far too boring.'

'I think you're anything but boring.' Lottie smiled at him, her heart a little lighter for telling him about Elliot. 'Which is why I bet you've got a whole raft of stories you could tell me about your life.'

'What do you want to know?' he said. 'I've lived a pretty normal life in lots of ways, I guess. Though maybe it hasn't quite turned out as I imagined it would.'

Lottie snuggled into his chest again. 'In what way?' she asked.

'Well, I'd have thought I'd have had at least two or three of my five-a-side team of kids by the grand old age of thirty-four,' he said. 'I'm going to have to get going if I don't want to be an old-aged pensioner by the time I'm kicking a ball around with child number five.' Lottie smiled, but sensed there was more he wanted to say. There was a pause, but then he started talking again. 'And I always thought I was going to be a doctor. From the age of about eight or nine it was all I ever talked about when people asked what I wanted to be when I grew up. Ross would change his mind and say "astronaut" or "fireman" or "chef" depending on what day of the week it was, but I got it into my head from early on that I wanted to be a doctor, and then it just kind of stuck, like I didn't even think about it, it was just part of who I was.' Lottie nodded and waited for him to go on. He pulled his knees up to chest, meaning she had to reposition herself on her side of the bed before he continued. 'And then I moved down here with Mum and Dad when I was seventeen and I found it hard starting again and I just kind of stopped caring so much about doing well academically and so, predictably, I didn't get the A level grades I needed. I even took a year out and sat them again, but I still only got Bs where I needed As. And just like that, I knew I could never be a doctor, and it kind of changed everything I thought about myself.'

'But could you not have done a medical degree after you'd graduated or something?' Lottie asked.

'Maybe. I think by that point I couldn't face any more exams and lectures and I just had to make the best of it. I've been lucky that I've had some great jobs and I like what I do. I guess I just don't have the passion for my career that someone like Ross has.'

'Why, what does he do? Don't tell me he became a doctor?' She frowned.

'No, no, he didn't. But he does work in the charity sector and what he does really matters. I'm not sure delivering projects for an engineering company really makes that much difference, but *his* work actually does. And maybe a bit of me thinks it should have been me who was the one who had that kind of job, I don't know. Maybe I think so much about both the past and the future that I sometimes forget to live in the present. Sorry, I haven't ever really said any of this out loud before, and I've just realized it makes me sound like either a total weirdo or a spoiled brat!'

'No, it really doesn't,' Lottie replied, shaking her head. 'I totally get it. I know what it feels like to be the one who isn't quite as good, the one doing fine but nothing special, the boring, average one.' Her cheeks flamed as she realized what she'd said. 'What I mean is . . . I don't think that you're boring and average – far from it. Just that I know what it feels like to feel that way.' She took Leo's hands and looked up into his eyes. His gaze was so intense it seemed to burn into her own, but she squeezed his hands a little and immediately felt him relax, and a small smile formed on his lips. Lottie wasn't aware of seconds or minutes, just the thump of her heart in her chest. Then Leo moved his lips towards her and she gave herself entirely to him.

'I can't believe we've only been together for eleven weeks,' she said a while later. 'And since you've already made me a solemn promise never to become a priest, we're already in a better position than I was five years into my previous relationship.' She mirrored her smile to Leo's, and thought once again how beautiful he was, inside and out.

'And I always keep my promises,' he said, reaching for her hand again. 'Eleven weeks, eleven months, eleven years – who cares. For once I'm going to live in the present. You know all the important things about me now. And I know that you are the most loyal, genuine person I've ever met. I know that I love you, Lottie Brown.'

'What did you say?' she whispered.

'I said I love you, Lottie Brown.' Her heart began to thud and she felt every emotion but couldn't put a name to any of them. If she hadn't been able to physically feel Leo's hand in hers, she would have felt like it was happening to someone else.

She swallowed and looked into his soft blue eyes. 'I love you too, Leo Sinclair.'

PART TWO

FOUR MONTHS LATER

Chapter Twelve

'I've pushed the boat out,' Annie announced as she carefully placed their drinks on the table in the pub and then produced three packets of crisps from under her armpit. 'I've gone for sweet chilli flavour – Alf said he's just started stocking them and wants to know what we think, so he did me a buy-one-get-one-free deal. But I also got a packet of cheese and onion, in case they're gross.'

'Good work, Annie. Come on, let's give them a try.' Lottie smiled, taking a pack of the chilli-flavoured crisps and ripping it open. 'Mmm, not bad, not bad at all.'

'Alf will be glad you approve! Open the others, too, Em, I'm starving.'

'Here you go,' Em said, splitting the packets open and laying them in the middle of the table. 'How are things going, Annie?'

'Good, I think,' she replied. Lottie noticed a look pass between her sisters, but before she could try to process what their expressions could mean, Annie had started talking about a big presentation she was putting together to show the results of an experiment she'd been working on for the best part of the last year.

Lottie tried to concentrate on what her sister was saying, but all too quickly her mind started to wander away from T cells and drug company office politics in favour of daydreaming. Specifically, daydreaming about a life where the man she'd fallen in love with was still very much alive. Despite it being four months since Leo had died, she seemed to be spending more and more time recently living in her parallel dream world, as it was much more preferable than the reality she was actually faced with. In her daydreams, she was sipping a glass of wine in Leo's house – or rather, the house they now shared. Sometimes, she was watching Leo cook something delicious in the kitchen while she 'helped' with the occasional stir; other times they were sitting elbow to elbow, planning a blow-the-budget trip to New Zealand's national parks.

She hadn't told her sisters about the revelation at Leo's funeral that he had known about his heart condition before he died. She'd wanted to tell them, but even four months on, she was still reeling from it all herself. She felt stupid for not putting two and two together before the funeral when Ross told her Long QT was a genetic condition. That meant, of course, that it was likely another family member had been diagnosed with it and Leo had therefore known he either had it or was likely to have it. Yet he'd never even mentioned it to her. She'd wished countless times over the last few months that she could ask Leo why he'd kept it from her, and sometimes she'd even found herself imagining his response. *'I was planning to tell you really soon, Lottie, I promise, but I just didn't want to worry you. I only want you to be happy.'* Her mind drifted back into her daydream, Leo by her side, clinking his glass of wine against hers.

She was brought back into the real world by Em brushing her arm. 'I said, how's your work going, Lots?' she said.

'What? Yeah, yeah it's fine,' Lottie said quickly. Keen to move the attention away from her, she said, 'How are the boys?'

Em sighed. 'Alex is almost at the end of his "settling in" period at St Swithin's, and although he's "in" I'm not sure how "settled" he is. This afternoon he had a proper tantrum. The only thing that would calm him down was me reading him one of his long-discarded picture books while he sucked his thumb.' She pulled a face. 'Then Dante started copying him and sticking his thumb in his mouth, and I had to step in. Inevitably there were tears – and not just from the boys. Poor Luca barely got more than a "Brilliant, you're home!" before I was out the door to come here, bless him!'

'Surely days like today make you reconsider that no alcohol rule you have?' Lottie said, taking a deep glug from her own glass. Wine had become Lottie's best friend of late. She tried not to think about quite how much she'd drunk on her own in her flat over the last few months, never mind at the pub with her sisters or workmates, as they all tried to 'cheer her up'.

Em laughed good-naturedly. 'It's not a "rule". You know I just don't really like the taste. Anyway, it sounds like all those tantrums have worn the kiddos out – Luca texted me before to say they both went out like a light, bless them. So he's cooking a ragù and speaking to his parents and Nonna with La Liga in the background.'

'God, I sometimes wonder if Luca is literally a mirage from planet Perfect Husband,' Lottie said. 'And he's insanely handsome to boot. You choose very well, Em.'

'Er, Luca didn't too badly himself, Lots!' Annie butted in. 'And "man looks after the kids he fathered then cooks the tea" is hardly headline news – women are allowed a social life too, you know.'

While their older sister had resolutely kept her maiden name – and subjected anyone who dared address her and Charlie as Mr and Mrs Gannon, including the master of ceremonies at her wedding, to a curt lecture about feminism and the patriarchy – Em had changed her name to Ricci as soon as she'd married Luca. Lottie was as much of a feminist as the next person, but she had to admit that Emilia Ricci had the perfect ring to it. Plus she could never imagine Em upsetting the apple cart when it came to her in-laws' expectations. In fact, they loved her almost as much as Luca did, and whenever Lottie met them at family get-togethers at her sister's palatial country home, they would tell her how much they adored the mother of their grandchildren and how perfect their little family was. Perfect was a word people often used when talking about Em.

'You're right, of course, Annie,' Em laughed. 'But I also know that I *am* lucky. Luca is definitely one of the good ones.'

'I think we can all agree on that,' Annie replied warmly. 'And I'm sure Alex will settle into St Swithin's really soon. He's a clever kid, like his mum and dad.'

'I'm sure you're right. He's probably just tired out by all the excitement, poor thing. Talking about excitement, what have you been up to this week, Lots? Let me live my life vicariously through you please! The most excitement I get at the moment is working out whether the huge grin on Dante's face is because he's just filled his nappy or because he's found the craft scissors and tried to give his poor unsuspecting little playmate a new haircut.'

'That does not sound like the angelic nephew I know and love,' Lottie laughed. 'But I'm afraid I don't have much excitement to offer you. Today at work we spent two hours discussing exactly how we should define the word "pandemic" because Reg was convinced the WHO website was wrong, even after the last few years. It took the whole lexicography team to convince him to finally give in. Is that the kind of excitement you're looking for?'

'Erm, not exactly – though I'm sure your work is actually really interesting,' Em added hastily. 'And how are you doing otherwise, outside of work I mean?'

Lottie saw Annie glance across at their little sister and raise her eyebrows a fraction, but Em's gentle smile remained. Lottie played with the stem of her glass. 'I'm fine.' Then when both of her sisters continued to look at her, clearly wanting more, she blurted out the thing she thought they'd most want to hear. 'I've been on a date with a friend of Rachel's.'

They both leaned forward and Annie immediately prodded her. 'You've been on a date with someone else already? Are you sure it's not too soon?'

Lottie felt her hackles immediately rise. She'd only said something to get them off her back. She knew they meant well, but it felt like Annie could never be pleased for her.

Thankfully, Em quickly swept in. 'Oh! Is he nice? What's his name? Does he know about ... ? Though obviously you don't have to tell us anything, Lots. We just know that it's a big step after what happened with— well, after what happened.'

Lottie swallowed hard, then shrugged. 'He's called Ian. He's nice, tall, works for a tech firm and, er, goes to the gym quite a bit,' she offered.

'Doing better than Charlie already, then.' Annie smiled. 'He sounds great. And he's a friend of Rachel's, so she must have vetted him first, right? Presumably he's not a massive shagger on the side.'

'Annie!' both Lottie and Em exclaimed.

'What? It's best to know these kind of things upfront, isn't it? Has he warranted a second date?'

'He's great, but to be honest I think you're actually right. It's all a bit soon, you know?' Lottie took another gulp of her drink and tried not to read her sisters' expressions. She couldn't help but feel she'd somehow let them down, whether by going on the date in the first place only four months after Leo, or not being very enthusiastic about the date after all. 'But you never know, we're still messaging, so we'll see,' she quickly added, smiling brightly.

'Good! That's good,' Em said encouragingly. 'You've had such a tough time lately, but it's good to see you enjoying yourself and trying to move forward.' She squeezed her arm. 'We just want you to be happy, Lots. We've been worried about you.'

Lottie squeezed her hand back. 'I'm fine, really. You don't have to worry about me, I promise. Now, hadn't you better be getting home to that yummy ragù Luca's making?'

Em laughed as she reached for her jacket and Annie rolled her eyes good-naturedly. 'I left Charlie step-by-step instructions on how to make the chicken tray bake I've planned for dinner, so I'm hoping the kitchen won't be a complete bombsite when I get home.'

'Fingers crossed – for his sake, anyway,' Lottie said.

Half an hour later Lottie had pedalled her way around the throngs of students and tourists and made it out the other side of Oxford to her flat. She heaved her bike into the hallway where it only just fitted, then crossed into the kitchen and opened the fridge. She blindly reached for one of the stacked ready meals without even glancing what it was, before thrusting it into the microwave with a sigh. While she waited for the ping to tell her it was ready, she removed her bra, breathing a sigh of relief, and stepped into her pyjamas, which were still on the sofa from last night. Minutes later, sitting on the sofa with a rapidly congealing lasagne, watching a reality show that seemed to consist of people stripping off in front of each other before choosing which randomly naked man to go home with, she briefly paused to wonder what on earth she was doing with her life.

But then her brain reminded her it didn't have to be like that and she could retreat into her imaginary world if she wished. So for the next few minutes she was able to pretend the pasta on the plate in front of her was in fact a home-made lasagne cooked by the gorgeous, thoughtful man sitting next to her, who was taking the mick out of the people on the TV.

'How bad does it have to get before you apply to go on a dating show where you're literally judged on the size of your tadger?' Daydream Leo laughed.

'Any woman will tell you it's not just about size,' Daydream Lottie replied.

'Ah, it's what you do with it, right? Honestly, I can't believe how cocky – pun intended – this guy is when it's pretty obvious he's never got close enough to a woman to find out what you're supposed to do with it.'

'Oi, don't be mean! At least he's got the balls – however small they are – to go on national telly and at least try,' Lottie pointed out. 'I don't see you stripping off and parading your body in all its naked glory for the world to see.'

'That is very true,' he conceded. 'I was just being horribly smug since I happen to be sitting next to the most beautiful woman in the universe, who also just happens to be the woman I'm going to marry one day.'

'Is that so?' Lottie said, raising her eyebrow. Suddenly, the Leo in her imagination wasn't laughing any more. He grabbed the remote control to turn the TV off and knelt down on the floor. The room seemed to swim before her eyes and her hand shook as Leo reached for it and began speaking.

'Darling Lottie Brown, will you do me the honour of becoming my wife, who I will love and cherish in sickness and in health, forsaking all others – and maybe even obey sometimes. *Please* say you'll spend the rest of your life with me. And I'm not just saying that so I don't have to go on a naked reality show. I mean it.'

Half crying, half laughing she whispered, 'Is this real, are you really asking me to marry you?'

'I mean, sure, I didn't quite envisage doing it while watching a load of naked people check each other out on the telly, but I couldn't stop myself. I've been thinking about it for months. I've even asked Annie and Em for their permission, as obviously we couldn't get married without their support – I'm too scared of Annie for one thing! I'm blathering – Jesus, I haven't even shown you the ring! Here, what do you think?'

Lottie raised her hand to her mouth as she stared at the twisted silver band adorned with diamonds and emeralds. 'Leo, it's beautiful! What ... how ... I don't know what to say!'

'Erm, yes, maybe?' Her daydream Leo was so vivid that she could picture his bright-blue eyes staring into hers, and in that moment Lottie felt like she could see his soul, pure and shining.

'Yes, then. Yes, Leo Sinclair, I will be your wife. Now come here and let me kiss you!'

Lottie opened her eyes and realized her cheeks were wet with tears. There was no one on the sofa beside her, her ready meal was discarded on the coffee table and her solitary wine glass sat empty and alone.

Chapter Thirteen

Lottie woke the next morning, her eyelids swollen, her cheeks raw and her under-eye shadows black. Jabbing her phone and seeing the time, she hauled herself out of bed and into the shower. Then she applied just the right amount of make-up to stop people at work asking if she was ill. She was glad she wasn't seeing her sisters that evening; little got past Annie's forensic stare or Em's sad frown. But thankfully she had the whole evening to herself, so she only had to get through eight hours in the office of acting like everything was normal.

It had been Annie who'd encouraged her to put on an act a few weeks after Leo's death, and 'fake it till she made it out the other side' of her grief. And, almost four months later, although Lottie definitely hadn't made it anywhere, she did feel like a career on the stage might not be totally out of reach should she need a change of job. Maybe it was that people *wanted* to believe that she was 'over' Leo dying, or maybe it was because they couldn't believe that she could ever truly have loved him after only knowing him for eleven weeks – either way, Lottie was grateful that both her family and her workmates had chosen to believe her when she told them she was fine. While she still sometimes saw her sisters exchange a look if she cranked the acting lever up too far, most other people seemed to have presumed she'd moved on as quickly as they had, and not even Em and Annie seemed to like mentioning the words 'Leo' and 'died' in front of her.

Lottie had kind of been telling the truth when she'd told her sisters she'd been on a date with a friend of Rachel's – with the emphasis on the 'kind of'. Rachel had been doing her level-best to babysit her over the last few months, constantly inviting her out after work or turning up at her flat with tickets to a new comedy night, so she'd barely had a minute to herself. And after a few weeks' grace, Rachel had taken to nudging Lottie whenever she spotted a hot man in whatever bar, theatre or comedy club they were in, nodding meaningfully at her, even though Lottie had reminded her every single time that she wasn't looking to date anyone and wouldn't be for some time.

'And I totally understand that, of course,' Rachel had soothed, adding with a cackle, 'And I'm a married woman, but that doesn't stop me appreciating a handsome man when I see him, does it?'

Lottie knew her friend meant well, and Rachel had long been obsessed with trying to match her with any even slightly eligible male in the vicinity. For the last few years, Lottie had managed to convince her friend that she was just

picky about who she went out with and when her friend
had started mentioning setting her up with her husband's
cousin who was 'totally gorgeous but totally unattached!',
Lottie had found herself inventing a Tinder date that would
then 'fizzle out' a few weeks later in order to get her off her
back. It wasn't that Rachel meant to be so scarily full-on,
Lottie knew, it was just that she wanted her friends to have
the same kind of happiness she did with her husband – who
she'd met on a dating website and who had turned out to be
just as kind, thoughtful and handsome as the friend who'd
written his profile said he was. And when she saw a woman –
or man – unattached, Rachel made it her mission to attach
them to someone else immediately. There wasn't a bad bone
in her body – just far too many romantic notions in her brain.

All of which was why Lottie had agreed to go for a Friday
night drink with Rachel and Guy after work five weeks earlier. She'd been turning down more and more of her friend's
invitations, but knew there were only so many nights out she
could cry off before Rachel saw through her fake 'I'm fine!'s
and tried a different a tack; a tack that would likely be much
worse than a few drinks on a Friday night.

The evening had been going OK. The three of them
had shared a bottle of wine and Rachel had done most of
the talking, while Guy kept them both entertained with
his wicked impressions of Reg, so Lottie hadn't needed
to expend too much energy. When Rachel went off to
get another bottle and Guy nipped to the loo, Lottie had
allowed herself to admit that she was actually enjoying

herself, chatting, laughing and being normal. She'd even managed not to place Leo front and centre of every thought for a good part of that evening, though as soon as she'd realized that was the case, she'd instantly felt guilty. She'd sighed, scrolled through her WhatsApp messages, tapped out a quick response to her sisters' conversation about how to make the best roast potatoes, then looked up to see Rachel coming towards her grinning.

'Look who I bumped into at the bar! Lottie, you remember my mate Ian, don't you? He was at my birthday drinks last year at that weird Mexican-themed place I booked. Epic fail! Anyway, Ian is here with a few of his workmates too – they might come over later.'

'Great!' Lottie had smiled, trying to pretend she was excited. 'How are you doing, Ian?'

He'd grinned back, placing three clean wine glasses on the table. 'Good, really good. It's a nice bar this, isn't it? Better than that place Rach chose for her birthday. And fewer sombreros, which is always good. Hopefully see you later, Lottie.' He'd grinned again, then headed back into the throng of people. Rachel had jabbed her in the ribs, and Lottie had braced herself for the onslaught of her friend's hot man speech, but thankfully Guy had chosen that moment to come back to the table, complete with a story about watching two men snort coke off a very grubby-looking toilet cistern, and Ian had been thankfully forgotten. It wasn't until Lottie herself had been making her way to the bar to buy yet another bottle of wine that she'd even remembered Ian.

The next few hours had blurred into a glass-always-topped-up-with-wine haze. She vaguely remembered Rachel telling her she was going to go home and suggesting Lottie came with her. When Lottie chose to stay, Rachel had given her a worried look and told her she'd make sure Guy kept an eye out, since he was still at the table chatting to a couple of mates who'd turned up. But Lottie didn't remember seeing Guy again that night and, several hours later, full of red wine and little else, she had been giggling her way back to Ian's house share. As she glugged back even more Cab Sav sitting on Ian's sofa, she'd pushed any murmurings about what she should or shouldn't be doing out of her mind and had instead done exactly what Rachel had been instructing her to do for weeks – she'd enjoyed herself.

When she'd come to the following morning, Lottie had felt like her brain was banging on the inside of her skull, while her stomach swirled angrily, and her tongue seemed to have doubled in size and developed a fur lining. She'd pushed herself onto her back and as her eyes focused, she'd realized it wasn't her own Artex ceiling above her. At the same time, she'd become aware of the man lying next to her. Despite the nausea threatening to overpower her, Lottie had forced herself into a sitting position.

'Ian?' she'd croaked.

'M-huh?' the mound of duvet next to her had replied. 'Urgh, I feel like shite!' He'd heaved himself over, grunted, then smiled at her. 'But *je ne regrette rien*, as they say.'

Lottie had tried to return his smile, but she'd known it was probably more of a grimace as she battled the sickness in her stomach, which was half alcohol-induced, half regret-induced. 'Am I okay to grab a shower?' she'd managed to say, and fled gratefully to the bathroom.

As the water cascaded down on top of her, Lottie had tried not to let her mind drift to anything except the scalding torrent hitting her reddening skin, but with only nausea for company, she was powerless to stop herself running through her memories of the night before. She could remember Ian suggesting they take the rest of the wine bottle into his room and the fierce, urgent sex that followed. Her cheeks pinked to match the rest of her body, and she felt her muscles ache in all her most private places. She could also picture fragments of them making love more slowly, as he told her how beautiful she was. But she'd quickly shut down those memories as they seemed to make the whirlwind in her tummy even worse.

She'd spent the next hour trying to leave Ian's house as politely as possible. Her whole body had been telling her to get dressed and bolt immediately, but she'd forced herself to smile and drink the coffee Ian had made for her. She agreed they'd had fun and let him kiss her goodbye in a way that left her in no doubt how much he'd like to carry on that fun again very soon. She hadn't been able to bring herself to let him down gently or otherwise, so she'd grinned and agreed again that they'd had fun, and then set off on the long walk into town to pick up her bike and cycle back to her own flat. Once home, she'd run a bath and lain in it until the cold water lapping at her arms forced her into her pyjamas and into the sanctuary of her own bed. Then, finally, she had allowed herself to slip back into the safety of her dream world, where Leo told her he loved her and he'd be there for her always.

That had been over a month ago, and now on her way to work, Lottie realized that she wasn't feeling the familiar twisting pain in her abdomen that she was so used to getting each month as regular as clockwork. Instead, only unease gnawed at her stomach.

Chapter Fourteen

The pregnancy test lay on the bed beside her, the box still unopened. It had been three days since Lottie had sat on the bus and checked the calendar on her phone, then realized her period was over a week late.

It wasn't as if she could blame Ian. She could vaguely remember assuring him that she was on the pill and that they didn't have to use any other protection. And she *was* on the pill – she just hadn't been that good at remembering to take it recently. She hadn't exactly had the need. Yet now here she was, possibly staring impending motherhood in the face.

Like most women, she'd spent a fair few sleepless nights in her late teens and early twenties worrying she could be pregnant after a condom had split, or after she'd taken the morning-after pill and was anxious it wouldn't work for some reason. But when you were thirty-three and your sisters and friends were all talking about having kids, or trying to have kids, then the thought you could be joining them in the family way was a slightly different prospect.

Over the last three days, Lottie had done a whole lot of thinking. Those first few hours when she'd registered that a tiny human could be growing inside her had sent her into shock. But as she'd listened to Rachel openly talk in the office about how she wanted to be 'up the duff within the next year', and read Em's stories of little Alex and Dante on the sisters' WhatsApp group, she'd realized that she wanted some of that too.

One morning in bed, wrapped in each other's naked bodies, she and Leo had talked about what they'd call the five kids he had confessed he wanted, and how they'd bring them up without iPads or screens and take them on adventures by the coast to their candy-coloured beach hut, and how they'd go skiing when they were tiny so they would grow up effortlessly gliding over the snow in Switzerland each season.

And during those first twenty-four hours, when she'd thought she might be pregnant, Lottie had allowed herself to dream about what might have been.

'Leo, I know you said you wanted five, but what if we started with one?'

'One what?'

'One baby. He or she could be our centre forward.'

'Oh my God, Lottie, are you serious? Are you really pregnant? Oh, clever, amazing you! We're going to be a family!'

Lottie had stayed in her daydream as long as possible, but real life had crept its bony fingers inside and she'd woken up to the loud, insistent voice in her head berating her for wasting time in a land of make-believe. The harsh reality was that she and Leo would never get the chance to live the life they'd dreamed of for themselves and their children.

Over the next couple of days, she'd mechanically got up, gone to work and come home each day, barely registering any moment beyond those she spent lying in bed, turning everything over in her mind. She did most of her thinking in the small hours of the night, counting the lines in the Artexed ceiling above her. She couldn't seem to get past the fact that her dreams of a perfect family with Leo had been smashed, but in a small corner of her thoughts, she'd started to ask herself whether she could still have a family.

If she did turn out to be pregnant, *could* she have this baby? Maybe Leo's death was a sign that she should live in the moment and take chances when they came. Was it crazy to think maybe this baby was the chance she needed? And maybe Ian was too. Sure, he wasn't Leo. But then no man ever would be, she knew that now – all men would be second best to him. But Ian seemed nice, kind and he was good-looking. He hadn't pressured her after their evening together and had been nothing but a gentleman, suggesting they see each other again, but only if she wanted to. Even when she'd texted him to say she needed to take a step back and wasn't in a place to have a relationship, his reply had been very understanding.

But surely this was crazy to even contemplate? Where would they live, for one? Neither of their flats would be big enough for all the baby paraphernalia. And how would two people who barely knew each other decide on how to parent a child? Maybe Ian would be a great dad, and not one of those men who looked at a nappy cluelessly or refused to do their share of night feeds. Or maybe Ian wouldn't want to be involved at all, and Lottie would raise the child herself – she could do that, couldn't she?

A jumble of thoughts hurricaned through her mind for three days, but by the time she found herself sitting on her bed staring at the pregnancy test next to her, Lottie felt she had some semblance of a plan. That morning she'd messaged Ian to say that, actually, she'd love to go for dinner with him and they'd arranged to see each other in a few days. She'd decided she'd have to tell him about the baby if the pregnancy test confirmed what she felt she already knew.

Lottie picked up the box from the bed and tipped the contents out onto the duvet. The leaflet explained that all she needed to do was pee on the stick and a blue plus or minus sign would appear in the window a few minutes later. Easy. So why was her hand shaking so much? Maybe she needed a cup of tea – but were you supposed to drink caffeine before doing the test, she wondered. She briefly considered the bottle of wine sitting in her kitchen cupboard, then discarded the thought almost immediately – she already felt horribly guilty about the amount she'd drunk over the past five weeks. She'd not had a drop of alcohol in the last three days, though and, coupled with everything swirling inside her head, it had meant she'd found it even harder to sleep and she now felt dog-heavy with tiredness. It was something she'd have to get used to as a new mum, she supposed.

She picked up the stick, but her hand was still shaking and her chest was thumping, and she knew she couldn't do it on her own. She picked up her phone.

'Em? I don't suppose Luca is around, is he? No, it's not him I want, it's you.' She paused, then rushed out, 'I think I'm pregnant and I'm about to do the test, but now I'm scared. Can you ... can you come?'

An hour later and Lottie was still staring at the unused pregnancy test on the bed, but now Em was sitting next to her, holding her hand and looking worried.

'I don't understand, though, Lots. How can you think you might be pregnant?' she asked gently. 'Leo passed away four months ago and there ... there hasn't been anyone since, has there?'

Lottie looked at her sister, willing her not to judge. She knew Em loved her unconditionally, but she also knew that, with her charmed life, complete with perfect husband who worshipped the ground she walked on, she could never understand what things had been like for Lottie lately.

'I slept with Rachel's friend,' Lottie replied quietly, and then added defensively, 'There's no law against it.'

'Of course not, sweetheart,' Em soothed. 'I'm just ... surprised, that's all. But of course you can see whoever you like, and why shouldn't you?'

Lottie fought back the words on the tip of her

tongue – 'Because I still love Leo' – and merely nodded her head.

'So how long ago was that?' Em asked.

'Nearly five weeks ago. I'm twelve days late, and you know me, I'm hardly ever late, even when I miss a few days of the pill.'

Em took a deep breath. 'OK, well, you did the right thing calling me – and buying the test.' She squeezed Lottie's hand. 'Have you thought what you're going to do if the test is positive?'

'Yes. I'm going to have the baby,' she said fiercely.' I'm meeting Ian on Tuesday, and we can raise the baby together. Or if he doesn't want to be involved, I'll raise it myself. But I think he will want to be.' She could see that Em was trying to look supportive, but she wasn't able to hide her shock. 'Don't worry, he's nice, Em, you'll like him. And I'm sure he'll be a great dad. We could be a proper family, like you and Luca and the boys. Maybe we'll even get married once the baby is old enough to toddle down the aisle.'

Em's eyebrows shot into her hairline and she reached for Lottie's hand again. 'Lottie, sweetheart, without being rude, you barely know this Ian, and now you're talking about getting married and having his child—'

'You and Luca have done it, and Annie and Charlie are trying to do it, so why shouldn't I?' Lottie interrupted angrily. 'Just because I'm poor little Lottie who can't keep a man from turning into a priest or even . . . even fucking dying, doesn't mean I can't have what you both have, you know?'

'Lots, come on, that's not what I'm saying,' Em said, her tone even and quiet. 'But having a baby with someone – a child who you'll be responsible for their whole lives – isn't something you can just decide to do. And I'm not saying you haven't thought about it properly, but it's a massive decision. And have you thought about what Ian wants? A baby would be a huge shock for him I imagine.'

'It's been a shock for me, for God's sake! And, like I said, if he doesn't want to be involved, that's fine. I know I can make this work.'

'And of course that's true, but starting a family is never a straightforward decision for anybody, let alone in this kind of situation.' Em took a breath. 'Also, Lots, we don't even know if you are pregnant yet – your period could be late for loads of different reasons, especially after the tough time you've had lately. We might be worrying about something that's not even happened. Why don't we do the test now?'

'I know I'm pregnant,' Lottie replied stiffly. 'And I'm going to have this baby.' She could see the worry lines on her sister's forehead deepen, so decided it was her turn to reassure her. 'I'll be fine, Em, really. Please don't worry.'

'Maybe we should call Annie,' Em said brightly. 'I think she said she and Charlie weren't doing much this weekend.'

'No!' Lottie answered immediately. 'I mean, let's not disturb her. Fine, let's get this test done and then you can tell me what I need to know about this pregnancy malarkey.' She attempted a grin, and Em gave her an uncertain smile in return. 'So, I literally just wee all over the stick, right?'

'Pretty much. You go to the bathroom and I'll read the leaflet and tell you exactly how long we need to wait and what it all means.' Em squeezed Lottie's hand again, then gave her a gentle push towards the bathroom.

Lottie grabbed the stick and trailed her feet out of the room and across the hallway. Sitting on the loo, willing her bladder to give up the large volume of liquid that just a few minutes before had been pressing down painfully, she marvelled at the human body and its ability to push a baby out. She'd seen enough TV shows to know that labour was anything but a walk in the park – though Em had seemed to sail through both of hers – but it was almost impossible to picture doing it herself.

She sighed and her bladder sighed in unison. Quickly, she thrust the stick under the flow, soaking her hand in the process – it seemed she couldn't even do a pregnancy test properly. She placed the stick on some tissue on the side, then washed her hands extra thoroughly and walked back into the bedroom, holding the stick away from her on its tissue bed.

'Well done,' Em said. 'Now we wait for three minutes. Maybe put it down on your dresser and then come and sit on the bed with me so we're not tempted to look before then.' She patted the space on the bed next to her and when Lottie had sat down, she smiled. 'Have you watched that documentary on Netflix I was telling you and Annie about the other day, the one about the ice caps melting? You should totally watch it, it's insane. I ended up having a bit of an argument with Luca about how rubbish he is at sorting the recycling.

I know it's only a small thing, but all that rubbish going into landfill means even more greenhouse gasses, and if we all just did our bit – including Luca – then it would make a difference.'

'I can't imagine you and Luca arguing about anything,' Lottie said distractedly, knowing Em was unsubtly trying to keep her mind off the time bomb lying two metres away. 'Em, can I ask you something?' she said, her gaze still on the stick.

'Of course,' Em replied immediately.

'What's giving birth really like? I mean, how do you actually get a baby out of that tiny hole? Unless I have an abnormally small vagina, I just can't see how that would work.'

Em laughed. 'With great difficulty! Of course, lots of women end up having have a C-section, either through choice or because the doctors say it's the only way the baby's coming out, but that's not exactly the easy option either. Poor Abbie in my NCT group got an infection and could barely pick little Ollie up for weeks.'

'But your births went really well, didn't they? I remember you just being really serene with both the boys, and Luca was so excited he was like a little child bouncing up and down all the time.'

'Well, I was lucky, yes. But I'll never forget those first few weeks after having Alex. How painful it was to sit down. And how utterly exhausted I was for so, so long afterwards. Then with Dante, I had contractions for three days straight before the midwives said I was dilated enough to come into the unit. At that point, I was so broken I didn't have much idea what was going on. Those first few days with him are a total blur.'

Lottie tore her eyes away from the dresser and turned to stare at her sister in astonishment. 'But ... but, I don't remember you being like that at all,' she stuttered. 'You were this perfect earth mother with both the boys from the start. I remember you being so calm and happy, even when they were teeny-tiny and screaming. You were amazing.'

'Ha! I definitely wasn't.' Em laughed mirthlessly. 'But maybe I spared you some of the worst details – probably because reliving the birth was the last thing I wanted to do. And it is true that once you hold that tiny bundle of blankets next to your chest, all the pain and blood and, erm, other bodily fluids are totally worth it.'

Lottie felt dazed. She cast her mind back to Dante's birth just a few years ago and she truly did remember Em popping him out and being back home mere hours later, inviting Lottie to come round for a cuddle. She shook her head to try to clear all the thoughts crowding in, and her eyes automatically returned to the test sitting on her dressing table. 'Is it time?' she whispered.

'Yes, it's definitely been three minutes,' Em replied gently. Lottie tried to stand up, but it felt like her limbs were frozen, and she fell back onto the bed. Neither of them said anything for a few seconds, until Em whispered, 'Do you want me to look for you?'

Lottie swallowed hard. 'Yes please.' She briefly shut her eyes and when she opened them again Em was standing next to the dresser.

'Ready?'

'R–ready,' she replied, shakily.

'It's negative, Lots. It's negative.'

Chapter Fifteen

It felt like the walls in Lottie's bedroom were moving in, trying to crush the life out of her, only for them to recede at the last minute and move away again, the process repeating itself in a nausea-inducing pattern, like a child's constantly rotating kaleidoscope. She opened her mouth, but no words would come out.

'Lottie, did you hear what I said? Are you OK?' came the faint sound of Em's voice from what felt like miles away.

The room stilled for a moment and Lottie managed to say, 'Negative? But that can't be right,' before the spinning and nausea started up again, only this time even more strongly.

'Sick. Bathroom,' she panted, and felt the comforting arms of her sister guide her across the landing again, where she promptly threw her guts up, and all her emotions came pouring out. As she heaved and gasped and sobbed, she struggled to take in the reality. She wasn't pregnant. She wasn't having a baby. She didn't have a new family.

She didn't know how long she sat on the floor of the

bathroom, Em's arm a familiar weight around her middle, keeping her physically together while her heart broke. When her body had finally stopped convulsing and had given up all of its tears, she felt Em shift a little. 'I'm going to run you a bath, sweetheart,' her sister whispered. 'Then I'll make us a hot drink and some toast and you can see how you feel.'

Lottie nodded numbly, happy to let her sister's soothing voice take charge and tell her what to do. She climbed into the tub and let the warm water hug its way around her aching limbs. She could hear the sounds of Em boiling the kettle and locating mugs in the kitchen and she tried to focus only on those noises and the comforting familiarity of the step-by-step process needed to make tea and toast.

'It's ready when you are, Lots,' Em said softly from outside the door. 'And I've left some clean pyjamas on the bed for you.'

'Thanks, I'll be out soon,' she croaked in reply, her voice juddering in her throat. Even the thought of heaving herself out of the bath was exhausting, but the lure of fresh pyjamas and a milky drink tempted her to shakily stand up and reach for her towel.

'There you are.' Em smiled at her as she came into the kitchen. 'Here's your tea and the toast won't be a sec. Go and sit on the sofa and I'll bring it into you.' Lottie did as she was told and was shortly presented with hot, buttery toast, which she nibbled cautiously.

'Good, you've got a bit more colour back in your cheeks

at least,' Em said. 'Annie said she should be here in a few minutes.'

Lottie looked up. 'You called Annie?'

'Yes, sweetheart. I know you said not to, but I really think you need looking after by both of us.'

'So you can *both* try to talk some sense into me, you mean?' Lottie said wryly.

Em didn't answer, just smiled serenely again. 'Will you eat another slice of toast?'

'No, I'm fine. Thank you, though. And thank you for . . . this.' She gestured at her drink and pyjamas.

'I'm your sister, Lots. You'd do the same for me and Annie. You don't need to thank me.'

Lottie nodded and sipped her tea. Desperate not to think about the negative test, her brain snagged on their earlier conversation about how hideous Em had felt after giving birth to both of her sons. Because Lottie hadn't really been there for her sister then. Nor had she really checked in on Annie enough through all her fertility treatments. It just felt that Em and Annie were better at all of that. They were the ones who had their lives sorted and their futures mapped out. They were the ones who people turned to when they needed advice or help. Lottie's life was a mess, and the only people who asked her for advice were her colleagues trying to decide whether they should include millennial slang in the definition of the word 'sick'.

The doorbell interrupted her thoughts and Em went to let Annie in.

'Hey, Lottie. How are you doing?' Annie asked coming into the room and enfolding Lottie in a hug. She allowed herself to be scooped up and held tightly, glad that Annie didn't seem to expect an answer. When she finally released her, Annie said gruffly, 'I know it's Saturday night, but instead of wine I brought us some posh hot chocolate and an M&S biscuit box.'

'Excellent thinking, Annie,' Em said, beaming. While her sisters busied themselves frothing milk and murmuring quietly to each other in her kitchen, Lottie was left alone on the sofa, steeling herself for the inevitable conversation they were about to have. She knew her sisters would want her to talk through her feelings and try to make sure she was OK, but now that all the adrenaline had left her body, she just felt numb. All she wanted to do was sleep, but she knew her sisters weren't going to leave until they were satisfied she hadn't completely lost the plot.

'Hot chocolate and a selection of biscuits, as promised!' Annie announced as she and Em came into Lottie's lounge, laden with mugs and plates. 'Dig in, everyone.'

Lottie let the gentle hum of her sisters' chatter warm her spirit as the frothy drink warmed her throat. But all too soon Annie signalled it was time to get down to business. 'So, Lottie darling, what's been going on with you?'

Lottie swallowed and gave a resigned smile. 'Well, I'm sure Em has filled you in.'

'Yes, she told me what happened this afternoon with the test and everything. But she also told me that you'd built up a whole scenario about settling down with this Ian guy and bringing up a family together even though you've only met him once. And that doesn't sound like the Lottie we know and love. Em was worried – and so am I, to be honest. So talk to us. Please?'

While Annie's little speech was typical Annie in its directness, her voice had taken on a new tenderness that wriggled its way into Lottie's heart, catching her off-guard. Tears pricked her eyes again. 'I-I don't really know what to say,' she replied unsteadily. 'My period was late and I thought I was pregnant, and I spent the first few hours crapping myself and wondering what the hell I was going to do. I thought about having a termination and read up all about it online, and it sounded okay and straightforward – or as straightforward as these things are – and thousands of women go through them every year and don't suffer complications, especially at such an early stage.'

'But then you changed your mind?' Annie prompted.

'I couldn't get the thought out of my head that this could be my only chance to have a baby.'

'And is that something you want, sweetheart?' Em said.

'Yes,' Lottie said immediately. 'Well, I thought I did maybe.'

'Did you and Leo ever talk about it?' Annie asked softly.

Lottie swallowed and tried to marshal her thoughts into something that made sense, but gave up and just let them all tumble messily out. 'I haven't thought that seriously about having kids for years. But then I met Leo and he said he wanted as many babies as we could have, and suddenly it felt like maybe that whole family thing was something I could have after all. And I hadn't thought that was really possible after everything that happened with Elliot. I know it had only been three months, but what Leo and I had was the real thing, I know it was. But then he died.' Lottie's voice caught in her throat and she came to an abrupt stop.

'And when he died, you felt like your chance to have a family disappeared too?' Annie said, her voice laced with so much emotion it caused fresh tears to fall on Lottie's cheeks.

She scrubbed them away and nodded. 'I think when my period was late, I kind of got it into my head that this was my second chance at it all. But I know you're both right that I jumped far too far ahead, trying to plan a future with a man I hardly know.' She took a breath. 'And on top of everything, I felt guilty for even thinking about a future without Leo. Like I was cheating on him.'

'No, Lottie, you can't—' Annie butted in, but stopped when Em placed a hand on her shoulder. 'Sorry, Lottie, go on.'

'It's just . . .' Lottie paused and glanced anxiously at her sisters, willing them to understand. 'I talk to him. Leo, I mean. In my head, sometimes.'

Lottie saw frown lines appear on her sisters' faces. She felt utterly exhausted with the effort of trying to explain and understand all these feelings. Her words began to dry up, and she knew she didn't have much left in her tonight, so she tried to bring things to a conclusion. 'But then the test showed I'm not pregnant, so neither of you need to worry any more. I'm not going to be a new mum whose relationship is only just older than my baby, and neither am I going to be a single mum having to deal with it all on my own. I just had a moment of madness and I'm sure my period will probably come tomorrow and this is all just weird PMT.' She forced herself to smile brightly at them. 'So as I said, I'm fine and you can stop worrying, really you can.'

She watched as her sisters exchanged the faintest glance with each other, and she knew they weren't going to be so easily satisfied. She curled into the sofa even tighter as Em began to speak.

'Sweetheart, I know you don't want to hear this, but have you thought about seeing your GP?'

'I thought we'd established I'm not pregnant,' Lottie snapped more viciously than she'd intended.

'No, not about that,' Em said quietly. 'About how you're feeling in general. About how you're dealing with your grief.'

'I'm fine!' She bit her lip, hating herself for shouting at Em of all people, and forced herself to remain calm. 'I am, really, Em. I'm fine. I'm not saying the last four months haven't been tough, because they have, but I'm trying to move forwards. I was thinking about having a baby with another man, for goodness' sake!'

She could see that Annie was trying to hold back, but she clearly couldn't stop herself. 'There is absolutely no shame in asking for help, you know, Lottie,' she said, her voice lower and softer than before. 'You've been through a lot in the last few years. The man you thought you were going to marry called things off to follow a greater love, and then the guy you fell head over heels for suddenly disappeared from your life in the saddest possible circumstances.'

'Rub it in, why don't you,' Lottie said with a weak smile.

'This isn't a joke, Lottie!' Annie flung her hands out in front of her in frustration, but Em put a hand on her knee and took over.

'We don't want to tell you what to do, Lots. We just think it might be worth you talking to someone. As Annie said, you've been through some horrible things and it takes time to process it all. You're obviously still grieving, but it feels like you've also got a lot of anger inside sometimes.' Lottie's expression must have been showing her indignation because Em added, 'Of course, maybe we're wrong about that, but it would still be good to speak to someone. It doesn't even have to be a doctor or whatever. We're always here to listen, aren't we, Annie?' she said, nudging her sister, who nodded vigorously. 'Or maybe there's someone else you can talk to. What about Leo's cousin? We obviously never met Leo so it must be hard for you to talk to us about him, but they were like brothers you said. Maybe it would help to talk about him and share your memories of him with Ross, and he could share his with you too.'

Lottie shook her head vigorously. She knew her sisters were trying to help, but they could never understand.

'No, that's not going to work, sorry,' she said. 'He's up in Scotland anyway. I just want to remember the Leo *I* knew.'

There was a moment's silence, and Lottie realized that

Em looked as exhausted as she felt. But after a few seconds, Annie started talking again. 'I remember when I first met Charlie. I was in Boston for a conference about kidney disease and he was there on some insane banking jolly. He and his team were using up what remained of the hospitality budget, buying everyone in the bar glasses of champagne like the posh, privileged dickheads most of them were — it definitely wasn't love at first sight, let's put it like that.' Lottie smiled despite herself. She vaguely remembered Annie had met Charlie at some work thing, but over the years she'd forgotten the details. 'Anyway, he handed me and my friend a glass and stayed to chat. And over the next few hours I found out that, although status and money were important to him, he was also funny and interesting and generous and thoughtful. We ended up sacking off our respective reasons for being in the city and instead spent the next five days together exploring in a blissful couple bubble. I look back now and can't believe I missed pretty much the whole conference, but I came home thinking I'd learned so much — not about kidney disease maybe, but about Charlie. If I'd applied to go on Mastermind at that point, Charlie would have been my specialist subject.

'It wasn't until years later that I realized how naive I'd been. If I'd actually sat in that big black chair and been asked questions about Charlie, I would have scored one, maybe two points. Because while I might have known his favourite food or what he thought about American politics, I had no idea about all the different jigsaw pieces that fit together to make him ... him. It wasn't until I'd got to know his friends and seen him around his family, and hit rock bottom and felt him lift me back up from the depths again, and seen the utter joy on his face when singing along horribly out of tune to The Killers at Wembley, or watched him cry when he first held his sister's newborn daughter, that I could ever say I knew him properly. And even now, every day I learn new things about him – like the annoying way he eats the porridge he's decided he *has* to have each morning, or that he still refuses to buy his shirts from anywhere except this one shop in Cambridge where his dad always got his from, even though we live nearly a hundred miles away. And maybe some of these jigsaw pieces irritate me or make me angry – and when I say "maybe" I mean "definitely do" – but when I look at the picture all the pieces make when they're put together, I realize that's what I love, who I love.

'Anyway, I suppose what I'm saying, Lottie, is that if Leo was still alive, you'd have met his family and many of his friends by now, and you'd have been through some highs and lows together, and you'd have started putting together his jigsaw puzzle, working out which pieces you liked and which you didn't. You'd have had time to decide whether you definitely wanted to invest more time in trying to finish the puzzle. You only knew him for such a short time and you barely got to start the jigsaw. But you could maybe find more pieces by talking to Ross – and in turn you could provide more pieces of Ross's version of the puzzle and help him too.'

Lottie stared at her sister. What she'd just said was the most un-Annie-like thing she thought she'd ever heard – and Em was clearly surprised too; she was sitting back in her chair gazing at Annie thoughtfully.

'But what if I find pieces of the jigsaw I don't like,' Lottie blurted out.

'But, darling, nobody is perfect. Not Leo, not Charlie, not even Luca!'

Lottie smiled briefly as Em laughed and nodded hard. Then she said out loud the sentence that had been spinning around in her brain for four months. 'Leo knew. He knew he had a heart condition that meant he could die, and he didn't tell me. And Ross knew too,' she spat, on a roll now. 'But even after Leo was gone, Ross didn't bother to tell me the truth. So, you're right, I am angry. Of course I'm angry. What kind of person does that?'

Lottie's sisters stared at her.

'How long have you known all this?' Annie eventually asked.

'Since the funeral,' Lottie admitted. 'I overheard some of Leo's friends talking about it and then his mum said something too. She must have thought Ross had already told me.'

Annie frowned heavily, her mouth set in a straight line. 'And you didn't think to mention this to us until now?'

Lottie couldn't bear to see the frustration on her older sister's face, nor the hurt and sadness in her younger sister's eyes.

'I can't believe you kept all of this to yourself. We could have helped you talk things through,' Em said quietly. Lottie stared at the floor. 'Have you spoken to Ross about it at all?

Did you ask him why he didn't tell you or why he thinks Leo didn't?'

Lottie hugged her knees and shook her head, readying her defences against the inevitable 'Don't you think you should?' question.

But before Em could say what she was obviously thinking, Annie cut in. 'You seem to be pretty angry with Ross in all of this. Don't you think you might be being a little unfair? Surely it was Leo's place to tell you what was going on, not his?'

'Leo was going through something terrible – a life-changing diagnosis – no wonder his head wasn't in the right place!' Lottie shot back immediately. 'I don't blame him for not telling me. But Ross should have said something – as soon as Leo died, he should have told me. I even asked him on the phone if Leo had known he had a heart condition, but he chose not to answer, and I was too caught up in my grief to push it. Ross decided I wasn't important enough to know all the information because he thought he knew best and decided to play God. But Leo loved me and I loved him, and no matter how much Ross doesn't want that to be true, it is.'

Annie's frown intensified. 'Maybe he thought Leo had told you – as you say, you loved each other so it's fair to think he'd have told you something like that.'

Lottie stared at her sister, fury rising in her throat, before Em stepped in and said gently, 'I think what Annie means is that, while it's of course understandable that you're angry, from what you've told us, Ross was under a lot of strain organising the funeral and the post-mortem and trying to make sure everyone was OK. Maybe he didn't hear you ask him, or perhaps he thought you already knew about Leo's heart condition. But whatever happened and whoever should have told you, Lots, it's really not healthy to hold on to this much anger.' Lottie watched her sisters exchange a glance before Em continued. 'Both Annie and I have been worried about you, sweetheart. It doesn't feel like you're dealing that well with everything that's happened – totally understandable, of course, it's been completely overwhelming.' She took a breath. 'But I wonder whether all of this anger you've been holding on to is a bit of a smokescreen so you don't actually have to deal with the most important part of all: that Leo's dead. I'm sorry, Lots, however much none of us want it to be true, he isn't coming back.'

Chapter Sixteen

Lottie didn't know how to reply to her sisters. She was emotionally drained, and she felt angry at herself for speaking her thoughts out loud; she should have just continued pretending she was fine. So she told them she wasn't feeling great and needed to go to bed.

Even so, it was almost another hour before she was able to get rid of Annie and Em. They insisted on doing the washing-up and tidying the kitchen, and kept suggesting that one of them should stay the night. Eventually, they agreed to leave her to sleep off her exhaustion on the proviso she call them if she needed anything at all.

When Lottie was finally able to sink under the duvet and shut out the world around her, she found she couldn't sleep. As she lay there cocooned in the darkness, she tried to force her thoughts away from everything that had been said and done in the last few hours. Instead, she tried to imagine that Leo was in bed next to her, comforting her. But somehow it felt all wrong. Whereas just a few weeks ago she'd been able to conjure his warmth whenever she needed it, tonight she struggled to remember the feel of his arms around her and the touch of his breath on her neck. Without him physically there beside her, she was well and truly alone.

Despite claiming to her sisters she didn't blame Leo at all for not telling her about his diagnosis, in the black of night she was able to admit to herself that, underneath it all, she *was* angry with him. Angry and disappointed. This was a man who'd told her he loved her, but he hadn't felt able to tell her that his life might be in danger. And if he hadn't told her *that* . . . She shook her head to chase the thought away, but still she couldn't settle – because there *had* been times when his mood had suddenly changed and he'd seemed prickly and almost secretive, but she'd shrugged them off, determined not to let the incidents ruin their otherwise perfect relationship. She shook her head again, but continued to toss and turn. Eventually, she grabbed her phone from her bedside table. Without pausing to let herself think, she opened a new message and typed:

Hi Ross, hope you're doing OK. Just wondered if you had a few minutes to talk at some point. My sisters think it would be good for me to talk about Leo with someone who knew him too, so I'm sending you this message. No worries if you are too busy though. Thanks, Lottie

The following morning was Monday, and, telling herself it was no surprise Ross hadn't replied in the early hours,

Lottie forced her exhausted body into work. She had never been more thankful Rachel was on holiday for a few days. Normally, she'd moan how long the days felt without her friend's constant chat messages pinging up on her computer, and their discussions about when and where they should go for lunch, which started five minutes after they'd finished their first coffee of the day and often coincided with the start of their hour-long morning editorial meeting.

But today, Rachel's absence was what had stopped Lottie calling in sick. Other than her sisters, Rachel was the only person who said 'How are you?' and actually wanted – even insisted – to know the truth. All of her other work colleagues, as friendly and lovely as they were, would let her get away with 'I'm fine, thanks. How was your weekend?' even when the black circles under her eyes were so heavy her whole face looked grey. Even Guy, when she finally made it in and sat down her desk, just said, 'You don't look very well this morning, Lottie, are you sure you should be here? You don't want to pass a bug on to everyone in the team.' He'd then launched into a story about a woman at his old place of work who'd infected everyone with a twenty-four-hour sickness just as they had to hit an important deadline, but was thankfully forced to stop when Reg appeared next to Lottie's desk.

'Are either of you coming to this morning's meeting, or have you decided you don't need to bother for some reason this week?' he asked icily.

'S-sorry, we lost track of time. We were discussing some

ideas we'd had for the site, weren't we, Guy?' Lottie managed to say brightly.

'Oh, yes, Lottie's got some great ideas,' Guy replied immediately. As Guy sauntered off towards the meeting room and Reg followed, Lottie gathered up her pen and notebook, shooting them both daggers. Monday mornings were always a bit of a stretch ideas-wise, and today was even worse, especially as she knew that after Guy's unhelpful comment, Reg would be expecting her to come up with something brilliant.

As predicted, after boring on for a few minutes about productivity and budgets, Reg turned to Lottie just as she was sneaking another peek at her phone's home screen for signs of a message from Ross, and said, 'Lottie, why don't you share the great ideas you've had with the rest of the team?'

She took her sip from her water bottle, buying herself another vital few seconds. 'Umm, I was just saying we should do some spotlights on the site on . . . ' She looked around the room, desperately hoping for something – anything – to spark an idea in the half a second she had left before she looked like an absolute idiot in front of her boss and whole team. 'On the weather?' she said desperately, as the sun came streaming into the room through the window and bounced off the very bald and shiny top of Reg's head.

'Weather? Right,' he said, clearly less than impressed. 'We've done quite a lot of features on the weather over the years – in fact, you've probably written most of them, Lottie. What spin on it did you have in mind?'

Lottie reached for water bottle again and took a long glug,

willing the cogs in her brain to turn even a tiny bit. Usually she could come up with at least two passable ideas to bring to their meeting while she walked the twenty steps from her desk to her chair in the meeting room. But today she had nothing at all. She fixed pleading eyes on Guy, and he gave her a wink that said, 'Fine, I'll dig you out of this one, but you are *so* going to owe me!'

'I think what Lottie means is that with an Indian summer apparently coming this week we should do a feature about the etymological origins of some of our favourite words and sayings about sunshine and heat,' he said, then added with a grin, 'You know, like "make hay while the sun shines" and "bring the heat" and the verb "to beek".' Reg's face began to redden and perspire in a way that could only mean he was trying to work out whether or not "beeking" was something he should be worried about.

'Yes, that's exactly what I meant. And beeking basically just means sunbathing, so that would fit in really well,' Lottie said quickly, in an attempt to earn some much-needed favour from their boss.

Reg removed a handkerchief from his pocket and dabbed his face. 'Hmm, OK, fine. Anyone else got any good ideas?'

Once she was out of the line of fire, Lottie's mind immediately began to wander away from the editorial meeting. The last thing she'd promised her sisters the previous evening when they'd called to check on her was that she'd break things off with Ian if she wasn't interested in a relationship with him. It was only fair on him, they'd said. But even in her completely exhausted state, she'd been able to see through their concern for a man they'd never met, and realized they didn't think it was healthy for her to keep messaging him after what had happened. She was half-tempted to do the opposite, just to go against what Annie and Em had decided was best, but frankly she didn't think she had the energy. She spent the rest of the meeting composing her message to him in her head. She only realized the meeting was over when she felt a dig in her ribs from Guy, alerting her to the fact that people were closing their notebooks and pushing their chairs back.

'Lottie, can I have a quick word?' Reg said before she could join her colleagues filing out of the room. Guy gave her a sympathetic glance and a thumbs up as he closed the door behind him.

She tried to smile across the table at her boss, but he was staring resolutely at the paper in front of him. He didn't look up as he started to speak, and Lottie couldn't help but notice his head was even pinker after an hour sitting in a direct line of sunlight beating through the window. All she could think of was the word 'porcine'. Despite everything that was going on at the moment, she could feel her mouth twitching. She forced herself to look down at her notepad to distract herself from all the pig-like images filling her brain, and tried to focus on what Reg was saying.

'As you know, Lottie, advertising hasn't been great recently and our audience figures are not going in the right direction at the moment, so I'm under more and more pressure not only to grow the site but also to cut budgets.' Reg paused, and Lottie's heart beat a little faster. One half of her brain was absorbing what Reg was saying, but the other half merely fed her snorting pigs and hogs snuffling for truffles, and she had to bite her lip hard.

'And frankly, Lottie, I've noticed that you've not been on top of your game recently. I know you've had some, er, medical issues and things going on in your private life, but I need you to be bringing more to the party.'

'Oh, right, of course. You're right, Reg. Sorry. I promise I'll do better,' she managed to say before run-walking out of the room and straight into the ladies' loos, where she finally gave into the swirl of laughter rising in her throat. But after a few seconds, she realized the sounds coming from her mouth had become sobs not giggles. She seemed to have no control over what her body was doing, and it was that that frightened her more than the possibility she might lose her job. She threw her hand over her mouth to stifle the sounds and used all of the deep-breathing techniques she'd picked up from the yoga classes she'd attended a few years back. Gradually, her breathing began to return to normal and she felt safe enough to emerge from her cubicle. Glancing at the mirror, she was glad no one was around, as what she saw staring back at her scared even Lottie herself.

By the time she'd removed the mascara that had made its way to her chin and in the process had also taken off all of the tint from the tinted moisturiser she'd slapped on that morning, she resembled a very pale but slightly less frightening version of herself. She hurried back to her desk, afraid she was going to be subjected to twenty questions by the rest of her team, but thankfully, they'd all become involved in some argument between the tech and marketing departments that simmered on for the rest of the day and took any spotlight off her.

She checked her phone yet again, but frustratingly there was still no message from Ross. Sighing, she sent Guy a quick chat message to thank him for getting her out of a tight spot (that *he'd* created, she didn't forget to mention), and managed to side-step his offer of lunch with a quick 'Better not, Reg is SOOO on my case at the moment!' so was largely left alone to look into sixteenth-century methods of harvesting hay in the sunnier months.

She arrived home hot and pretty bothered after a sweaty and arduous cycle ride. But instead of immediately stripping off and jumping in a cold shower, she stood in her living room, allowing the sweat to pool under her armpits while she furiously typed out a message.

Hi Ian, I'm so sorry to mess you around, but I don't think I can make dinner tomorrow after all. I think I probably have too many things going on right now for it to be fair on you, but I'm sure I'll see you around at something with Rachel at some point though. Take care, L x

She pressed send before she could even read back the words, then tapped out a quick message to her sisters saying she was fine but knackered after work so she was going to get an early night, then she turned her phone off to stop her constantly checking it. Next, she got a bottle of wine out of the cupboard, and a large glass, and poured herself a generous measure. Only then did she walk into her bedroom, glass in hand, and take off her damp clothes.

Later, she sat on top of the duvet, her laptop resting on her knees as, between sips of wine, she read back through every page she'd ever looked at about Long QT syndrome. She'd been doing the same thing at least once a week for the past four months. She wasn't even sure what she was looking for any more, but she didn't seem able to stop. When she hadn't drunk half a bottle of wine, she was able to recognise that a part of her was still searching for answers. She had so many questions still, for Leo, for Ross – who hadn't even bothered to reply to her message – and maybe even for God or whatever higher being she or anyone else chose to believe in.

But when she had drunk half a bottle of wine, like tonight, she kept clicking and reading and sipping. It wasn't long before she exhausted everything the internet had to say about the heart condition that had killed the love of her life. After refilling her glass, she turned her phone back on and saw Ian had replied with a nice, if bland message. She heaved a sigh of relief that at least he hadn't been a dick about things even though she'd messed him around. There was no reply from Ross.

She turned back to her laptop and whiled away another hour scrolling through the tabloids' gossip pages online, before bringing up a new window on her computer and typing the words 'lexicographer job UK' into the browser. She had no real expectation of finding anything other than the entry-level jobs she usually saw advertised, but her conversation with Reg that morning had worried her enough to see if there were any possibilities should the worst actually happen. When it threw up nothing more than a few assistant positions paying peanuts and wanting fluency in five different languages, she widened her search to include all jobs to do with language and editing.

Approximately five thousand results flashed up and she began scrolling aimlessly, still sipping her wine. But her eye suddenly snagged on one particular advert. A literacy charity in London was looking for a Head of Outreach. Though she'd barely admitted it to herself, Lottie did want a bit more out of her career than writing three hundred words about Tudor sayings for a website that might soon let her go anyway. But this job would mean leaving Oxford for the Big Smoke and being the new girl among some very clever and important people. That kind of success was for the Annies of the world, not her. For the last few years she'd decided she was better off staying as a bigger fish in a small pond, surrounded by people she knew and liked. But as she read through the list of responsibilities and desired qualities, Lottie wondered if maybe they were all skills she already had, even if she didn't get that many opportunities to show them off. Before she could overthink it, she located her years-old CV from a folder on her computer that she hadn't so much as opened for the last two years, added a few grandiose statements to the top of it and uploaded it to the application system, clicking the 'Apply' button with the kind of force she usually reserved for emailing her landlord or her mother.

Realising that her legs were burning from the heat of the laptop, she flung it to the floor – briefly wondering whether she'd regret that in the morning when she came to check if it still worked – and threw herself back onto her pillows, suddenly exhausted and wishing the September heatwave everyone else seemed so excited about would calm down.

She checked her phone yet again for a message from Ross, but the screen still just showed the same photo of her and Leo grinning at the camera, with no message notifications. She lay on her bed fidgeting, too hot to pull the covers over her, but too uncomfortable to sleep without them. Her head was starting to pound and she could feel a dragging pain in her stomach. The amount of alcohol she'd drunk tonight would normally be enough to make her pass out, but she knew her mind was still too active, so got off the bed and went for a pee. She slid down her knickers and, even in the low light from the streetlamp outside the window, she could see blood. The final proof that she wasn't pregnant. A wave of emotions broke over her – sadness, regret, guilt, and finally relief.

Chapter Seventeen

Lottie couldn't remember when she'd last been so tired. It felt like she'd just been going through the motions all week, exhausted and zombie-like during the day but unable to sleep at night as her head filled with unwanted thoughts. And even Rachel seemed to sense the need to tread carefully when she came back from her holiday with her husband in the New Forest at the end of the week. She didn't push Lottie too hard to come for 'just one' after work on Friday and even kept her comments about Ian to, 'Maybe I won't invite him to my birthday drinks next month then!'

Lottie had come up with an excuse to miss pub club that Wednesday as she just didn't have the energy to pretend she was *absolutely fine* to her sisters – the only way to stop them giving her those piercing looks and worried glances. She was furious with Ross for not bothering to reply to her message, and she couldn't help but be annoyed with her sisters too for pushing her into texting him in the first place. It had clearly been a terrible idea.

But now it was the weekend and she had two long days of nothingness stretching ahead of her. She should have been pleased she could just lie on the sofa in front of the TV, but she found she was restless and irritable, and itching to *do* something.

Her phone lit up with a notification from the sisters' WhatsApp group, and Lottie wondered if they could see into her brain after all. It was from Em, inviting them both to Sunday lunch at her house, and suggesting that Lottie came that afternoon and stayed over. Lottie's immediate response was to make another excuse as to why she couldn't go, but the quiet of the flat buzzed around her and she realized she was going mad inside the echo chamber of her own head. She would just have to go back to faking everything was okay to convince her sisters – and maybe at some point pretending things were okay would eventually make things *feel* more okay too.

She slowly tapped out a reply to Em and added that she'd supply the wine. Mentally scanning the alcohol cupboard in the kitchen to see if she had a couple of bottles still in there, she was suddenly assaulted by the memory of drinking an entire bottle a few nights earlier – and applying for that job in London. What on earth had she been thinking, she wondered now. Her heart raced at the very thought of moving her whole life away from her family and friends to a dark and dingy studio flat in somewhere like Brixton; or worse, subjecting herself to a house share with complete strangers who probably smoked weed and had all-night parties. It seemed red wine – or at least, a whole bottle of red wine – had a lot to answer for.

Lottie retrieved her laptop from the bedroom floor and saw the 'Thanks for applying for the role of Head of Outreach' tab was still open. She dreaded to think how embarrassing her application was, fuelled as it had been by an overload of Shiraz and misplaced bravado. She shook her head again and quickly deleted the tab, then searched for the name of the head of HR at the charity on LinkedIn. She fired off a polite but firm email stating that her circumstances had changed and she no longer wished to pursue her application, then breathed a sigh of relief that she'd remembered in enough time to perform damage control.

Galvanised by her sudden spurt of activity and seeing her joggers lying discarded on the floor, she suddenly decided that maybe what she needed to bring her mood levels up was to go for a run. Em was always mentioning how helpful she found running and yoga, while Annie loved lifting weights in the gym with Charlie, so every few months Lottie resolved to be more healthy herself. Today could be the start of all that. She heaved herself into her sports bra and grabbed her headphones. It was still gorgeously sunny but thankfully nowhere near as hot as it had been a few days before. However, after precisely five minutes outside – at least three of which had been spent stretching – Lottie was reminded why she never normally did this: she just wasn't made for running. She felt the urge to walk just a hundred metres along her road, even though it was downhill, and by the time she'd turned the corner, she was already sick of the Beyoncé song she'd chosen for its motivational qualities, but couldn't seem to jog and jab at her phone at the same time so she was stuck with it.

She continued walking, only half-heartedly picking her feet up a bit higher when another jogger came into view. But when she realized that the whole of Oxford appeared to be out running, she lost all interest in even pretending she was one of them. Then, of course, the heavens decided to open, so she was left with little choice than to actually run back home. As she jog-walked back up the hill, she was passed by at least two yummy mummies running faster than her despite pushing prams, but still her lungs felt like were about to explode.

Two hours later, Lottie still felt wheezy, but she had managed to have a shower and wash her hair, and there was definitely something to be said for the satisfied, smug feeling that came from being able to tell her sister she'd been for a run earlier. Maybe the whole thing had been *almost* worth it.

By the time she arrived at Em's that afternoon, even climbing out of the car made her legs protest, and half an hour of giving Alex and Dante piggybacks around the garden meant that her arms would also be killing her in the morning. But for the first time in weeks, Lottie felt something close to contented as she helped Em put the boys to bed, and then chatted to Luca while he knocked up a lasagne so delicious she knew she'd be dreaming about it for days.

'It's nice to see you smile,' Em commented as Luca stood

up to clear away their plates and Lottie helped herself to the crusty bits of pasta stuck to the lasagne dish with her fingers.

'Yeah, well, I know I haven't been a laugh-a-minute lately,' she replied, adding a grin to show her sister she was joking.

'You've had a tough few months,' Em agreed. 'But it's good to see you looking forward and not backwards again. How are things at work?'

Lottie allowed Luca to poor some more wine into her glass but quickly put her hand up to stop him from being too generous. 'It's all fine,' she replied, inwardly wincing at her less than truthful answer. 'Though Reg mentioned user numbers were down and budgets were being tightened, so I'm not holding out much hope for a promotion in the near future.'

Em scrunched up her face in concern. 'Oh, that doesn't sound good. Do you think your job is safe for now?'

'I'm not sure. Though God knows what else I could do round here, so let's hope so!'

'I'm sure you'd find something else in Oxford – maybe at the uni?' Em said.

Lottie couldn't help but think it was easy for her sister to say that from the safety of her charmed, ladies-who-lunch-because-we-don't-need-to-work life in the Cotswolds. 'There aren't many lexicographer jobs around anywhere, to be honest.'

'I'm sure something will turn up if it comes to it,' Em said cheerfully. She paused, then added shyly, 'I'm thinking about running some Italian classes locally, and when I mentioned it to some of the other mums I was surprised by how enthusiastic they were. A few even talked about me teaching the kids the basics, too.'

'Yes, I can imagine parents wanting little Henry to be fluent in Italian by the time he's six!' Lottie laughed snidely. Then, immediately feeling horrible for being so dismissive of her little sister, she quickly added, 'And you'd be a brilliant teacher, Em, especially for the little ones. You're so patient with Alex and Dante – although they're obviously both child geniuses already.'

'Of course they are, with Emilia as their mother.' Luca beamed as he rejoined them at the table and leaned over to kiss his wife on the lips. Lottie couldn't help but smile at the pure happiness that seemed to radiate from them.

But when she woke up the next morning, Lottie couldn't quite dismiss that needling feeling that Em had no idea how lucky she really was. Her youngest sister had effort-lessly glided through her life. At school, she'd been good at everything, rather than great at English and rubbish at maths like Lottie, or a high flier in the sciences she loved and just okay at the more creative subjects like Annie had been. And people loved Em. She was the girl everyone wanted to be friends with, from the too-cool-for-school illicit cigarette smokers to the always-in-the-library over-achievers. Her blend of nice but not boring, beautiful but not vain and kind but still funny won people over. By the time she'd got to university, girls wanted to be her and boys wanted to bed her. Then she met Luca during her year abroad as part of her Italian degree and, ten years later, she and Luca were just as head over heels for each other as they had been then, while Alex and Dante were the most gorgeous boys Lottie had ever laid eyes on. Em and her family were perfect in every way.

Lottie's mood wasn't helped by the fact that she had slept badly. Whether it was too much rich lasagne or the overuse of her muscles the day before, she'd lain awake most of the night. And now her brain seemed overloaded with thoughts about her sisters, her job and, of course, Leo. She'd tried to spend less time in her imaginary world recently, but often, in the small hours of the morning, she gave in and allowed herself to step inside her alternative universe again. And this morning, she just wanted to stay there, cocooned and safe with the man of her dreams.

Unfortunately, her two small nephews weren't going to let that happen and, on the dot of eight o'clock, they both ran into her room.

'Auntie Lottieeeeeee, wake up!' Alex shouted. 'We've been waiting for you to stop sleeping for yeeeeeears, but Mummy said we had to wait for the little hand to reach eight before we could come in but now it is so we're here! Can you ask Mummy if we can have chocolate toast for breakfast? Me and Dante have had some krispies but we're still hungry.'

'Sleepy-ed!' piped up Dante, jumping onto the bed and putting his hands on Lottie's head. 'Polpol, Auntie Lottie?'

'He means Calpol,' Alex translated, rolling his eyes at his brother in a manner he could only have picked up from an adult, and Lottie laughed despite her exhaustion.

'No, I don't need Polpol, Dante. Thank you for asking,

though,' she replied, gently removing his hands, which were now poking her eyes. 'And yes, I'm sure we can go and ask for some chocolate toast. In fact, why don't you let Mummy know that I've ordered a cup of tea and some chocolate toast for my breakfast? I'll be down very soon.'

The boys ran off joyfully and she got dressed. Lottie reminded herself, as she did whenever she spent any length of time with her nephews, that she should try to be more like them and find happiness in the little things in life.

Her better mood lasted most of the morning. They all went for a walk and the children delighted in jumping in puddles in their little wellies. The picture-perfect family drew admiring glances from everyone they passed. But Lottie couldn't help but wonder whether people assumed she was the kids' nanny or home help; she didn't exactly exude the same aesthetic beauty as Em and her photogenic boys. Then they came across a couple of other families who Em and Luca knew from Tots Rugby and St Swithin's, and Lottie felt strangely invisible. The parents chatted about their tiny offspring's achievements, arranged playdates and agreed they 'really must' book that pampering session at Soho Farmhouse they'd been talking about. To be fair to Em, she tried to bring Lottie into the conversations, but as soon as the other women established she didn't live in the area and didn't have children, she was ignored.

Lottie smiled and listened to Em's chatter on their walk back home, but mostly she found herself dwelling on the voices in her head, and the feelings of resentment and anger swirling inside her. What right did these people have to treat her like an outsider, a woman of low status and non-importance who was excluded from their clique? It wasn't as if she even wanted to be part of the kind of yummy-mummy life her sister now seemed to lead; it was more that it was assumed she wasn't important enough to be part of it because she didn't have all the trappings of wealth – and family.

'What time did Annie say she was getting here?' Lottie asked once they were back at the house, craving the balance their older sister brought to their dynamic.

'In about an hour, I think,' Em replied, gathering up an armful of potatoes from a veg box and handing Lottie a peeler. 'Fancy prepping the roasties?'

The pair worked in companionable silence, punctuated by appearances from the boys offering up their Lego creations for praise – as well as a near total meltdown when Alex 'whispered' to them that Dante's spaceship was 'built by Daddy really'. When the younger boy had been placated with a banana and Em had heaved a sigh of relief that all seemed to be quiet on the Western Front again, she said in what she obviously thought was a casual way, 'How did Ian reply to your message cooling things off?'

'He was fine,' Lottie answered quickly, hoping to shut down any kind of conversation about what had happened the last time she'd seen her sisters. It was hard to believe that it was only last weekend that she and Em had sat on her bed staring at a small but hugely important white stick. And Ian *had* been fine. Of course he had; he probably knew that getting involved with someone who had a ton of 'issues' wasn't a good move, even if he was too polite to say it. 'It's all in the past, and as you said, I'm trying to look forward now.' Lottie glanced down at the carrot she was vigorously peeling and quickly dropped it into the 'done' bowl. She took a breath. 'I was really grateful you came over last Saturday, Em.' She smiled at her sister.

Em waved away her words. But Lottie could tell by the determined look in her eyes that she still had something to say. 'Did you have a think about what we said about talking to Ross?'

'I texted him, actually,' Lottie replied, her tone more defensive than she'd intended.

'Oh, that's good!' Em said, clearly delighted.

'But he hasn't replied.'

Em's smile faltered a little. 'I'm sure he will eventually, he must have a lot on,' she said, before adding gently, 'But don't feel like you just have to rely on him. We could set up an appointment with a professional. I can help you do that, if you want?'

'I'm just not sure it's something that would help me,' Lottie replied, knowing Em meant well, but wishing more than ever that she and Annie would both just leave her alone. 'And I know how long you have to wait for these kind of things on the NHS – I'd be an old woman before I got my turn, and I'd only be taking a space from someone who really needs it.'

'Luca and I could pay for you to go private,' Em began, but before Lottie's brain could really process what her sister had just said, the door knocker clanked and they both jumped.

'That will be Annie,' Lottie said, slipping off her stool and storing the conversation away to be examined when she felt strong enough.

'Boys, come and say hello to Auntie Annie and Uncle Charlie,' Em called as Lottie queued behind her to hug their sister and brother-in-law.

After a cacophony of coat-taking, Lego-showing and pleading for Charlie to play cricket in the garden, the three sisters smiled at each other.

'Lunch is cooking and the veg is all prepped, thanks to Lottie, so I think we've earned a rest on the sofa,' Em said. 'How's your week been, Annie?'

They all flopped down, and as they chatted, Lottie wondered whether she should nudge her younger sister into opening one of the bottles of wine that stood on the kitchen side. Annie – who would normally have suggested they have a pre-lunch drink by now – didn't seem to be taking her usual cue. Lottie decided she'd wait for a lull in the conversation, so she didn't seem too much of a lush, especially since she'd drunk her fair share of Montepulciano the night before thanks to Luca's generous pouring. She tuned back into what Annie was saying.

'Usually I'd have dug my heels in and said that we couldn't make those kind of decisions about the project until next year, but under the circumstances, I just gave in. I think John had been all ready for a heated discussion about it so he was a bit taken aback!'

Lottie wished she'd heard the rest of the story because she had no idea what decision Annie's boss was surprised about, but at least Em seemed to have been listening. She nodded sagely and gave their sister a look Lottie couldn't read, then nodded again.

Annie cleared her throat and Lottie glanced from her to Em, confused.

'Actually, Lottie, now all of us are together, I have a bit of news,' her older sister said, her voice wobbling a little in a very un-Annie-like way. 'You know we'd decided to delay our last round of IVF for a few months? Well, then we had an appointment with our consultant and she told us we should actually probably get on with it sooner rather than later, so I started the injections and everything.'

'Oh, that's brilliant, Annie,' Lottie said, her heart constricting for her sister, knowing how tough she'd found the process last time, especially when ultimately it had all been for nothing. She also felt a twinge of guilt as she realized that her own pregnancy scare just a week ago must have raised so many emotions for Annie. Lottie hadn't even thought about what she must be feeling as she was so wrapped up in her own world. 'How are you feeling? When will you know if it's been successful?'

'Well . . . now, actually. I'm pregnant, Lottie, I'm actually pregnant!'

'What? Wow, that's amazing!' Lottie shrieked, launching herself at her sister. 'Oh my God, how many weeks are you, tell me everything. Oh, I'm so happy for you!'

'Slow down, Lots!' Em laughed. 'I'll let you two catch up while I get us some drinks. Do you want wine? And Annie, we have Seedlip, or fruit juice, or there might even be some alcohol-free beer if you fancy it?'

'Wait, you knew already, then, Em?' Lottie asked, frowning.

She saw her sisters glance at each other yet again before Annie waved her hand. 'Yeah, I had to tell someone as soon as we found out. I knew I'd burst otherwise! And you obviously had a lot going on, Lottie. We didn't know if the pregnancy would stick. But I had my three-month scan last week and it looks like you're going to have another niece or nephew come March!'

Lottie smiled along with her sister's delight as she told her how pleased the doctor had been with the eggs she'd had harvested, and how she and Charlie hadn't let themselves get too carried away, even when they put back two embryos that seemed really healthy. Then they'd done three pregnancy tests on the first day they were allowed and even then they still hadn't believed it. 'But don't worry, we're only having one! I'm not sure we could have coped with twins.' Annie grinned.

While her joy for her sister was completely genuine, Lottie couldn't help listening to the niggling voice in her head reminding her she'd been left out – *again*.

'I can't believe you've both known for weeks and are only just telling me now!' she said casually, with a laugh that sounded fake even to her own ears.

Em placed a glass of wine in her hand and squeezed her shoulder. 'As Annie said, you've had enough to deal with over the last few months.' She paused before turning her sympathetic gaze up a notch. 'And it's okay to feel a bit weird and even sad about it, especially after last weekend. We weren't sure how you'd react after everything, but I'm so glad you're happy for Annie.'

'We're all happy that we're all happy!' Annie laughed. 'Cheers, sisters!'

Lottie clinked her wine against their juice glasses, but then placed it on the table next to her, her hand shaking, the liquid almost spilling over the rim.

'Did you really think I wouldn't be happy for you, Annie?' she asked, trying to keep her voice level. The pause before either of her sisters responded was more than a beat too long, and something inside Lottie broke. 'Is that really what you think of me?' she shouted over their feeble protests. 'That I'm so self-centred I couldn't possibly be happy that my sister is actually pregnant after years and years of trying? I know I've been a bit wrapped in my own world – losing the love of your life will do that to you. But it's good to know how you both see me from your ivory towers. I'm sorry that my life isn't as perfect as yours and that I didn't bounce back from my grief as quickly as you think I should have done. But I don't need to see a shrink or "talk to someone". I just need the two people who are supposed to know me best in this world to believe in me. But if you actually think I'd make your news all about me, Annie, then maybe neither of you know me at all!'

Chapter Eighteen

Lottie's sisters begged her to 'talk about this sensibly' and 'please just listen' to what they had to say, but Lottie turned her back on them and headed for her room. She stuffed her clothes into her bag, unplugged her phone from the wall and went back down to the hall, where she retrieved her coat and furiously shrugged her arms into it. She could hear both of her nephews crying in the living room and her stomach twisted in guilt. She looked up at the sound of footsteps and saw Luca standing in the doorway.

'Lottie—'

'Luca, please could you drive me home?'

'Shouldn't you—'

'I can't, I'm sorry. Please give the boys a kiss from me and tell them I'm sorry if I scared them with my shouting. I really didn't mean to. I'll wait outside for you.'

As much as she usually enjoyed Luca's company, she was grateful he didn't try to talk to her during the forty-minute car journey. Instead, he put on some classical music, so

Lottie's fury was soothed by the sound of Einaudi's piano. But when they pulled up outside her flat and she reached for the door handle, Luca put a steadying hand on her arm.

'Em loves you, Lottie, and so does Annie. They would never do anything to hurt you, you know that. Please don't let this come between you, *mio caro*.' He kissed her on the cheek and she blinked back tears as she thanked him, then made for the safety of her flat where she let the tears fall freely. Grief, sadness and frustration all welled up inside her, but it was anger – even fury – that fuelled her sobs. Twenty minutes later, all cried out, she crawled into bed still fully clothed and fell asleep.

She woke later, her throat full of razor-blade soreness, unable to work out how long she'd been asleep. Her phone said eight o'clock, but, with the early-September sun only just beginning to set, it took her a few seconds to realize it was eight in the evening. It seemed unbelievable to Lottie that it was still the same day; still the same day she had made her nephews cry; still the same day she had found out Annie was finally having the child she had wanted for so long; still the same day she had realized how little her sisters thought of her.

She checked her phone and saw she had countless missed calls and messages, but she knew she couldn't deal with them, not yet at least. As she kicked off her jeans and pulled on her pyjamas, she was tempted just to slip under the covers and let sleep take her away again. But hunger gnawed at her stomach. It had been almost twelve hours since the piece of toast and Nutella she'd eaten that morning and her body was running on empty.

She made herself a huge bowl of pesto pasta and forked it into her mouth mechanically as she watched a shocked old lady on TV being told the brooch her late-husband had given her was worth ten thousand pounds. As the old lady began weeping with surprise and gratitude, tears leaked from Lottie's eyes yet again, and she flicked the channels until she found a suitably vapid action movie she could get lost in without fear the tap would turn on again. Ginger stalked into her living room, jumped up on the sofa and curled up beside her, his paws kneading her pyjamas as he settled into his favourite spot.

After the hero had saved the world, she turned off the TV, shooed Ginger out of her flat door, and shuffled into bed. Only then did she allow herself to peer inside the box that contained her sisters' words. Replaying the scene in her head was like rewinding a particularly upsetting Netflix show and hoping it would prove to be more watchable on second viewing. But it wasn't.

It was true that Lottie shouldn't have stormed out without letting her sisters speak. But it was also true that they seemed to have the lowest possible opinion of her if they thought she would be anything other than happy for Annie. She tried to examine her feelings as objectively as possible; but she *was* happy – in fact, completely, ridiculously happy – for her sister. She had hated having to watch Annie go through three cycles of IVF, only for each to end in a negative test, but she'd hated it even more when her sister had finished the fourth cycle and sent her and Em a photo of ten positive pregnancy tests in a line ('I had to make sure the first nine weren't false-positives, and I calculated the likelihood that all ten were incorrect to be one in five thousand, so I think we can conclude that I am definitely pregnant!') only for her to miscarry three weeks later.

But now that she could share in her sister's unbridled joy at finally getting the one thing she most wanted, it had been tainted. She shook her head sadly, turned out the light and sunk into the comfort of her mattress once again. When sleep didn't immediately come, she instinctively reached for her phone so she could scroll through social media, hoping she could tire out her eyes so they forced themselves closed, but then she remembered all of the message notifications she didn't want to look at and left her phone face down on her bedside table.

As she lay there in the dark, she attempted to ignore the thoughts snagging at the furthest reaches of her mind, like a small child tugging at its mother's skirt, but the more she tried to pretend they didn't exist, the stronger their grip became. Could she one hundred per cent honestly say happiness was the *only* emotion she felt at Annie's news? Or were there tendrils of jealousy and anger, and even shame, twisted into that happiness? Jealousy that now both her sisters seemed to have the perfect life in the perfect homes they owned with their perfect husbands and perfect children; anger that it all seemed to come so easily for Em, and even Annie, with her wealthy husband and ability to throw money at a problem until it was eventually solved; shame that she would never be as successful, well-off or even as happy as her over-achieving sisters. The awful truth struck her: she was *exactly* the mean-spirited person Annie and Em believed her to be.

Growing up, Lottie had always thought of herself as a just-above-average person – neither super clever nor totally stupid; not drop-dead gorgeous but not pig-ugly either; not the most popular but with enough friends that she felt part of something. As the middle child, she was used to constantly comparing herself to her sisters, but she had largely been happy with being the 'funny one' sandwiched between the 'brainy one' and the 'angelic one'. Her label helped to anchor her through her teenage years, tempering her expectations of how well she might do in her exams or what boys she might be able to pull on a Saturday night.

But through her twenties, she'd started to get to know herself better and give herself new labels – linguist, uncool music lover, stationery geek, high-heel hater, fiancée, potential mum – and she'd started to like the woman she'd become. But then Elliot had left her and her whole sense of self had crumbled. She wasn't who she thought she was after all. Sure, she still loved language and Elton John and note-books and trainers, but they began to feel superficial against her newest labels – former fiancée, single woman, one-bed-flat renter, childless thirty-something. She'd learned to live as this new person she barely recognised, because what choice did she have, really?

Then slowly, very slowly, she'd started to feel more comfortable in her new skin. Until, at the beginning of this year, she'd deleted the dating apps she half-heartedly scrolled through after one too many wines, and for the first time in as long as she could remember, she'd felt almost content with life.

But then she'd met Leo and the universe had shown her what she had been missing out on for the last five years. Despite Ross's best attempts to derail things, Lottie had allowed herself to believe that, thanks to Leo, she could have the friendship, the attraction, the love, and even the children, that her sisters had, and that she'd convinced herself she didn't need, but deep down she knew she craved.

Then, in the blink of an eye, all those dreams, all that expectation, all that happiness had been ripped away from her. It was as if the universe was taunting her like a quiz-show host telling a losing contestant 'here's what you could have won'. Except she wasn't leaving a television studio empty-handed and returning to normal life otherwise unscathed. She had been changed for ever by what had happened to her. Now, it seemed, she had changed so much she'd become a person who was jealous of – and even angry at – her own sister for finally finding the happiness she'd been chasing for years.

As she paced around her flat in the dead of night, what shocked Lottie even more than this realisation, was that her sisters had seen her for what she really was before she had herself. She knew Em didn't have a bad bone in her body, so for her little sister to acknowledge such shameful qualities in her was truly shocking. Her legs shook and she collapsed onto the sofa.

Lottie was still sitting staring into the gloom when the soft beams of the early-morning sun began to weave their way into her living room through the barely drawn curtains. The weak shards of light felt like they were piercing her sensitive flesh; her whole body ached and her head felt too heavy for her shoulders. She pushed herself upwards, staggered a little, then slowly made her way into the bedroom, with the gait of someone three times her age. She reached for her phone and sunk back onto the bed. As soon as she'd blindly thumbed out the briefest email to Reg saying she had a flu-like virus and didn't want to pass it on to the rest of the office, and an even briefer text to Rachel telling her not to worry, she pulled the duvet over her head and tried to shut out the world. She slept fitfully on and off, then woke up with a start, her heart racing and her skin clammy, though she had no memory of what she'd been dreaming about.

She forced herself out of bed and into the shower; the sensible side of her brain told her she needed to break the cycle she seemed to have fallen into over the last twenty-four hours of sleeping during the day and staying up all night. She pulled on fresh pyjamas, making a mental note to put some laundry on later, or she'd soon run out of the joggers and vest tops she only took off when she was forced to leave the house, and ate her way through a packet of jaffa cakes in front of back-to-back episodes of an American reality show about wannabe magicians. Life felt strangely unreal, as if when she opened her front door she'd find the world had stopped turning and that nothing really existed.

When her thoughts returned to what had happened with her sisters the previous day, she felt detached from it, like it had happened to another Lottie entirely. The only thing that made sense was the parallel world she allowed herself to wander into when the noise inside her head became too much, but even that felt disconnected and strange. Even after scrolling through countless photos on her phone, sometimes she found it hard to picture every detail of Leo's face and it scared her. So she'd often disappear into the comforting memory of that perfect night together where they'd stayed up talking into the early hours, listening to his heart beating strongly against her cheek, as she snuggled into his chest. Sometimes it was the only thing that kept her sane. But tonight it felt odd and wrong.

'Am I a jealous person?' she said into the empty air of her flat. She tried to imagine that Leo was in the room with her, and what he would say. She wanted to picture him telling her that she was perfect, the most unselfish, loyal, genuine person he'd ever met. But she couldn't conjure the words, or even the sound of his voice. Maybe it was because he'd never had the chance to find out if she was jealous or not during those three idyllic months they'd had together. Or maybe it was because she was none of those things she wanted to be: unselfish, loyal or genuine.

'Am I going mad?' she asked out loud again. She hadn't

spoken for over twenty-four hours and she felt her throat grind the words into the empty room. 'Is the first sign of going mad talking to yourself when you know no one else can hear you?'

As she found her voice, the sound of it bouncing off the walls around her began to feel strangely reassuring and real, so she kept going, standing up from the sofa and saying whatever came into her mind. 'Lottie, I put it to you that you are jealous of everything your sisters have that you don't. You shouted at them and stormed out of the house without letting them speak and you haven't answered any of their calls and texts since. How do you plead?' While the word *guilty* looped inside her brain, she couldn't bring herself to say it out loud.

'What's next on your self-destruction list?' she continued, her voice growing stronger. 'Handing your notice in at work? Rowing with Rachel and Guy?' She paused for breath and realized she'd been pacing the flat again. She stopped in front of her floor-to-ceiling mirror in the hallway and stared at her reflection. Her mousey hair hung lankly around her shoulders and her skin looked sallow and dull. 'Or maybe you could pick up the phone to your sisters and tell them you're sorry, that yes you are a bit sad about Annie's news, as well as madly happy for her, and that actually you're not as fine as you said you were. In fact, you haven't been fine since that moment four months ago when you answered Ross's phone call.' The face looking back at Lottie in the mirror was of a woman who was weighed down, exhausted, scared. But there was also a hint of something else burning in her eyes, however faintly: determination.

Lottie gripped her phone. She scrolled to the top of her recent calls list and her thumb hovered over Em's name. She glanced back at the mirror and this time the only thing she could read on the face looking back at her was fear. Hands shaking, she thrust her phone into her pocket and out of sight, and moved back into the lounge, taking up position on the sofa and playing the next episode of the reality show she'd been watching, like an addicted zombie.

Minutes, hours passed, time structured only by the length of each episode, until suddenly a foreign noise broke through the fog. Someone was knocking on her door. Lottie froze, so unused to anyone turning up at her flat unannounced that she almost forgot what to do. But then the knocker clanked again, and, reluctantly, she got up. It was only as she was turning the keys in the lock that she realized she was in no fit state – physically or mentally – to see anyone. But she'd already alerted whoever was on the other side of the door to her presence, and she was far too British to run down the hall and pretend she wasn't in.

The door was always a bit sticky, so she gave it a yank, and it flew open, harder than she was expecting, to reveal the last person she would have guessed her visitor to be.

'Lottie. Hi.'

She blinked. 'Ross, what on earth are you doing here?'

Chapter Nineteen

Lottie stared at Ross, her mind cycling through emotions so fast it couldn't land on any one thought. He stood there, also seemingly unable to put a sentence together, until the silence grew so uncomfortable Lottie felt compelled to repeat her question, not caring that it sounded even ruder the second time around.

'What are you doing here?'

'Sorry to turn up unannounced,' he said, his words tumbling over hers. 'Sorry, you go.'

'No, no, carry on.'

'Right, sorry. I was just going to say – I know I should have called before just turning up here, but I got your message and I wanted to talk to you and it didn't feel right to do it over texts. I tried to call you after the funeral but it went straight to voicemail and I didn't leave you a message, and well . . . ' He tailed off and looked at his feet. Lottie opened her mouth to fill the gap, but quickly shut it again when she realized she had no idea what to say. Ross took his hands out of his pockets and attempted a smile. 'But I agree, I think it would be good for us to talk. And I thought we should do it face to face.'

Lottie frowned. 'Face to face?' She tried to force her brain to actually make sense of what Ross was saying, rather than just parroting his words back to him.

'Yes. I was coming down anyway to see Leo's parents, and then I got your text last week . . .'

Lottie felt herself flinch at the sound of Leo's name, but the feeling was quickly replaced by a shot of anger. If Ross had really wanted to talk to her, he wouldn't have waited a whole week after she'd messaged him to tell her that! 'I'm a bit busy right now,' she answered, looking at him and daring him to contradict her obvious lie.

'Of course, and I'm sorry again for not calling ahead. I'm in Oxford for a few days. What about tomorrow night?'

'I'm busy then too, I'm afraid,' she replied immediately, cringing at how abrupt it sounded, but unable to stop herself. 'I mean, I've got a lot of things on with work and, you know, other things.'

'Other things?' Ross said, his eyebrows raised. Was that a hint of a smile on his face? Was he mocking her, Lottie wondered angrily.

'Yes, other things,' she shot back. 'I don't have to explain myself to you.'

'I wasn't suggesting you should,' he replied in an irritatingly mild voice. 'I just thought it would be nice to catch up, see how you are. Eddie and Margaret were asking after you.'

At the mention of Leo's parents, Lottie softened a little. 'How are they doing?'

'They're a bit up and down, to be honest. But they're doing OK, considering ... '

Lottie didn't need to fill in the end of his sentence. 'Send them my love, won't you?' He nodded and her heart twisted with guilt that she hadn't thought to send them so much as a card in the four months since their son's funeral. 'I could go for a quick drink tomorrow night maybe?' she said in a rush.

'That would be great.' Ross's face lit up. 'I could meet you after work, or wherever is easiest for you.' Lottie nodded, and they arranged a time and a pub. His smile was even wider now. 'I'll see you tomorrow, then. Bye, Lottie.'

Before Lottie could shut the door, Ginger strolled in as if he owned the place, but she didn't have the strength to pick him up and deposit him back outside. She locked the door and breathed out for what felt like the first time in hours. It was only as she trudged the six steps back to the safety of the sofa that she realized not only had she just made Ross stand on the doorstep without even thinking to invite him in, but that she had stood there in her oldest, most comforting pyjamas, which were once bright pink, but were now washed-out and threadbare to the point of indecent. Lottie threw herself on the sofa in abject embarrassment. Ginger glared at her and began kneading a hole in the sofa in protest. Lottie sighed. Not even her sisters had seen her wear these pyjamas for the last five years and she had just exposed them – and apparently herself – in all their glory to a man she'd last seen when she'd yelled at him at his own cousin's funeral. Excellent.

She'd half-decided to take the following day off work, too, thinking that if she went into the office and said her flu symptoms had magically disappeared overnight it would be another black mark against her name. She was fairly sure she was getting very close to the limit of how many black marks Reg was going to allow her to have. But she woke up at 6.30 a.m. and, knowing there was no way she was going to be able to get back to sleep – and that she couldn't face another day on her own in her flat, stewing and panicking about her impending drink with Ross – she bit the bullet and started to get ready for work.

She pulled on her favourite green midi-dress and plugged in her straighteners, deciding she might as well make the most of the extra time she had. She sniffed the air and glanced at her straighteners suspiciously, before realising that the burning smell was probably the layer of dust that had settled on them since she'd last bothered to use them. Giving them a cursory blow, she set to work on taming her painfully-in-need-of-a-cut hair into submission. She remembered how therapeutic and satisfying she had always found the process of dividing her hair into sections and straightening each part in turn until it was all glossy and sitting uniformly just above her shoulders. Not that she was making any kind of extra effort for her meeting with Ross later – she hadn't even decided she was definitely going to turn up.

Even after she'd faffed around with the coffee machine, topped her cereal with both chopped banana *and* strawberries, and watched a repellent breakfast-news presenter sneer at an equally repulsive politician, it was somehow still nowhere near eight o'clock. It was like time was operating in a whole different dimension. She picked up her phone and began composing a message to her sisters, but when she couldn't past 'Hi both', she admitted defeat and headed out of the house.

She couldn't bring herself to go into the office early and make small talk with any of her over-eager workmates, so she got off the bus before her usual stop and wandered into Christ Church Meadow. It was still too early for the whirlwind of tourists to be flying around, and the university term hadn't yet started, so it was mercifully quiet, other than a few shouts from rowers on the river beyond.

The morning sun was just beginning to unfurl and Lottie raised her face to feel the welcome heat. She sat down on a bench and opened her work emails, sending Reg a quick message to tell him the symptoms she'd thought yesterday were flu had turned out to be really awful PMT so she'd be coming in to work today after all. She wasn't a fan of falling back on the old 'women's problems' excuse, but she also didn't need Reg asking too many questions. Then, before she could think too much about it, she tapped out a message to her sisters saying she hoped they were both okay and that she just needed a bit of space but would see them soon.

Once she'd pressed send, she allowed herself to scroll through the many, many messages they'd both sent since

Sunday afternoon. None of them seemed to be written in the accusatory way she'd feared, and all of them said they were worried about her and just wanted her to be happy. Guilt curled its way around her body at the added stress she had caused them both, especially when Annie was anxious enough already. New messages from them both appeared within seconds, but despite their pleas, she still couldn't bring herself to reply with anything more than, *Please don't worry, I'm fine, speak soon x*. She knew that she should tell them that Ross had asked her to meet him this evening, as it would make them both happy, but she couldn't bring herself to. Maybe it was knowing she'd have to answer all their totally reasonable questions when she didn't have the answers, or that they'd inevitably bombard her with messages of support and advice that would make her feel even guiltier for her recent behaviour. She put her phone back in her pocket and tried to lose herself in the beauty of the meadow.

Glancing at her watch, she realized she'd dawdled too long and was now in danger of actually being late for work. Knowing that Reg would be watching her like a hawk, she broke into a trot as she made her way through the city centre and out the other side to her not-quite-so-salubrious office.

'You're back!' Rachel squealed as she walked in. 'Although you don't look great, I have to say. You're all red and sweaty and your eyes look a bit funny. Should you be here?'

'You don't look very well, Rach is right,' Guy said loudly from the other side of the office. 'You didn't look great the other day either. I hope you don't have the lurgy – I don't want to be ill before my trip to Oz. I'm going on Saturday, don't forget!'

'What Guy means is he hopes you feel better, Lottie, because he missed you yesterday. Also, no one's going to forget your trip, darling – you mention it at least five times a day.' Rachel laughed. 'Come with me to fill my water bottle in the kitchen, Lottie, and we can have a catch up.' Lottie gratefully followed her friend away from everyone's attention, fanning her still-red face.

'I just walked here a bit fast, that's all,' she said, taking the glass of water Rachel handed her and downing it immediately.'

'Are you really OK?' her friend asked, eyeing her beadily. 'I've been a bit worried about you recently.'

'Not you too!' Lottie replied, sighing and rolling her eyes. 'Em and Annie are obsessed with checking I'm all right as well.'

'And are you? All right, I mean. If your sisters are worried then I'm probably right to be as well. What was wrong yesterday?'

Lottie quickly weighed up whether the PMT excuse would wash with Rachel and decided, on balance, that it was better to go with something slightly closer to the truth. 'I just had one of those days. You know, when everything feels a bit shit and you just can't face the world?' Seeing her friend's worried expression, she quickly added, 'I was probably just hormonal, and I feel fine today anyway. How was yesterday – did anything exciting happen?'

Rachel gave her a long look, but then obviously decided not to push things. She launched into a story about Reg's foul mood and how he'd shouted at just about everyone in their Monday-morning meeting that their ideas weren't good enough – even Guy who he usually left well alone, preferring to focus his ire on the female members of the team, much to Lottie and Rachel's annoyance.

'He told me last week we needed to make some budget cuts,' Lottie admitted. 'Maybe he knows something about the dictionary's future we don't.'

'That's weird, he hasn't mentioned the cuts to me,' Rachel said, frowning. 'And to be fair, Guy was totally asking for it. He was being super annoying – you know how he gets weirdly argumentative and digs his heels in when anyone dares to suggest his idea isn't as good as he thinks it is. Oh well, let's not worry about that now. Did you hear that Chrissie in marketing got engaged?'

The day passed quickly as Lottie ploughed through her inbox and tried to suck up to Reg whenever she could, earning herself a vomit sign from Guy and a thumbs up from Rachel. She was still finishing her weather feature when she realized it was six o'clock and everyone else was heading for the door as quickly as they could. Grabbing her make-up bag, she went to the ladies' and stared at herself in the harsh lighting, examining whether her eyes still looked 'a bit funny' as Rachel had told her that morning.

At that moment, her friend barrelled through the door and caught Lottie with her mascara in hand. 'I knew you were up to something!' she said with a grin. 'I know you were all hot and bothered this morning, but I could tell you'd made an effort – you only ever wear that dress on special occasions. So, what is it?'

'What's what?' Lottie replied, trying to arrange her face into a picture of innocence, but catching sight of her reflection and realising she couldn't look more guilty if she tried.

'What's the special occasion? Oh my God, please tell me the only thing wrong with you yesterday was exhaustion after a weekend with a hot man who you're about to go and meet for round two.'

Lottie couldn't help but smile. 'Ha! Sadly, I was actually under the weather yesterday.'

'So, where are you going tonight? You know you want to tell me . . . ' she wheedled.

Lottie sighed. 'Believe me, it's not as exciting as you think. I've said I'll see Ross.'

'Ross?' Rachel paused, then frowned. 'As in Leo's cousin Ross? As in the guy who made you feel like actual shit when you first met him?'

'Yes, as in him. He wants to talk about Leo, and I guess I took pity on him. He has just lost his cousin, after all.' Lottie wasn't sure why she'd suddenly become so defensive about seeing him, especially as she'd been umming and ahhing all day about whether she was actually going to go anyway.

'Rather you than me.' Rachel pulled a face. 'I think I liked my imagined hot man date better, to be honest.'

'Ha! Me too.' Lottie forced an awkward laugh and felt

herself blush. What was wrong with her? 'Anyway, I better go,' she said before her friend could ask her any more questions. 'Wish me luck.'

'Just send me a *help!* text at any point and I'll call and invent a work emergency,' Rachel said, pulling her into a hug.

'Thanks, Rach. I'm not really sure what possible emergency an online dictionary could have at eight o'clock on a Tuesday night, but I'll leave that one for you to figure out.'

The streets of Oxford were full of tourists and locals alike, soaking up the unexpected September sunshine, and as Lottie made her way to the bar down the road, she managed to forget everything that was going on for a couple of minutes and just let the laughter and smiles and chatter envelop her. But as she walked through the pub, scanning the packed beer garden and finally spotting Ross waving to catch her attention, she had never wanted to turn around and run home as much as she did in that moment. What the hell was she doing?

Chapter Twenty

'I didn't know what you'd want to drink so I bought two pints of lager and thought you could throw one over me if you didn't want to drink it,' Ross deadpanned as Lottie reached the table. It wasn't what she was expecting him to say at all, and she momentarily frowned in confusion, but then he broke into a nervous grin. 'Or I could distract you and quickly down it to avoid a soaking.'

Lottie picked up the drink he'd slid across the table to her. 'It's cold and it's wet, so it sounds pretty good to me,' she said with a smile. 'God, I thought this ridiculous Indian summer had burned itself out, but it seems to have come back with a vengeance today.' She fanned herself with her hand as she sat down and took a huge sip of beer.

'It was even hot back home before I left – or as hot as Scotland ever gets, anyway. I'm not sure I'm built for heat-waves,' he said with a rueful smile.

Lottie took another long drink from her glass, both because she was as thirsty and hot as she'd confessed, but also to give her brain a moment to reconcile the person sitting opposite her with the practical, serious figure she'd seen at the funeral a few months before, and the snarky, unpleasant, arrogant man she'd encountered at their first official meeting.

'How long are you down here for?' she asked, trying hard not to seem rude as she wrestled with her thoughts.

'Till next Monday. My parents were coming down to stay with Eddie and Margaret and I didn't like the idea of Dad driving all that way, so I took a few days off work and suggested we share the drive. I'm planning on catching up with some friends for a few days and then spending the rest of the week with my folks.'

'Sounds like a lovely plan.' There was a pause as they both sipped their drinks again, but Ross didn't seem in any hurry to restart the conversation and Lottie wondered if she was the only one feeling awkward. Even amongst the hum of happy chatter all around them in the beer garden, she couldn't stop herself reaching for another silence breaker. 'Bet it's nice to have a week off work too.'

'Yeah, it's always nice not to be staring at my laptop. Although I am lucky to do a job I love, so most of the time it doesn't feel much of a chore.'

'What is it that you do?' she asked politely, having searched her memory in vain for what Leo had told her.

'I work for a water aid charity. It's not always the most exciting of jobs, but it can really feel like I'm making a difference, especially when I see the pictures of our schemes in action all over the world.' He smiled again and it struck Lottie that she'd never met a man who seemed so sure in his own skin – but not in an arrogant or smug way. It unnerved her how different he was from how she remembered – and how relaxed he seemed, when she was feeling uncomfortable and prickly.

'So what did you want to talk about?' she blurted out. 'Sorry, I mean ... I'm just finding this a bit weird,' she stumbled.

'Lottie, it's fine,' Ross said, touching his hand lightly against hers. She quickly moved her hands into her lap and started picking at a stray thread on her dress. If Ross took offence, he didn't show it. 'I just thought it would be good for us to talk. I hate that I upset you at the funeral. There was just so much going on that day.' For the first time since he'd waved to her across the beer garden, she felt his confident air falter a little, and his voice became quieter, whether consciously or not. 'I wanted to come after you and talk to you properly, but I had to look after my aunt and uncle and then when I looked for you, you'd already left.'

'Of course, your family had to come first.' Lottie nodded vigorously. Then trying to affect as neutral a tone as she could, she added, 'But you have my number. I didn't hear anything from you for four months, you don't answer my text and then you just turn up on my doorstep out of the blue. Talking didn't seem that high on your priorities before, so what's changed?' The calm demeanour she'd tried to channel quickly vanished and even she was surprised at the anger in her words. She took a quick breath and went to apologise again, but something stopped her. Because she *was* angry. Angry about the way Ross had treated her when they'd first met; and angry that she'd found out about Leo's heart condition not from her boyfriend, not even from Ross, but from other people at his funeral.

'I know, I should have tried harder,' Ross replied, his voice sounding even quieter after Lottie's raised tones, though his eyes didn't flicker from hers. 'But I've been trying to process Leo's death. You feel the same I'm sure.' Only now did he glance down at his drink, his voice almost a whisper. 'It's still hard to believe he's gone.'

Even a heart made from granite couldn't fail to be moved by the grief so clearly etched across Ross's face – he'd lost the closest thing he'd had to a brother, after all. But Lottie realized that, though she did of course feel sorry for him, the emotion at the forefront of her mind was still fury – even stronger than before. How dare Ross presume to know how she was feeling? He knew nothing about her, and nothing about her relationship with Leo. She tried to reach for the right words to show him how incensed she was, but her brain was a jumble of sounds that she couldn't join together, and a bolt of nausea coursed through her. She went to grab her glass to take a steadying gulp of beer, but she realized her hands were shaking, and she shoved them back onto her lap out of sight. It felt like her body was having an allergic reaction.

'Lottie? Are you OK, do you want me to get you some water or something?'

'I don't feel great actually, I'll just—' She finished the sentence by running inside the pub and into the ladies' loos.

In the cubicle, she rested her head against the cool tiles of the wall, not caring what awful bugs she might pick up, and tried to breathe away the sick, swirly feelings in her stomach as her legs wobbled precariously. She forced herself to concentrate on breathing through the next ten seconds, and then the next, and then the next ten, and after several minutes, she felt the adrenalin begin to subside.

It felt like she'd run a marathon – except one where she was being chased by bears the whole time. She briefly wondered if that was how Leo had felt in his final moments, but she grabbed the skin on her thigh hard and her pain receptors leapt into action, chasing the thought away. Her heart rate sped up again. What was happening to her?

She didn't know how long she sat hunched on the seat, her body firing off messages through her nervous system, making first her feet and then her hands tingle with pins and needles, her brain unable to hold on to any one thought. The quiet of the bathroom was periodically broken as the door swung open, letting in the gentle hubbub from outside. Then suddenly it was broken by a foghorn voice bellowing, 'Is there anyone called Lottie in here? Your man wants to know if you're all right!' Then came a knock on the cubicle door. 'Hey, you okay in there?'

'Y-es,' Lottie quickly stuttered. 'I'm just coming.'

'Good stuff, I'll go and tell your man. He was looking a bit worried out there all on his own. Hope you patch things up between you, babe.'

'And you,' Lottie replied automatically, before she had a chance to realize her response didn't really make sense.

The noise of the pub faded again as the girl swung the door back in place, and Lottie gingerly slid the cubicle lock back and peeped out. Thankfully, there was no one else there and she was able to stare at her smudged mascara and red eyes in the mirror without an audience. Not that she was able to do much about her appearance other than scrub at the black lines on her cheeks and smooth down her hair as much as possible. She scrunched up her eyes to block out her reflection then put her head down and opened the door. She could see Ross pacing up and down the carpet at the end of the corridor.

'Lottie, are you OK?' he said, his eyes wide. 'I was worried.'

'Sorry. I suddenly felt sick and came over a bit funny. It's probably the heat.' She tried to force her mouth into a sort-of smile. 'I think maybe I should head home, though, if that's OK.'

'Of course! You don't look very well. I've got the car so I can drive you home.'

'No, really, there's no need, I'm fine.'

'I insist. You can't walk home if you're poorly. I'm just in the shopping centre car park, but I can bring the car round here and pick you up from the side street maybe?'

'The car park's fine. I'm feeling a bit better already,' she lied. She couldn't think of anything worse than spending more time with Ross, but she also just wanted to get back to the safety of her own flat as quickly as possible, and the shopping centre was only a few minutes away.

They walked in silence, and even though Lottie could feel

him glancing at her in concern, she couldn't bring herself to reassure him she was fine again. Once they were in his clearly expensive car, and the air con and inoffensive radio station were providing a backing soundtrack, Ross seemed to relax a little.

'Feeling sick is the absolute worst, isn't it?' he said. 'I remember one time when me and Leo were kids – we must have been about seven or eight – it was a few days before the holidays ended and we decided we needed to do something exciting that we could boast about to everyone at school.'

As he talked, Lottie squirmed inside. She was torn: she knew her sisters were right that it could help to hear Ross's stories of the Leo she never knew, but she was also afraid that the memory of *her* Leo would fade even further. She was already struggling to fit together all of the pieces of him, and she was scared. Her thoughts crowded in on each other and she turned away from the sound of Ross's voice and stared out of the window, one part of her trying to shut out everything but the hum of the road, while the other followed Ross's words. If he noticed her discomfort, he didn't show it. He continued his story as if she were listening avidly.

'So we went to the woods near where we lived and spent the whole morning picking mushrooms and God knows what else to create some kind of "pie" that we'd decided we were going to cook over a fire. Leo had nicked some matches from his dad's shed. And before you ask, yes, we were obsessed with those old Willard Price adventure books. The thought of surviving on our own in the woods was the height of excitement! Obviously, it was back in the days when parents just let their kids go off for the afternoon and didn't really ask them where they were going and what they were doing. I'm pretty sure they regretted that by the end of it all. Anyway, we must have got bored when we realized we had no idea how to make a fire, so Leo started daring me to eat some of the mushrooms we'd found, in a sort of Russian roulette, thinking one of them might be a death cap mushroom, which someone in our class had said could kill you with one bite. I gnawed my way through these things but nothing bad happened, so instead we came up with this story to tell our mates that I'd eaten a poisonous mushroom and immediately dropped to the floor, and Leo had been the hero and saved my life, fishing out the bits of mushroom from my foaming mouth. You can guess whose idea that story was!

'But then a few hours after we'd got home that evening, I started throwing up horribly and, not to be outdone, Leo took one look at my mushroom vomit and started being sick too. He burst into tears and told his mum that I'd made him eat a poisonous mushroom and now he was scared we were both going to die – I think he suddenly got really frightened I was actually going to cark it. I was so sick, and pretty scared myself, that I couldn't even argue and just started crying too. I'll never forget how ill I felt for days afterwards. Plus I got a massive telling off from my parents about bullying Leo, even though he was the one who'd suggested the whole thing! I was so upset about the injustice of it all, but it was hard to stay mad at Leo for more than about five minutes, even back then.

I think he promised he'd swap me the Jürgen Klinsmann FIFA sticker I'd been after for weeks and all was forgiven. Neither of us have ever eaten mushrooms again, though.'

Despite herself, Lottie had found herself drawn into the story and couldn't help but smile when Ross came to an end. 'I knew he didn't like them, but I had no idea there was such a traumatic reason.' She paused, surprised at herself for engaging, before adding in a rush, 'It must have been tough when Leo moved so far away.' For a moment, she imagined being separated from her sisters and shuddered.

'It was. But it was the way things had to be,' he replied in a tone that made it clear the conversation was going no further. Lottie turned to look at him. She wanted to ask what was wrong. But his easy smile had disappeared and his closed expression reminded her of how he'd been the first time they'd met. She shut her mouth and her question remained unasked. They were both silent for the rest of the journey, except for when Lottie needed to give him directions to her flat.

They pulled up outside and she quickly reached for her bag. 'Thanks for the lift, and I'm sorry I spent most of the night in the loo and looking like I was going to throw up all over you,' Lottie said, immediately cringing inside and wishing yet again her brain had told her to shut up. It was like there was a second Lottie inside her, one she didn't know at all. She was so confused at how she was feeling.

Ross smiled and reached out his hand to touch her shoulder. 'I hope you're feeling better. At least it's a bit cooler now.' He took a breath and Lottie made to open the car door. 'Wait,' Ross said. 'Sorry, do you have a second before you go inside?'

Lottie's body screamed for her to say no, but politeness took over. 'Sure,' she replied stiffly.

'Thanks, I appreciate it. I should – I mean, I want – to apologise to you, Lottie. I should have told you before the funeral that we knew about Leo's diagnosis when he was alive. It was wrong of me not to and I've felt guilty every day since that you found out in the way you did. It wasn't Margaret's fault – of course she presumed that you knew, understandably. It was my fault, and I'm sorry.'

Lottie glanced at him for the first time since he'd started speaking and she saw pure anguish on his face. She quickly looked away again, but found herself angling her body away from the pavement and towards him a fraction.

'I'm ashamed to say I didn't tell you for selfish reasons,' he continued. 'I knew when you found out, you'd wonder why Leo didn't tell you himself. I hated the thought of you thinking any less of him because he didn't have the courage to tell you. At the time, I didn't see the irony in me chickening out of telling you too.' He grimaced. 'We argued about you, you know, me and Leo.'

Lottie frowned. 'Why?'

'I told him it was far too soon after his diagnosis to be going on dates and getting involved with someone new. He wasn't dealing with his diagnosis at all, just shoving his head in the sand and hoping it would go away. He hadn't even started taking the meds the specialist had prescribed – he kept saying he didn't need them, that he felt completely fine. He hadn't had any symptoms or anything, like his dad, and he didn't believe it was real. But obviously he didn't listen to me – typical Leo.' Ross smiled sadly. 'And he started seeing you anyway. And after a while I could tell how happy he was – I hadn't seen him that happy in years – and I couldn't take that away from him. It was clear how good for him you were, and he even said he'd started taking his tablets and booked in for another appointment with the specialist, and his parents were so happy he was finally starting to face up to things. But then he and I had another argument. I said he should tell you about his condition, that you had a right to know. He told me to butt out and asked me what I knew about relationships anyway – and to be fair, he had a point. And then a couple of weeks later, he was . . . he was gone.'

Ross swallowed and put his hand to his mouth, and tears pricked at Lottie's own eyes. She wanted to say something, but she was worried that if she tried, she'd just start sobbing, so she kept her mouth firmly closed. She was still staring determinedly out the car windscreen, but out of the corner of her eye she saw Ross's shoulders start to shake.

Not knowing what else to do, she slid her hand onto his knee. Then she felt him place his hand on top of hers, and the banging in her ribcage eased just a little. She allowed herself to glance at Ross again and her heart contracted to see him in such pain. She gripped his leg tighter and felt him squeeze her fingers in return.

Neither of them said anything, but she could hear Ross crying softly as the radio piped out the opening bars of a ballad she vaguely recognised. The car began filling with violins and choirs, and as the music reached its climax, Lottie felt something inside her come undone. Tears leaked down her cheeks and she felt Ross's fingers grip her tighter, until eventually the final chorus of the song faded out and was replaced by the abrasive sound of a car advert, and the moment was broken. Embarrassed and confused by what had just happened, Lottie snatched her hand away from under Ross's and quickly began rummaging in her bag. She pulled out a tissue and tried to blow her nose noiselessly. She could tell out of the corner of her eye that he'd moved his arm up towards his eyes, and she wordlessly thrust the tissue packet at him.

'Th-thanks,' he said a little shakily. There was silence for several moments while he wiped his eyes and Lottie tried to compose herself again. When Ross began speaking again, the warmth had returned to his voice again and he managed a smile. 'Leo was a wee bugger sometimes and could be so set in his ways. But I've realized that I can be too.' Now his smile was more rueful. 'I'm ashamed of the way I treated you that first day we met, Lottie. I was a bastard to you. I was so sure I was right and that Leo shouldn't be getting into any kind of a relationship, especially with someone he clearly felt so strongly about, and I tried to scare you away. I was an idiot, and a nasty idiot at that. I'm sorry and I hope you can accept my apology.'

He turned to face her and Lottie moved back slightly in her seat when she saw the intensity in his expression. Most of the time, Lottie tried to hide her emotions, embarrassed by her grief, but it seemed that Ross wanted her to see exactly how he was feeling, and it scared her, she realized. She quickly looked away and mumbled, 'You were only doing what you thought was right for your cousin.' Ross nodded but didn't seem in any hurry to speak, so Lottie, once again, found herself filling the silence. 'He often talked about how you were a brother to him in all but name,' she rushed out. 'He cared so much about what you thought.'

'Thank you,' Ross said. 'That means a lot.' There was another pause, and Lottie reached again for the car-door handle, but then Ross carried on talking. 'I don't suppose you'd like to come to Eddie and Margaret's for lunch on Sunday, would you? Mum and Dad will be there too. It'd give them an excuse to tell all the old stories about me and Leo when we were kids, which they'd love.'

Lottie's stomach lurched. She was assaulted again by her now familiar fear – did she want to hear the old stories about Leo when he was a kid? They were in the past, before *their* past. What if she found out something she didn't like? But glancing at the pleading look on Ross's face, the word *no* seemed to stick in her throat, and she heard herself agreeing. Ross's face lit up and he said he'd pick her up and text with the timings.

She let herself wearily into her flat, peeped through the window to make sure he'd finally driven off, then collapsed on the sofa. All of her emotions about the evening and the moment she and Ross had just shared in the car were jumbled together like a fistful of knotted jewellery, but she didn't have the energy to start unpicking it. Instead, she closed her eyes and opened the door to the place she knew she should stay away from, but still couldn't give up, especially when tonight he felt so real in her mind.

She dreamed that she was snuggled into the warm space on Leo's chest that felt like it had been made specially for her cheek, murmuring, 'Tell me what you were like as a kid. I bet you loved all that Boy Scout stuff, didn't you?'

'I think I probably preferred reading about it more than actually taking part in all that derring-do! I always made Ross be the one who jumped in the river or tested whether the rope swing we'd made was actually safe. I was always getting him into trouble.'

'Didn't he mind?'

'Nah, course not. He did whatever I told him to, it was hilarious. There was this one time, I even made him eat some poisonous mushrooms . . .'

Chapter Twenty-one

By the time Sunday arrived, it had been a whole week since Lottie had seen either of her sisters. It was incredibly rare for so long to go by without Lottie seeing them. Even when one of them was on holiday or busy at work, she'd catch up with the other one. They had been messaging a little here and there, but it hadn't gone much beyond, *Yes, it's boiling, this heatwave is too much! Hope you're both okay x*. Em had continued to send anecdotes about the kids – apparently Dante had told his nursery key worker she was an 'old lady' in his drawing, which hadn't gone down very well considering she was barely thirty – and Annie had texted to say the couple whose wedding she and Charlie had been to in Italy just a few months before were filing for divorce already. But there were none of the deeper thoughts and feelings they usually shared so easily with each other.

Lottie still hadn't told them about meeting Ross during the week and their emotional conversation, nor had she mentioned that she was supposed to be going to Leo's parents' house for lunch that day, or that she was horribly nervous and was considering calling Ross to cancel.

She and Ross had been messaging quite a lot over the past few days. He'd texted the day after their aborted pub visit to ask whether she was feeling better, and to tell her how grateful he was that she'd allowed him to apologise. He hadn't mentioned the moment they'd shared in the car, and Lottie couldn't decide if she wanted him to acknowledge it or not. She knew that if it had been her, she would have instantly sent a message saying how embarrassed she was for breaking down in that way and asking the other person to forget it had happened. Maybe Ross was so embarrassed he didn't even want to reference it. Or maybe he was so unembarrassed he didn't need to mention it. Lottie wasn't sure, and she wasn't sure what her reaction said about her either. She'd replied with a fairly bland message thanking him for his honesty.

What she hadn't admitted to Ross was how confused she now felt about Leo. When she thought of how humiliated she'd felt at the funeral, the anger she'd been feeling for the past few months was still right there on the surface. But now, instead of being aimed at Ross, it was Leo she was furious with. What Ross had said in the car had made her question everything. Why hadn't Leo had the guts to tell her about his condition? It wasn't as if her reaction would have been negative – it had never been Leo's *fault* that his heart didn't work properly, it wasn't something he chose to have. But he could have chosen to tell her, and he hadn't. Surely if he'd been as committed to their relationship as Lottie had thought he was – and as he'd said he was – he would have had to tell her at some point?

Lottie had found herself getting more and more frustrated and angry, going round and round in circles until it felt like her brain would explode. During the long, dark nights when her body denied her the comfort blanket of sleep and she found herself longing for the cat that wasn't her cat to snuggle on her bed with her, she had even admitted that her sisters might have been right when they'd said that the betrayal she felt about not knowing had taken over her whole grieving process. She wished she'd been able to talk to Annie and Em about it over the past few days, but there was still something stopping her. She knew she needed to make things right between them, but she also knew she had to do it face to face not over WhatsApp, and that felt like an insurmountable challenge right now. Her whole body still felt weighed down and heavy, every step a mountain to climb. She knew she needed to knuckle down and come up with some standout ideas at work, but her head seemed to be filled with fog and everything she wrote sounded robotic. And even though she could barely admit it even to herself, as she lay staring at the same spot of ceiling above her bed, she knew she needed to tell a professional about the dreamland she was once again allowing herself to spend far too much time in.

It was when her world came to a grinding halt at the weekend, when she didn't have the routine of work and the distraction of Rachel and Guy's chatter, that reality kicked in and reminded her all over again that it wasn't healthy to spend so much time either living in the past or in her head. She'd spent all of Saturday rewatching the detective series she and Leo had binge-watched one weekend, having sex and eating bacon sandwiches and Chinese takeaways between episodes.

But now it was Sunday and Ross was coming to pick her up in less than an hour. Logically, she knew it was too late to cancel now, but she comforted herself with the thought that she could always feign illness if she needed to. But as the clock ticked closer to the time Ross would be picking her up, she realized that chance was slipping away, and she really was going to have to go for lunch not only with Leo's parents, but Ross and his parents too.

Of course, they had all seemed genuinely lovely in the few minutes she'd spent with them at the funeral, but she couldn't shake the thought that they were going to be judging her – and her relationship with Leo. After all, today's lunch was a slightly macabre take on meeting the prospective in-laws for the first time. And although things had definitely thawed between her and Ross and she understood why he'd acted the way he had towards her during their first meeting, she still couldn't shake that image of him warning her away from Leo so aggressively. The doorbell rang, interrupting her thoughts and sending a shot of nausea from her stomach up into her throat.

'Hi!' she trilled, her voice artificially high and girly.

'You look nice,' Ross said, catching her off guard with a kiss on the cheek. By the time she'd pulled herself together, he was already walking towards the car and holding the door open for her.

As they made their way out of the suburbs and into the Oxfordshire countryside, Ross chatted easily about the friends he'd been staying with and Lottie tried to nod and laugh in all the right places, while also trying to keep her breathing steady, continually telling herself that she was just going for a nice lunch with some lovely people who'd been through a tough time. Ross did a pretty good job of keeping her distracted and calm, but as soon as they pulled into the driveway of a large detached house, Lottie's heart began to thump again.

'Here we are,' Ross said. 'Eddie and Margaret have been looking forward to seeing you all week, but I promise you they're just as nervous as you are. Even though there's no need for any of you to be nervous.' He smiled and made a show of rolling his eyes, and Lottie gave him what she hoped was a grateful smile but felt even to her like a grimace.

She grabbed the bottle of wine and bunch of flowers she'd thankfully remembered to bring with her and took a deep breath as Ross led her towards the front door.

It opened before they'd even got near enough to knock. Margaret immediately opened her arms and cried, 'Lottie, I'm so glad you could come!' and proceeded to envelop her in a hug like she was a long-lost relative.

Lottie thrust the now rather crumpled flowers at her, as well as the wine, and gabbled, 'Lovely to see you, Margaret. I brought you these. I don't know much about wine but I thought this one sounded nice and the man next to me in Sainsbury's said he and his wife love it, so hopefully you will too.' She bit down on the inside of her lip, clamping her mouth shut before she could continue waffling.

Margaret smiled gently. 'I don't know much about wine either, but if it's good enough for that man and his wife, it's good enough for us. Isn't that right, Eddie?'

'Of course, of course!' Eddie replied, emerging from behind his wife and grabbing Lottie's hand with both of his. Even though she'd barely spent any time with him at Leo's funeral, Lottie was immediately struck by how much older and frailer Eddie seemed.

She was led into the sitting room, where Ross's parents were waiting patiently to say hello. 'Lottie, wonderful to meet you properly,' Ross's mum said warmly. 'I'm Morag and this is James. I know we saw you briefly at the funeral, but it's lovely to have the chance to get you know you better. Ross has told us lots about you.'

'Has he?' Lottie turned towards Ross, her eyebrows shooting upwards. Her thoughts whizzed through all the things he might have told his parents about her, from all the reasons he didn't think she was good enough for Leo to the fact that she'd spent most of their meeting earlier in the week in the loo, before the more rational part of her brain kicked in. Leo's parents had invited her into their house, and everyone was smiling at her, so it was unlikely Ross had said anything too negative.

'Aye, his mum and me turned the thumbscrews on him

this week,' Margaret said with a playful glint in her eye. Then she added more seriously, 'And anyone who manages to win the approval of both Ross and dear Leo is always welcome in this house.'

Lottie had no idea how to reply to that, but thankfully Margaret bustled Eddie and James off to sort drinks and check on the food. 'It's nothing fancy, just roast chicken. And then I thought we could go for a stroll later to walk off the pavlova I've made for pudding. Nigella never lets us down with that one. Now, Ross darling, do you want to show Lottie the garden while Morag and I sort out whatever mess the men are making in the kitchen?'

'Will do, Auntie Margaret – and don't let Dad near the gravy or it will be full of weird lumps.'

Ross led Lottie back through the front door, so she could collect her shoes, and then down the side of the house, through a gate and out into one of the most beautiful gardens she had ever seen.

'Wow, this is amazing,' she breathed as she took in the rose bushes heavy with huge yellow petals, the pretty gladioli and the wispy scarlet cosmos flowers. There was an array of hanging baskets overflowing with petunias and fuchsia. 'It's like the Chelsea Flower Show!' she exclaimed.

'Oh my God, Eddie would love you for ever if you told him that,' Ross said with a laugh. 'The garden is his pride and joy. He used to try to get Leo to help him with the weeding when they first moved down here, though as a seventeen-year-old Leo was having none of it! But once he was older, he used to love helping his dad out here.' He smiled sadly. 'I think it's been a real solace for Eddie over the last few months. He's had to scale back some of the more active things he used to do because of his heart, but the docs said he could still keep gardening as long as he didn't do anything ridiculously energetic. So it's been nice for him to be able to get out here and do something he really enjoys.'

Lottie followed him as he walked over the huge lawn and up a couple of steps to a second much smaller rectangle of grass, which was surrounded by raised beds of fruit and vegetables. At the far side of the lawn, where a low fence separated the garden from the fields beyond, was a small rose bush that had just a few deep pink and golden yellow flowers dotted on its branches. 'This is Leo's rose,' Ross said with a sad smile. 'Margaret wanted to plant something in his memory and Eddie found this rose called "Leo Ferré" online, so it was clearly meant to be.'

'That's lovely,' Lottie said, trying to ignore the itch of emotion at the base of her throat.

'Yes.' They were both silent for a few seconds. Then Ross seemed to pull himself back from his thoughts and said, 'We'd better head back inside. I don't want to be responsible for lunch being ruined – Auntie Margaret would make her displeasure very clear!'

Chapter Twenty-two

Lunch was absolutely delicious, and as the wine flowed and everyone chatted, Lottie began to relax and allowed herself to sit back and watch the family's dynamic.

Ross gently took the mick out of his parents but was never anything but kind to his aunt and uncle. He made sure everyone had enough of what they wanted and teased his dad about how many roast potatoes he'd spooned onto his plate.

'Enjoy them while you can, James,' Eddie said with a small sigh. 'I've got Margaret here watching my cholesterol like a hawk.'

Margaret tutted good-naturedly and placed a soothing hand on her husband's. 'Lottie, I remember Leo told us you're a lexicographer,' she said. 'Is that right?'

Lottie took a sip of her drink and smiled. 'Yes, but I'm no Susie Dent off *Countdown*.' Her heart contracted as she was instantly transported back to her first date with Leo in the curry house, and she swallowed hard before adding, 'I work for an online dictionary based in Oxford.'

'That sounds interesting,' Morag said encouragingly. 'Do you enjoy it?'

'It is interesting – well, sometimes anyway. But I am thinking about looking for a job that's the next step up, probably in London.' Lottie hadn't known she was going to say that until the words were out of her mouth, and out of the corner of her eye she saw Ross look up from his plate at her. 'Well, maybe, we'll see,' she quickly backtracked.

'It makes sense to want to move up the ladder.' Eddie nodded. 'Would you commute into London every day from Oxford?'

'I'm not sure yet,' she replied, her heart racing suddenly at the thought of leaving her little flat and its proximity to her sisters for the bright lights of the capital where she knew almost no one. 'I grew up in Oxfordshire. My parents have moved abroad, but my sisters live nearby and I see them all the time, so it would be strange to move away.'

'That must be lovely having your sisters so near,' Margaret said. 'Are they older or younger?'

'Annie is older and Em is younger – I'm in the middle,' Lottie replied warmly. 'I'm so lucky to have them close by. We see a lot of each other.' She swallowed quickly, all too aware of how close to a lie that was right now.

Morag smiled. 'Aye, it's good to have family around you. Ross and Leo were as thick as thieves growing up, weren't they, Marg?'

'They were. It was hard on both of them when we came down here, but we had no choice.' The atmosphere around the table grew heavy, and as much as Lottie wanted to ask why Leo and his parents had been forced to move from Scotland, she felt like it was somehow inappropriate, though she wasn't sure why.

Thankfully, Eddie broke the silence. 'Luckily, someone invented email and those message board things the boys were so into, eh? And it helped us old fuddy-duddies get with the programme and get our heads around it all.'

'I'm still not sure I've got my head around any of it,' Morag said. 'What was that thing you showed us last night, Ross? Chatsnap or something?'

'Snapchat, Mother,' Ross said with an exaggerated roll of his eyes.

Lottie laughed. 'I'm not sure *I* even understand that properly. And I think my nephew probably knows more about YouTube than me – and he's four years old. He can find a *Paw Patrol* video in two clicks.'

'Ross and Leo loved a cartoon about two dogs at about the same age – I can't remember what it was called now, but I do remember them spending every waking hour for weeks on all fours pretending they were puppies.'

'Thanks for that, Mum!' Ross said, throwing a smile Lottie's way. 'I'm sure Lottie doesn't want to spend all day talking about Leo's and my early dog-acting abilities.'

Before Lottie could reply to the contrary, Margaret had butted in and said, 'Maybe not, but I'm sure she'd love to see a few photos of you both when you were little. They were adorable!' she added, winking at Lottie. 'Come and sit next to me and you can have a proper look.'

Ross grumbled and rolled his eyes again but clearly felt

he couldn't deny his aunt her little pleasure, so went to fetch the photo albums, which he then carefully laid on the table between Lottie and his aunt. 'Fine, but I can't sit here and watch you take the mick out of our terrible haircuts, so I'll clear the table and get the pavlova ready, shall I?'

'You are a love.' Margaret smiled at him. 'Right, Lottie, where shall we start? What about these ones from when we went up to Loch Ness. The boys must have been quite wee at that point, around six or seven maybe, Morag?'

'Aye, about that. Young Leo got into a few scrapes that week, I seem to remember!'

'When didn't he?' Margaret laughed. 'Do you remember he frightened poor Ross half to death with all his stories about the Loch Ness monster coming out of the lake at night and searching for little boys to eat?'

'I'm sure I was only pretending to be frightened, Auntie Margaret!' called Ross from the kitchen.

'Och, you always were the more sensitive one, Ross darling,' she replied fondly. 'That's why you complemented each other so well. We used to call him Leo the Lionheart, didn't we, as he was always leading you both off into battles and adventures. Left to his own devices, he would have grown up half feral, but you helped soften him out and stopped some of his madder schemes.'

'And he helped make sure I didn't retreat into the shy, quiet, self-conscious boy I might otherwise have become,' Ross said softly from the doorway, and he shared a sad smile with his aunt.

'Aye, Leo certainly had spirit in those days,' Eddie said before the moment of silence could become awkward. 'Too much spirit at times, mind. I don't think I've ever quite recovered from finding the two of you passed out in the shed.' He turned to Lottie. 'They decided their first proper taste of alcohol should be the fifty-year-old single malt I'd been saving for years. And the worst part,' he said, glancing back at Ross, 'was that you chose to do it when Margaret and your mum were away on that health farm weekend and me and James had to try and sort you out before they got home and tore a strip off us for not minding you properly!'

'That was *definitely* Leo's idea.' Ross grinned. 'Now, enough of telling Lottie all about our misdemeanours – who's for pudding?'

When they'd all put away as much pavlova as they could, Margaret declared that a stroll was very much in order, otherwise the fuddy-duddies would likely fall asleep. 'And by fuddy-duddies, I mean Eddie,' she whispered to Lottie. 'Goodness, I'm glad the heatwave has broken at last.'

'It's so much nicer now it's cooler,' Lottie agreed as they set off for their walk. She found herself falling into step with Eddie, slightly behind the others, as they made their way through the field at the back of the garden. 'You have such a lovely view out here,' she commented, glancing back at the house.

'Aye, we're very lucky,' Eddie replied. 'We were used to having so much space in our village in Scotland, so when we moved down here the garden and the countryside were a huge selling point.'

'Your garden is stunning,' Lottie said, smiling as Eddie beamed with pride just as Ross had said he would. 'It must take a lot of work though.'

'It does, but we did most of the hard work back in those first few years after we moved down here. I couldn't do any of that back-breaking stuff these days. Now it's just about keeping it all looking good and maybe putting in a few new plants here and there to spruce it up when needed.'

'Ross showed me Leo's rose,' Lottie said, glancing at Eddie. She didn't want to upset him, but she also didn't want to not mention it. 'It's beautiful.'

'Thank you, hen. It's only small now, but it should grow into quite a sight, hopefully. I put it at the back against the fence – we still gets lots of sun there and in a few years it should start peeking its head over the top and it'll be seen from this far away. We took some of the earth from the burial site and mixed it into the rootball, so it feels like there's a bit of Leo there too. I rather like the idea not only of people being able to see the plant from afar, but that Leo can see out into the world too.'

Lottie found she couldn't speak. The unexpected tenderness of his words had blindsided her, and she knew that if she opened her mouth she would find herself sobbing. Without thinking, she reached for Eddie's hand and gave it a gentle squeeze, which to her relief he returned. 'Och, I'm a sentimental fool I know, but these things help sometimes.'

Lottie swallowed as hard as she could and managed to say, 'They do,' giving him a watery smile.

'Ross has been an absolute rock to us through all this – and to his parents,' Eddie continued gruffly. 'He's such a good lad, he really is. He always looked out for Leo – there wasn't anything he wouldn't do for him. This has all been so tough for him, poor lad. He took Leo's death pretty hard. His problem is he's always checking on me and Margaret and making sure his own parents are OK, and no one's checking on him.' He stopped walking and Lottie turned in surprise. He fixed her with a beady stare and said, 'He needs someone to look after him – and someone he can look after too, you know, hen.' Then he carried on walking and Lottie was left staring at his back completely confused.

A few hours later, the time came to say their goodbyes.

'You'll come again soon, won't you, Lottie?' Margaret said, giving her a soft kiss on her cheek. 'It's been so nice for us to get to know you a little. Leo seemed so happy during his last few months and it was clear you two had something special. He'd even talked about bringing you home to meet us soon. It's just a pity he wasn't here today to see it.'

They both blinked and then smiled at each other as tears gathered on their lashes.

'Of course I'll come again, if you'll have me,' Lottie replied, determinedly forcing the emotion back. 'I'll help you out with a bit of weeding too, Eddie, although my fingers don't have a hint of green on them, so you'll have to show me what to do.'

'You may live to regret that offer!' Margaret laughed, as Eddie placed a protective hand on her shoulder. 'He'll have your fingers worked to the bone, whether they're green or not.'

'I might go easy on you – to start with anyway, hen!' Eddie smiled.

Once Lottie and Ross were back in the car and pulling out of the drive as all four parents waved them off, Ross smiled at her.

'They loved you. Almost sickeningly so!'

'Margaret and Eddie are so lovely. And your parents,' she added quickly. 'They're obviously really close.'

'Yeah, they are. Though none of them are getting any younger. And I think the physical distance between Scotland and Oxfordshire feels even bigger at the moment. I was thinking of suggesting that Eddie and Margaret move back up north, but Eddie would never leave his garden, especially now he's planted Leo's rose. And he's only just got used to all of the doctors and his cardiologist down here, and I know he wouldn't take too kindly to a whole new group of medics pushing and prodding him. He's not the easiest patient.'

Lottie laughed. 'Why *did* they move down here when you were teenagers?' She glanced across at Ross curiously and was shocked by the look on his face. It immediately took her back to the first time they'd met. Now, the look hit her even harder, because, while she wouldn't go so far as to say she and Ross were friends, she had allowed herself to think that he was at least starting to like her. During the past week, they'd shared a couple of big moments together; big to her anyway. Now, as he continued to stare angrily at the road in front of him, she felt a blast of fury burning through her stomach and up into her throat. 'What?' she blurted out, her voice booming into the silence. 'Why are you looking at me like that? What have I said?'

'What?' he echoed, frowning even harder. 'I was looking at the road, not you,' But before Lottie could say the retort forming in her mind, he seemed to collect himself. 'Sorry,' he said. 'I didn't mean to snap. It's not your fault.'

'What isn't my fault?' Lottie asked, shaking her head in confusion. 'You were laughing and joking a minute ago. I don't understand.'

'You asked me why Leo and his parents moved down here, and I guess there's no easy answer, really,' Ross said quietly.

'Wh—' Lottie bit back another question and instead took a breath and said in the same quiet tone Ross had used, 'Only tell me if you want to.'

'The problem is it's Leo's story to tell, not mine. I don't pretend to know everything about your relationship with Leo, but I can see how much it meant to you and I don't want to take away from that or change how you felt – or still feel – about him.' He glanced across at her and she could see the pain etched into the lines around his eyes.

Lottie could feel her heart banging in her chest and a snake of unease slithering around her lungs. A part of her wanted to forget all about this conversation and to rewind her life to five minutes before when they were pulling out of Leo's parents' drive all smiles and waves. But the other part, the part she'd been pushing away since Leo's death, wanted to know; wanted to know what could possibly have made Ross react in this way; wanted to know what could possibly make her feel differently about the man she loved.

'But Leo isn't here to tell his story,' she said unsteadily. 'So you're the only one who can.'

There was a moment of quiet. The only sound was the noise of the countryside swishing behind them as they drove towards the outskirts of the city. Then Ross said, 'I will tell you, but can we save it for another time maybe? Sorry, it's just been a busy few days.'

'Of course,' Lottie said immediately. The part of her that had wanted to rewind time pushed its way to the front and relief flooded her body.

'Thank you.' He paused and the car filled with quiet before he said, 'Tell me about your sisters. It sounds like you're really close.'

Lottie felt wrong-footed. 'Erm, yeah, we are. Most of the time anyway.'

'Most of the time? Do you find you're often the peacekeeper as the middle child?'

'Ha, no! That's Em. I guess I'm not a typical middle child in that way. Em's always been better at knowing exactly the right thing to say. She's just one of those people who everyone really likes and wants to be friends with. I know I'm biased, but I genuinely have never met a nicer person than her.' She smiled as she spoke and a feeling akin to homesick-ness washed over her.

'She sounds wonderful,' Ross said warmly. 'And what about your older sister?'

'Annie? Well, she's very … Annie! She's one of the most interesting and intelligent people I know. She's a research scientist and works in a lab with test tubes and pipettes and things, but definitely not Bunsen burners – she took the mick out of me when I asked her that a few years ago! She can be a bit intimidating, and she's definitely a bit bossy, but when she tells me to do something, I generally do it because I know she not only has my best interests at heart, but she usually tends to be right. But don't ever tell her I said that, obviously.'

'Obviously.' He smiled. 'So you like being in the middle then?'

'I guess, although it's not as if I have much choice! And I think maybe it's sometimes held me back from "reaching my true potential" as my schoolteachers would have said. I've always found it hard to work out exactly who I am. I'm not the clever one, the successful one or the pretty one – I'm something in the middle, I suppose. Anyway, sorry you don't want to listen to me boring on. You just need to turn left at the traffic lights.'

Ross flicked his indicator on and the rhythmic clicking gently soothed Lottie's embarrassed squirming. She wasn't sure why she had gone from chatting about her sisters to detailing her personal existential crisis. As they turned into her road, Ross said quietly, 'I was interested in what you were saying, and you weren't boring on. And, anyway, you're all of those things – clever, successful, pretty.'

He said the last bit so quietly, it took Lottie a few seconds to even register his words. But before she'd had a chance to process them, he'd pulled up in front of her flat and was speaking again. 'Thanks so much for coming today, Lottie, I know Margaret and Eddie, and my parents, will have appreciated it so much – as do I. I'll drop you a message during the week.' He leaned over, kissed her on the cheek and waited for her to clamber out of the car. Then he waved and pulled away.

It was only when she closed the front door behind her that Lottie realized he would be going back to Scotland the following day and she had no idea when she would see him again. The thought gave her a very odd feeling.

Chapter Twenty-three

Lottie was exhausted. She felt like her brain had been whirring constantly and over the last few hours it had spat out truths she wasn't even aware were in there. Talking about her sisters with Ross and his family had brought home to her how off-balance she felt having not seen or spoken to them for a week. Despite her huge lunch, her stomach panged like it was empty.

She ran herself a bath and hoped the almost scalding water would act as the warm hug she craved. While she and her sisters had squabbled over toys and friends as kids and bickered over clothes and make-up as teens, as adults they'd almost never argued – and certainly never spoken to each other in the way Lottie had shouted at Annie and Em the previous weekend. Tears pricked her eyes and she reached out a dripping hand for her phone, which she'd left on top of her towel. Praying she didn't drop it in the water, she thumbed out a message to her sisters.

Sorry for being such a selfish cow. I know it's only Monday
tomorrow, but don't suppose both of you could do pub club,
could you? No worries if you can't make it, or even if you
just don't fancy it, but it would be good to see you. Hope
you're okay xx

Then she threw her phone face down on the chair and resolved
not to look at it until she was out of the bath, however much
she wanted to. She knew she needed to apologise to them both
properly in person, but she also knew that they had every right
to not want to see her after how she'd behaved. She just had to
hope they were better people than she was. As she added more
hot water to the already almost overflowing bath, steam filling
the bathroom as she hadn't bothered to open the window, it
wasn't just the bathwater making her face wet.

She tried to focus on her breathing and let her mind clear,
like all of the calming apps she'd downloaded and opened
only once told her to do. But her brain was having none of
it. She gave in and grabbed her phone again – but the screen
was blank; there were no notifications. She jabbed at the
screen and checked she had actually sent the message, but of
course she had. Maybe it had got lost in the ether somehow?
She swiped left on the message and while it seemed Annie
hadn't read it yet, there were two blue ticks next to Em's
name. Her little sister had read the message fifteen minutes
ago and hadn't replied. Lottie lay back in the water and
squeezed her eyes shut, not allowing herself to contemplate
what that might mean.

The One

She spent the next ten minutes concentrating intently on washing her hair, applying a conditioning mask and then slowly rinsing it off, steadfastly not thinking about her sisters, about Leo, about Ross. Instead she mentally listed all of the things she needed to do at work the next day and how long they might take her; what she was going to wear each day of that week; what days she would wash her hair; when she would do her laundry; and what bin she needed to put out on Wednesday. As she dried herself slowly and deliberately and slathered on moisturiser, she even managed a light chuckle – she could launch a meditative app that prescribed writing to-do lists instead of 'square breathing', 'mindful gratitude' and 'asking the universe to provide'. She could call it *Listfulness*. Only once she had applied night serum, hair serum and the hugely expensive cellulite serum she knew she shouldn't buy but always added to her basket as soon as she got paid each month, did she allow herself to look at her phone. Her heart raced as she saw three notifications.

Sorry, had to work some childcare things out, but yes, I'm def up for an early pub club! Normal place/time? Emx

Only just seen this – been at the longest Sunday lunch at Charlie's parents, but yes, all good with me. Ax

Brilliant! Looking forward to seeing you both (and you're not a selfish cow, Lots!) xx

Lottie breathed out properly for what felt like the first time in hours. Her sisters *were* better people than her. Now she just had to worry about what she was going to say to convince them she was truly sorry. There was so much to catch them up on, but she also needed to make sure the spotlight shone on Annie and her pregnancy. She had so much to make up for there.

She choked down the lump forming in the back of her throat, determined not to give in to the tears yet again. Instead she grabbed her laptop and lost herself in scrolling through news websites, social media loops and even the spam folder on her email. She never understood people who had 15,233 unread messages in their inbox, she actually found it therapeutic to delete emails that were clearly from hackers and scammers.

As she clicked away, her eyes snagged on a message declaring an email she'd sent was undeliverable. Frowning, she tried to place who on earth Sue McNally was, and then remembered she was the HR person she'd emailed after accidentally applying for the job at the literacy charity. She scrolled up the spam list, checking for any other strange messages, and then two from the top, she saw an email dated two days ago. It was from the charity. Frowning, she scanned the email and her heart sped up. She had been offered an interview for the role of Head of Outreach.

Chapter Twenty-four

Lottie arrived at the Rope and Anchor sweating slightly, and not just because she'd cycled faster than normal to get there having left work late. For the first time ever, she was nervous about seeing her sisters. Spying their usual table was free, she dumped her bag on the chair and gratefully peeled off her jacket that was now sticking damply to her skin.

'Lottie!' Em cried from several feet away, drawing glances from neighbouring tables, many of whom stopped to stare longer than strictly necessary at Lottie's tall, blonde, beautiful sister. 'You're here! God, it feels like forever since I've seen you.' She threw herself at Lottie, who was only too glad to bury her head in her shoulder and hug her tightly.

'I know, me too. Sorry I was such a dick.'

Em gripped the tops of her arms and gently pushed her away. 'You weren't a dick,' she said forcefully. 'You are human and you're hurting. That's allowed.'

Lottie gave her a watery smile. 'Maybe instead of standing

here arguing about whether or not I was a dick – and I was, OK? – shall I get us some drinks?'

'I'll get them,' Em insisted, finally letting her go. 'Your usual?'

'Actually, I'll join you both on the softies tonight, I think. I've decided to give the wine a rest for a while. Could I just get a Coke, please?'

Lottie went to sit down, but before she could shove the coats and bags out of the way to make room, Annie's voice boomed across the pub, making people stare again – though Lottie couldn't help but notice the men that had been openly leering at her little sister were a little more intimidated by her big sister.

'Lottie! How *are* you?' Annie beamed at her and pulled her into such a tight hug that Lottie was instantly worried about being able to breathe. Thankfully, her sister released her a few moments later and, as she was removing her coat, Lottie took the opportunity to take a few deep breaths of sticky pub air.

'Annie, I'm sorry. I hate that I said those things to you and Em. I didn't mean them, I promise. Please forgive me. I truly couldn't be happier for you and Charlie. And I can't wait to be an auntie again. It's so exciting! How are you feeling?'

There was a beat of silence; Annie had her head down and was fumbling with something in her bag. Lottie realized she was holding her breath. But when her sister finally looked up, she fixed Lottie with determined eyes. 'There's nothing to forgive. But promise me that you'll stop bottling everything up and talk to someone? It doesn't have to be me or Em, but it does have to be someone. You've been through the shittest of shit times and you can't expect to be the same person afterwards.' Her eyes softened and she reached for Lottie's hand. 'I don't pretend to know how you're feeling, Lots, but I do know what grief feels like. You know we lost the baby at three weeks last time? Well, I was pregnant once before that.' Lottie widened her eyes but didn't want to interrupt her sister. 'It was two years ago and it happened naturally, by some miracle, but then eleven weeks in, I started bleeding. I was due to have my first scan the following day, but instead of seeing my baby for the first time on the sonographer's screen, I was having a conversation with the midwife about whether or not I should let the tissue pass out naturally.' She paused and Lottie instinctively raised her hand to her chest in shock. 'Anyway, the only way I could process what had happened was to talk to someone. Yes, I talked to Charlie, of course, but I also had some counselling. And it helped so much, Lottie, it really did. I'll never forget my baby, but it meant I was strong enough to go on and try again with IVF. And when that also ended in miscarriage, I was still able to find the strength to try one more time. And now I'm fourteen weeks into growing this one. And I couldn't be happier. So all I'm saying is talking can help.'

'I'm so sorry that happened to you, Annie.' Lottie took a couple of deep breaths to swallow the tears that always seemed so close to the surface at the moment. But if her older sister could stay strong enough to talk about it without crying, then so could she. 'I can't imagine how awful that must have been. I wish you could have talked to me,' Lottie said quietly.

'It felt too, I don't know, too much maybe to talk to you and Em about. Which I know sounds silly, but I suppose I didn't want you to feel even a fraction of the pain I was going through. You're my sisters, I wanted to protect you from that.'

Lottie nodded and squeezed her hand, not daring to open her mouth in case all that came out was a sob.

'So all I'm saying is, yes, you can always talk to me, Lottie – and I mean always – but I also know there are some things that are too painful to share with us. And that's when therapy can help. I mean, I know I'm hardly one for spirituality woo-woo nonsense, but sometimes self-care does have to be at the top of your list. Promise me, Lots, promise me you'll talk to someone – whoever you feel most comfortable with, but someone?'

Lottie made a face but nodded. 'I promise,' she whispered.

Annie squeezed her hand. 'Good.' Then she smiled a little shyly. 'I didn't show you this the other day so I wanted to do it now. It's from our first scan – meet your niece or nephew!'

Lottie took the shiny piece of paper Annie had thrust at her and stared in wonder at the blurry image.

'Sorry, I had to queue for ages at the bar – Alf was chatting to someone about starting up a quiz night instead of actually serving any drinks! Anyway, here you go – Coke for you, Lots, and Seedlip and tonics for you and me, Annie.'

'Thanks, Em,' Annie said. 'Cheers, sisters!'

Lottie raised her glass. 'Cheers. Look, Em, it's our niece or nephew!' she said, waving the scan photo. 'I think she's a girl, definitely. Can they tell the sex at this point?'

'No, not for another few months,' Em said, laughing. 'And even then they might not be able to tell, or Annie might decide not to find out.'

'Er, this is Annie we're talking about, of course she's going to find out!' Lottie said.

'Oi, I am here, you know. But, yes, we are going to find out the sex at the twenty-week scan, and yes, you will both be the first to know. OK?'

'Cheers to that,' Lottie said. Then she took a deep breath and tried to keep the wobble out of her voice. 'I just wanted to say again now much I've missed you both. I feel ashamed by what I said, even more so because you were right, Em. I was jealous of your lives. If I'm honest, I still am. You both have things sorted – you live your lives like proper adults, whereas I don't feel like a grown-up, with my one-bed rented flat and slightly weird job on the outskirts of town. I've not got or done any of the things that make someone a proper grown-up. I don't have a wine rack, and I never have more than one bottle in at one time. I don't have a proper house with a proper garden, an actual career, a life plan of any sort. No, let me finish, Em,' she said, seeing her sister open her mouth, but also throwing her an apologetic smile. 'But I think those three months with Leo made me realize that maybe I could have all that. When I was with Elliot I always somehow felt like we were two five-year-old kids playing "house" – and it turned out I was right in some ways. But then meeting Leo gave me a taste of what I could have. And then it was all taken away in the blink of an eye. And, yes, I admit I am angry about that. But I'm not angry with you two, and I should never have taken it out on you. So I'm sorry.'

Lottie had had no idea she was going to say all of that before she'd opened her mouth – maybe it was Annie's demand that she talk to someone, or maybe her brain had actually been able to start processing everything a bit more since talking to Ross. But what she did know was that, once her words were out there, she suddenly felt a lot lighter.

Both her sisters tried to talk at once, but Em immediately acquiesced to Annie. 'I think I speak for both of us when I say your apology is accepted – it was accepted fifteen minutes ago for God's sake! – so none of us is ever going to mention it again. But I do think I need to tell you that I definitely do not have being a grown-up sorted! And I'm sure Em feels the same. Yes, I have a house with a garden, but the garden is so overgrown it's verging on a jungle. Yes, I have a wine rack with more than one bottle of wine in it, but that's only because I've been completely off booze for the last three months, and then hardly drinking before that with all the IVF stuff. And, yes, I might have a career of sorts, but I certainly don't have a life plan, whatever that is, and who knows what's going to happen when this little one comes along and throws a newborn grenade into our lives! But that's fine, because that's real life.'

Em then jumped in. 'Yes to everything Annie just said. We don't "have it all", Lottie, I promise you – whatever "it all" really means. We all drop the ball every day and are just trying to muddle through as best we can. And I definitely don't have a career, or even a job, for goodness' sake!' Lottie frowned at the very un-Em-like tinkly laugh that came out of her mouth.

'But you have the boys, and they're such a credit to you, Em,' Lottie reassured her.

Her sister nodded. 'I know, and I'm very lucky. But that doesn't stop me sometimes thinking *what if* and maybe wondering if I shouldn't have something to show for all those years of hard study at uni,' she said, and Lottie noticed her hand shook a little as she reached for her drink. Lottie's brain whirred. Em had never mentioned any of this before and she didn't quite know how best to respond, so she glanced at Annie for help.

Her older sister caught her look and said encouragingly, 'Loads of companies would be chomping at the bit to employ someone with your kind of language skills, Em. There are lots of jobs out there, I'm sure, if that's what you wanted.'

Em nodded and smiled, but didn't look wholly convinced. Hating see her little sister look less than her usual easy, happy self, Lottie blurted out, 'There do seem to be lots of opportunities around at the moment. Even I have applied for a new job.'

'What—'

'Where—'

Her sisters tripped over each other in their haste to find out more, and Lottie put her palms out in a *woah* gesture. 'Calm down! I really don't think anything will come of it. It's an amazing job and loads of people will apply who have a ton of proper experience. I don't know why I even mentioned it.'

'What is it, where is it and why not?' Annie demanded.

'I said calm down!' Lottie laughed, but she quickly became serious, biting her lip as she said quietly, 'It's working for a charity called Literacy For All. It's based in London, heading up their outreach programme. They focus on young people who leave school without great reading and writing skills. Obviously, I'm not at all qualified for the job and I'm never going to get it, but—'

'Why wouldn't you?' Annie butted in again. 'Of course, it will be tough to get an interview, but if you did and you had the chance to showcase your skills and your passion, then you'd have a great chance.'

'They've invited me for an initial interview on Zoom next week,' Lottie said, even more quietly.

'Well then, that's amazing! You're a shoo-in,' Annie almost shouted in excitement, before Em put a warning hand on her arm.

Em fixed her with the same fierce gaze she'd given her when she'd walked into the pub earlier, and Lottie realized she wasn't going to get off easily after all. 'Lots, you have emailed them back to say yes to the interview, haven't you?' she asked, eyeballing her even more closely. When Lottie didn't immediately answer, her eyes grew even steelier. 'You just said that it was an "amazing" job. You wouldn't even need to move if you didn't want to, you could commute from here. You do want this job, don't you?'

'Yes,' Lottie replied meekly.

'Then you need to put yourself forward and go for it!'

'Have you been spending too much time with Annie recently?' Lottie eyed her suspiciously.

'Oi!' both her sisters shouted together, and they all laughed.

'But in all seriousness, Lots, you don't want to look back and wonder what might have been,' Em persisted. 'You've got past the first hurdle. They must think there's a chance you might be the right person for the job, otherwise they wouldn't waste their time interviewing you, would they?'

'Maybe,' Lottie mumbled.

Before Em could say anything else, Annie was apparently unable to contain herself any longer and burst out, 'Lottie, for God's sake you need to email them back right now!'

'Well, not right now.'

'Yes, right now. I've got my laptop here and you can log in to your email account. Come on, what's your password?'

Lottie looked at Em for help, but her little sister just raised her eyebrows and shrugged. 'To be fair, Lots, I wouldn't argue with a woman full of hormones if I were you.'

Lottie looked from one to the other again and then sighed in submission. 'God, being the middle child is so annoying sometimes. Fine! Let's email them now, but I'm doing the typing, OK, Annie?'

Chapter Twenty-five

There was no denying the huge weight that had been lifted from Lottie's shoulders once her relationship with her sisters had been restored. But now, as well as trying to keep her current job, she apparently had an interview to prep for.

She spent most of her evenings mainlining rubbish TV to avoid thinking about her career – or her grief. She especially didn't want to think about the fact that her daydreams with Leo were bringing her far less comfort than before. They'd begun to feel stale and repetitive, but she couldn't bring herself to examine what it might all mean, so she buried herself in reality shows that could transport her into someone else's life. By her third straight season of *Married at First Sight Australia*, though, even her tired brain was craving something different, so when Ross messaged her a couple of days later asking if she was free for a call that evening, her stomach fizzed with both anticipation and apprehension.

'Ross, how are you?' she said, answering her phone after just two rings.

'I'm good, thanks. Wishing I was back in sunny Oxfordshire – you wouldn't believe how much colder it is here.'

'Give me sunshine over snow any day!'

'Hmm, well, not sure you'd last long up here then, though thankfully even Scotland draws the line at snow in September – at least I hope so!' He paused and Lottie was about to ask him how his week was going when he started speaking again. 'I've been thinking about what you said – you know, about me being the only one who can tell Leo's story now, and you're right. I wish I'd told you face to face when I had the chance, but if you have time this evening . . .'

He tailed off and Lottie realized that whatever story he had to tell must be a big deal for him. Her stomach flipped with nerves as she tried to imagine what on earth Ross was going to say. 'Of course, that's fine,' she replied. 'But only if you want to. I feel like I've forced you into this.'

'You haven't and I do want to,' he said. 'But it needs to be your choice, too. As I said, Leo isn't here to give his take on things, but what I've got to say might . . .' He paused while he clearly tried to search for the right words, ' . . . make you see him a little differently, and I want you to be prepared for that.'

'I am,' Lottie replied, far more confidently than she actually felt.

She heard Ross take a deep breath. 'OK. Well, as Margaret mentioned at the weekend, Leo was a bit of a daredevil when we were little,' he began. 'But as we started to grow up a bit, he knuckled down at school and started getting top grades and playing a lot of rugby. Our school was really into sport, as well as exams, and it quickly became obvious that Leo was pretty good. While we saw each other a lot during classes and with our parents, he began to spend a lot of time with the other rugby boys, especially at the weekends when they'd go away for tournaments and things. I had a few really good friends, but I wasn't really into going out and drinking. The summer we were sixteen, I hardly saw Leo the whole holiday because he was away on a training camp. He came home full of stories about all of the things he and his teammates had got up to – drinking till they were sick and pulling as many girls as they could and keeping tally.'

'Urgh!' Lottie said without meaning to. 'Sorry, Ross, I didn't mean to interrupt.'

'Don't worry, and I don't disagree. It probably sounds even more awful when I retell it now, and Leo was never the worst of them – he just tended to get swept up in the moment, I think. At the time, I confess I was envious – not about the drinking, but about the girls. I hadn't exactly had much experience at that point. And I think my jealousy was a big part of why I told Leo that maybe the rugby lads were a bad influence and that he should be spending more time studying for his Highers with me. We had a bit of an argument and we did make up afterwards, but things weren't quite the same between us for a while.

'I went to the pub with him and his mates a few times, but I hated the whole laddish culture, downing pints and wolf-whistling at girls. It was mostly just boys' bravado, but I never felt like I fitted in. And then when we turned seventeen, I became the designated driver. I was one of the first in our year to pass my test and Dad got me an old banger at a car auction, so I ended up driving everyone around and not drinking. A few months later, Leo passed his test too, and my parents suggested we both share my car and halve the costs to make it cheaper. Which made sense in theory, but in practice it meant Leo demanded to use the car whenever he wanted to show off to some girl and then persuaded me to drive him around when he wanted to go drinking with his mates.'

Ross paused for breath and Lottie had to bite her tongue to stop herself butting in. Thankfully, Ross then continued, though his words came faster now, almost spilling into each other. 'Then one night in April – the night of Saturday, April 10, 2004 to be exact – Leo invited me to the pub. He and the rugby guys had finally persuaded the landlord to do a lock-in after months of them nagging him. I was flattered he'd invited me – I hadn't been out with him for a few weeks – but before I'd even said yes, he started talking about what an amazing night we were going to have and how absolutely bladdered everyone was going to be, adding, "Except you, Ross – you'll be driving!" I was pissed off that he'd just assumed I'd be happy to chauffeur him around without even thinking to check with me first, so I told him I couldn't come because I had "other plans". Leo knew full well I didn't have any plans, so he tried to

274

talk me round. He even promised to put in a good word with a girl he knew I liked. But I wasn't having any of it. He ended up storming out and taking the car. He said I was probably just going to spend the night being a sad bastard watching TV with my mum and dad – which was exactly what I was planning to do, obviously, but I wasn't going to tell him that.

'I sat in our living room that evening and drank three cans of lager watching some crap film with my parents, wishing I was in the pub talking to that girl I liked. Then I went to bed at eleven o'clock, feeling woozy. The next thing I remember is Mum waking me at three o'clock in the morning, saying there'd been a terrible accident. Leo's car had crashed and several people were badly hurt. I knew instantly, deep in my belly, that it had been Leo driving, and that he'd likely been over the limit – and that he might be dead.

'The next few hours are a blur. I know Mum went to the hospital to be with Margaret and I stayed at home with Dad waiting for news. I kept promising myself – and even God, who I didn't even know if I believed in – over and over again that if only Leo was okay, I would drive him wherever he wanted to go for ever, no questions asked. I didn't tell my parents about our argument – I didn't want to get Leo into more trouble – but I felt so guilty. If only I'd agreed to be the designated driver, as I usually did, then none of this would have happened and Leo would be back in his bed at home with his parents right now. And the guilt only grew the longer we waited.

'Finally, Mum called and told us that Leo was okay – he'd been knocked out, but miraculously he just had minor cuts and bruises – and his friend Matthew had broken his leg, but was otherwise pretty much all right. But the other boy in the car, Carl – he hadn't been so lucky. Doctors had to put him in an induced coma because they were worried about the swelling around his brain, and he'd broken his sternum and lost a lot of blood. They weren't sure he would make it till morning.'

Lottie put her hand over her mouth and her mind whirred with questions she both wanted and didn't want to ask.

'When Mum came home a few hours later,' Ross continued, 'she said the last thing she'd been told was that Carl was stable but still in an extremely serious condition. Leo had been discharged and was back home, but apparently he hadn't uttered a word. Eddie and Margaret suggested we let him sleep for a bit and then I should go over and see if he'd talk to me. They knew the police would want to be involved, but they wanted to find out from him what had happened. That afternoon, he still hadn't spoken a word to anyone, so I went up to his room – I remember my hand was shaking so much I could barely knock on the door.

'I found him sitting on the floor, his back against the bed, just staring at the wall. I sat down next to him, but even after spending almost every day of my life with him, I had no idea what to say. We stayed silent and both just stared at the wall in front of us. It was filled with rugby programmes, gig tickets and photos of us at every point of our lives. Then I felt Leo begin to cry. His whole body crumpled next to me and all

I could do was put my arm round him and hold him. I was more scared than I'd ever been in my life, and I desperately wanted to run downstairs and get our parents. But I stayed there in his room with him, and eventually he stopped crying enough to tell me what had happened.

'He said that, at first, he hadn't drunk even a drop of alcohol. But once the lock-in started, his mates had taken the piss out of him and kept daring him to do some shots. So in the end, he did, and then followed it up with some vodka Red Bulls. When they all decided to leave some time after one o'clock in the morning, they could only get one taxi to come and get them, so the others got in and left Leo, Matthew and Carl. They didn't know what the hell they were going to do, and didn't want to wake Leo's parents and ask for a lift, so he told the other two the fresh air had woken him up. He insisted he didn't feel drunk and was fine to drive home. They were both much drunker than him, so I guess they agreed without too much thought.

'And everything was fine until they got on the B road. It didn't have any streetlamps and at that time of night there was hardly anyone else around, so it was pitch black. A deer or some other animal jumped out of the trees, and Leo swerved and then skidded, and he lost control of the car. It ended up on its roof on the other side of the road. Matthew was the first to come round and he managed to drag himself out of the car and call an ambulance.'

Ross's voice cracked a little, and while Lottie wanted to give him the space to get his story out, she couldn't stop herself from saying, 'Are you OK, Ross? Do you want to take a minute?'

She heard him take a shaky breath in. 'No, I'm fine. I think it's easiest for me to try to do it one go, if that's all right?' He paused, but when he continued his voice was a little stronger. 'So, I didn't know what to say. I just kept telling Leo that everything would be all right and I was sure Carl would be fine, even though I knew deep down that nothing would ever be the same again. Then Leo said that the police had breathalysed him in the hospital and while he'd been pretty close, he was just under the limit, but he was so scared he was going to go to prison. I think something kicked in inside me then. I knew that no matter what happened, he couldn't go to jail. It would not only break Margaret and Eddie, but it would break him too.

'I forced him to promise me that the story he was going to tell the police was that he'd had one vodka Red Bull at the start of the lock-in and that was it, and although it might have been a pretty strong one because they hadn't been using a measure, he'd only had Coke after that. I made him practise his story out loud until I was happy he would remember it, but he still couldn't stop crying. It was the worst afternoon of my life. Then the doorbell rang and Margaret came upstairs and said the police were here and wanted to talk to Leo.

'We sat on the sofa in the living room and the police questioned him, thankfully pretty gently. I couldn't even hold my cup of tea, I was shaking that much. I have no idea how Leo got through it, but he stuck to our story and the police seemed to accept it. But for months afterwards I was so scared they were going to come back and arrest him. Leo and I never spoke about that afternoon again. We barely even spoke about the accident, to be honest. It was clear Leo wasn't coping and it didn't help that the whole village and school were talking about it for weeks. He became more and more withdrawn and wouldn't even speak to me, let alone his rugby mates.

'Then, one evening, when I got home from school, Mum sat me down and told me Leo and his parents were going to move to England and try to make a fresh start. I was seventeen, but I cried like a baby. I think I cried for the closeness Leo and I had, for the end of our childhoods, for poor Carl, for poor Leo. It must have been so hard for Mum having her sister move so far away when she'd been just down the road for so long, but at the time I couldn't see past me and Leo. It's only been in the past few months that me and Mum have really talked about it and she told me how upset she was and how powerless she felt.' He stopped and Lottie heard him take some deep breaths.

'I can't begin to imagine how awful all that must have been for everyone involved,' Lottie said. 'I can totally understand why Leo and his parents felt that moving away was for the best. Did your parents think about moving down here too?'

'I think with their jobs and everything it just wasn't doable. And Mum thought it was important that we held our heads high in the community. She kept telling everyone that it was an accident and no one was to blame. And then there was Carl to look after too.'

'He didn't d— He was okay then?' Lottie said, her voice rising in hope.

'No, no he wasn't okay,' Ross replied sadly. 'The accident left him in what doctors call a permanent vegetative state. A few months after it happened, he was able to breathe on his own and open his eyes, but he couldn't move or speak or show any response to anything going on around him. Leo and I went to see him in hospital about a month after the accident and Leo just couldn't cope. He was sobbing, almost hysterical. Carl's parents, John and Helen, never publicly blamed Leo for what happened, but they asked him not to come again because they found it too upsetting. That broke Leo. It was soon after that they decided to move down to Oxfordshire.'

'God, that is so awful – for Carl's family and yours.' Lottie felt tears welling in the corners of her eyes.

'I actually think John and Helen said it for Leo's own sake,' Ross said quietly. 'They knew that if Leo kept coming to see Carl, and kept being so physically reminded of what had happened, he would never be able to move on. They are such lovely people and they just didn't want another young man's life to be ruined. At first, they tried to stop me going to see Carl for the same reasons, but eventually they relented when I turned up at the hospital after school every day for a week. I was lucky enough to get to know them pretty well over the next few years, and they always asked after Leo. They were really upset when I told them he'd died, and they sent Margaret and Eddie the kindest letter a few weeks after the funeral.'

'What happened to Carl?' Lottie asked, already fearing the worst.

'After about a year, John and Helen had their house specially adapted and brought him home from hospital. They had carers with him all the time, but Helen was determined to look after him as much as she could, while still trying to be there for their daughter Eilidh. And she did look after him for five years, but then he got one too many chest infections and sadly passed away. It took them a while to come to terms with his death, Helen especially. She had to grieve for him all over again. But they're doing OK, and now Eilidh has two little ones, and they've got a new lease of life playing the doting grandparents.'

'I'm glad,' Lottie said. 'They sound like nice people.'

'They are,' he said. 'I just wish I'd known them under better circumstances.' Lottie thought he sounded exhausted, which was hardly surprising. There was a beat of silence before he continued. 'Thanks for listening, Lottie. I've not told anyone about all of this for a really long time, and I think I'd forgotten how much of who I am is still tied up in it all. Even though, as I said, it's not really my story, it's Leo's. We didn't really talk about it, and he certainly didn't speak to his parents about it for fear of upsetting them, but I know how heavily it still weighed on him. I always called him for a chat on the anniversary every year to make sure he was OK. Neither of us actually acknowledged the date or its significance. But I knew that he knew. I always hoped that one day he would find someone special enough for him to open up to about it all, so he didn't feel he had to deal with it all on his own. It sounds like, given a bit more time, you could have been that person, Lottie. I just wish he was still here to tell you himself.'

'Me too,' she said quietly.

'I think he was with you when I called him on the anniversary this year. It was only a few days before he died, and at the start of the call he sounded happy and excited, and then I went and ruined everything.' He sighed sadly. 'I'm not sure I'll ever forgive myself for that.'

Lottie's brain whirred and she thought back to the gorgeous bike ride that had changed so quickly after Leo had taken Ross's call. She opened and then closed her mouth, unsure of what to say. 'Oh, I s-see,' she stuttered. 'I thought you'd called to warn him off me again.' The minute the words were out of her mouth she wished she'd kept it shut. 'I mean—'

'Then I regret it even more,' he said sadly.

'You shouldn't – regret it, I mean,' she replied quickly. 'You were just checking in on your cousin on what you knew would be a tough day for him.'

He sighed again. 'Look, I'd better go, or neither of us will get up for work tomorrow. I'm sorry – I feel like I just dumped all of that on you, which really wasn't fair of me when I'm so far away.'

'I asked you to. Please don't apologise,' she said. 'And

thank you for trusting me with your and Leo's story. It means a lot that you shared it with me.'

'I'm glad I did. Sleep tight, Lottie, and don't be a stranger.'

'You too.'

She ended the call and sat staring into the darkness of her living room. Whatever she had imagined Ross was going to tell her, it certainly hadn't been that. All she could think of was just how sad it was. Carl had been the ultimate victim and lost his life, and the rest of his family had had to deal with a long and drawn-out grief over several years. It must have felt to Ross like he'd been cut adrift from Leo at the very point in his life when his cousin needed him most, and then Ross had had to cope with the fallout of the accident when Leo and his family had moved away. Their parents had lost the support networks they'd relied on for the last two decades. And Leo was a victim too. He'd almost lost everything. He'd been given the chance of a fresh start, but he'd had to live with the knowledge of what he'd done.

Lottie thought back to when she herself was seventeen. She'd definitely done some thoughtless, even reckless, things that in hindsight she wished she hadn't, especially when she'd felt pressured into things she really wasn't sure she wanted to do. Seventeen was such an in-between age – not a child, but not yet an adult. But even the worst of those times, when she'd had to call Annie, thankfully home from university for the summer, to come and get her from the house party she'd ended up at where she was hopelessly, scarily out of her depth, had caused no real lasting damage – and she'd learned to never go off with grown men she barely knew on their motorbikes again.

But for Leo, that thoughtless, reckless thing had caused unbelievable lasting damage.

Chapter Twenty-six

Over the next few days, Lottie found herself struggling to concentrate on anything for more than a few minutes at a time. She and Ross had taken to texting each other several times a day, and they'd had another couple of calls since. She tried to limit how many questions she asked him about Leo – she found she still both wanted to know and yet didn't – so they chatted about work and weekend plans. But when she was lying in bed with nothing but her own thoughts, she couldn't stop turning over everything Ross had told her in her mind. At least a few things finally made a bit more sense now, like Leo's change in mood after Ross's phone call during their bike ride, and his extreme reaction to the boy-racer who had narrowly missed hitting them when they were walking home from the burger restaurant. But there were still so many things she didn't know about how the accident had affected Leo in the immediate aftermath and in all of the years afterwards. She only knew what Ross had told her, and she so wished she could curl up with

Leo, stroke his mane of hair and listen to him as he opened up about how he felt.

One night, she threw off the duvet and desperately tried to conjure up a daydream of Leo. But although, if she concentrated hard enough, she could take herself back into that one moment where she snuggled her cheek into his chest, that's where her dreams now started and ended, it wasn't enough. Tears pricked the corners of her eyes as she felt Leo slipping still further away.

Without the crutch of alcohol, Lottie slept fitfully, and she knew the little work she was doing was below par. Reg had been keeping an even closer eye on her than usual, and it was only thanks to Rachel and Guy covering for her and pointing out her mistakes that she hadn't been hauled into another meeting with her boss.

She was glad she was seeing her sisters again that evening and could tell them everything.

'Carl's poor, poor parents,' Em said, shaking her head. 'I just can't even imagine losing one of the boys.' She shivered. 'It's awful.'

'It's the kind of tragedy that affects everyone involved for the rest of their lives, isn't it?' Annie agreed soberly. 'Did Ross say whether he and Leo ever talked about it when they were older?'

'He said they never mentioned it again after he made Leo promise to tell the police he'd only had one drink. I think Ross tried to get him to talk about it a few times over the years, especially when Carl died, but he said Leo kind of shut down,' Lottie replied. 'Leo was happy for Ross to be in contact with Carl and his parents, but he didn't feel he could engage with them himself. I think he tried to just get on with his life down south and reinvent himself.'

Annie frowned. 'It feels like Leo got off pretty lightly, considering. He was allowed to run away from the situation and pretend everything was fine and dandy and have this great life at uni, but what about Ross and his family stuck back up in Scotland?'

'I don't think it was quite like that,' Lottie protested. 'He still had to live with what he'd done.'

'Did he? It sounds to me like Ross was the one who had to live with the consequences of his cousin's actions,' she said.

Lottie stared at her sister, but bit back the retort that was on the tip of her tongue – because, although she had barely allowed herself to acknowledge it, that very thought had been niggling away inside her for the past few days. She hadn't allowed herself to pick it out and examine it for fear of what she might find. Instead, she turned to her younger sister. 'What do you think, Em? Do you agree with Annie?'

Em took a sip of her drink before she replied, and it was clear she was choosing her words carefully. 'I agree that it certainly looks like Ross bore the brunt of the aftermath, and it sounds like Ross stepped up to the plate admirably. I can't imagine many young men acting in the way he did. He sounds like a very kind and loyal person.'

Lottie nodded. 'And Leo?'

Em sighed. 'Look, it's hard to say, isn't it? And he's not

here to give you – or us – his side of the story. I'm sure he had his reasons for distancing himself from the whole thing. It was his parents who made the choice to come down to Oxfordshire, so you can't really blame him for that, and once that had happened, I imagine it was quite easy to shut himself away from it emotionally. To close that door and never have to open it again.'

Lottie felt a heavy ache in the pit of her stomach as a realisation suddenly hit her. 'He did the same thing with his heart condition,' she said slowly. 'He buried his head in the sand about that too. I think that might be why he didn't tell me – he thought it would just go away. But it didn't. Just like the accident never really did. When Ross told me the story, he was still so emotional about it, but maybe Leo never really faced up to his own emotions because he didn't have to.' Her sisters nodded and squeezed her hands. And now she'd started speaking, Lottie found she couldn't stop her thoughts spilling out. 'At the funeral, Ross talked about Leo being brave and courageous, but what if that wasn't always the case? Do you think he'd have ever told me – not just about his diagnosis, but about the accident? When I opened up and told him about Elliot, he was so supportive. But I told him that the hardest thing for me to deal with after Elliot left was that he'd kept this big secret from me, and even then, Leo didn't flinch about his own secret.'

Tears flicked across her eyelashes and she smiled a watery thank you at Em as she passed her a tissue. 'I don't think Leo was a bad person,' Lottie continued, 'and I don't want either of you to think that either. I wish more than anything that you'd met him and been able to see how kind and funny he was, how we just fitted together, how he made me feel truly me. But without him ever being honest with me about who he was, maybe our relationship just couldn't have lasted. Maybe it would always have ended somehow.'

Her sisters cocooned her in hugs and supportive words, then spent the next few days checking in on her all the time and telling her how proud of her they were. Despite her tears, Lottie had actually found that getting all of her thoughts out in the open had helped clear her mind a little, and while she knew she still had a lot of emotions to work through, it had somehow allowed her the space to concentrate on other things. Which was lucky, as her Zoom interview was fast approaching.

After their visit to Leo's parents' and their emotion-filled call, Lottie found herself messaging Ross more and more. There were some topics they avoided, but their everyday exchanges quickly became long, in-depth chats. When Lottie told him about her interview, he'd immediately offered to help her prepare. The charity he worked for was much more medical-based, but he told her that organisations operated in similar ways across the charitable sector. It was only when they had a FaceTime call a couple of days later that Lottie realized just how little she knew about budgets and funding and targets and press releases.

'Erm, Ross, I may be able to write six hundred words

about the etymology of the phrase *hair of the dog*, but I know nothing about KPIs and trustees,' she'd said, forcing herself to laugh but convincing neither of them.

'You don't have to,' Ross had replied. 'Because I can coach you on all those things. Plus they're never going to *expect* you to know it all. They know your experience comes from the language side – they'll have your CV in front of them – but they still wanted to interview you, so any knowledge of the mechanics will be a bonus. You just need to focus on getting across your passion for language and how important you think it is that all young people and adults have access to reading and writing tools, so they have the same opportunities in life as more privileged people do.'

'Are you sure you don't want to do this interview instead of me?'

'No, because you are going to wow them by being you. And I'm only repeating back to you exactly what you told me the other day in your messages.'

Lottie didn't quite know what to say to that, but she meekly agreed and asked him to repeat what he'd told her about government grants.

With Ross's prompts jotted down in the notebook in front of her as a safety blanket, Lottie had felt her video interview hadn't gone nearly as badly as she'd feared it would. And a few days later she was rewarded with an email asking her to come to a second interview, this time in person at the charity's London office the following week.

Now, staring at the glazed faces all around her on the packed Tube, she wondered if she would soon be staring intently at her phone to avoid catching anyone's eye on a daily basis. She jiggled her leg up and down as nerves shot around her body, earning her a sigh and a frown from the commuter next to her. Today she had to give a presentation about her 'vision' for the charity's outreach programme. A video interview was one thing, but she knew it was a whole other ball game standing up in front of people and telling them how brilliant she would be at the job. Plus she wouldn't be able refer to her notes to read verbatim the lines Ross had given her.

She was glad she had listened to Em's suggestion to dress as herself and not in some stuffy suit or heels that made her feel uncomfortable, but she'd also taken Annie's advice to dress as a polished, sparkling version of herself, and wear some jewellery that could act as a talking point. So now she was making her way stickily across London in a long-sleeved navy jersey dress, which was fine in the autumn breeze above ground, if not in the seemingly endless tunnels below. She fingered her gold Tatty Devine necklace in the shape of a typewriter, then smiled at the lady opposite who seemed to be surreptitiously checking it out, too.

She finally arrived outside the charity's headquarters, but even with a Tube change on top of a long train journey, she still seemed to be an hour early. Having already glugged a strong flat white before she even got on the train, she wasn't sure she should have another – caffeine plus nerves usually equalled shaky hands and embarrassing things coming out of her mouth – but spying a coffee shop down the road, she treated herself to a muffin and a decaf latte before opening her laptop and mouthing her way through her presentation yet again.

She'd scoffed her muffin and drained her coffee and was on her second read-through when she started to panic. She was far too inexperienced to even be speaking to these people never mind presenting her ideas about how to run their business to them! It had always been there, this doubt, ever since she'd pressed send on her application over a month ago, but she'd managed to keep the feeling to a low mutter – until now. Now it began to grow in strength, drowning out the words of her presentation and dominating her thoughts.

Lottie glanced at the time on her phone. She only had twenty minutes until she'd be standing in front of two almost-strangers, talking them through the muddle of meaningless words on the slides in front of her. She swiped her finger across her phone screen and quickly brought up her sisters' WhatsApp group. She looked at all their 'you can do it, Lots' and 'you'll wow them – just be yourself' messages, but their words sounded faint and far away as she read them back to herself. Instead, the voice in her head boomed, *What the hell are you doing? Just pack your bag and get the next train home. This job isn't for you. You work for a tiny online dictionary, what would you know about helping people read and write?*

Without really stopping to think, but knowing she needed to speak to a real-life human to stop the voice in its tracks, Lottie clicked into her recents menu and pressed call.

Ross answered on the second ring. 'Hello? Lottie, are you OK? Aren't you supposed to be in your interview?' he asked, his voice full of concern.

'I-I don't think I can,' Lottie said, her heart pounding in her chest. 'I'm a complete fraud and they'll see through me straight away. Why bother putting myself through it? There's no point.'

'Yes, there is, there's every point. Lottie, stay on the line, OK? I'm going to go quiet for a moment, but just give me a second and I'll be back. Lottie, did you hear me?'

'OK,' she whispered. Every part of her body was telling her to give in to the inevitable and get back on the train. Sweat was pooling in the small of her back. But just as she was about to give in, disconnect the call and pick up her bag, Ross's voice came back on the line.

'Lottie, are you still there?'

'Yes.'

'Good. OK, what's your earliest memory of you as a child?'

'What? I don't know.' She frowned. 'Look, Ross—'

'Think, Lottie, what do you remember about being little?'

Lottie puffed out her cheeks and shrugged, but then gave in and let herself be transported back to a time when everything was less complicated. 'I remember one Sunday morning, me, Annie and Em were sitting on my parents' bed,' she said. 'They were downstairs, but the three of us were propped up against the pillows and Annie started reading us a story about an owl and some animals that lived in a wood. She must have been about six and I can't even remember what the book was exactly about, but I do remember that me and Em loved it when Annie did all the voices of the animals like she'd learned from her teacher. There was this tiger in it and sometimes I got a bit scared and would hold my hands over my eyes when I saw him on the page. And every single time Annie would try to explain that he was a good tiger in the story, but I wasn't having any of it. And then Em started copying me, even though she didn't know why, and we'd both sit there with our hands over our eyes whenever the tiger was on the page. And then as soon as Annie turned the page and the tiger wasn't there any more, we'd put our arms down and hold each other's hands underneath the bedcovers while the owl got her happy ending.' Lottie blinked in surprise as she finished speaking. She hadn't thought about that book, or Annie doing the voices, or her and her sisters holding hands, for years, and she was shocked by how vivid the memory was.

'I'm always suspicious of tigers that sound too good to be true,' Ross said, and although she couldn't see him, she could tell he was smiling. 'But, Lottie, can you see? *That's* why you need to go this interview. You experienced the power of reading and words from a very young age. It created bonds between you and your sisters. But what if Annie hadn't been able to read? What if you'd never had the opportunity to get a good education? A few days ago, you told me you passionately believe that every adult and child deserves a chance to shine – and to be able to shine they need to be able to read and write. That's why you need to go and deliver that presentation you've worked so hard on.'

There was a beat of silence while Lottie tried to absorb everything he'd just said. 'OK,' she said quietly.

'Good. Now be yourself – and don't forget to breathe.'

'I won't, but I don't want to shower them with my coffee breath either, so I'll keep the deep breathing to a minimum. I actually managed to throw half my flat white down my front on the train. Thank God I didn't wear that white shirt you suggested.'

'What are you wearing?' Ross asked.

'This isn't some kind of sex chatline, you know!' She put on a seductive, breathy voice. 'I'm wearing a fitted white waitress shirt, just unbuttoned enough to give a flash of the sheer black bra beneath—' Ross sniggered in her ear and Lottie stopped abruptly, suddenly acutely aware that quite a few people in the coffee shop were staring at her. People who could possibly work at the charity office two hundred metres away. She also registered that she'd just said those words down the phone to Ross, but before she could process the awfulness, self-preservation kicked in. She started shoving her laptop into her bag one-handed and, very much in her normal voice, added, 'Anyway, I better go, Ross. But thank you, I-I don't know what I'd have done if you hadn't answered.'

'You don't need to thank me, Lottie,' he said quietly. 'And I'm not going to wish you luck, because I firmly believe you make your own luck. Go wow 'em.'

An hour later, Lottie emerged blinking back into the daylight. The last sixty minutes had whizzed past in a blur, and she was already struggling to remember everything she'd said and everything the interviewers had said to her. She thought she hadn't let anything too embarrassing come out of her mouth (she definitely hadn't mentioned sexy waiting staff outfits, which was a plus) and while there had been a question about how she would cope with working in such a different sector, she managed to recall a few of the sentences Ross had coached her on, and they'd seemed to nod and smile in the right places. She breathed out a long sigh of relief – at least it was all over and she hadn't made a complete idiot of herself.

The journey back to Oxford in the rain seemed to take for ever and with each mile, Lottie began to feel frustrated and disappointed with herself. She should have been more confident, she should have answered the interviewers' questions better, she should have asked them better questions. She knew she'd been reluctant to have the interview initially, but now she was so far through the process, she realized she wanted the job with a fierceness she'd never felt before. Of course she'd been happy when she'd got her first position out of university, and her job at the online dictionary, but she'd never felt like this before – that getting this job felt like the key to changing everything, not just in her own life, but hundreds of other people's too.

By the time Lottie let herself and a mewling Ginger into her flat, she was both soggy and deflated. Outwardly, in her texts to her sisters and Ross, she kept to the 'what will be will be and there'll always be other opportunities' line, and they all messaged back to agree. Her sisters reminded her that at least it was now out of her hands and she could relax. But inwardly, Lottie felt anything but relaxed.

Later that night, as she lay in bed debating whether she should get up and throw away the ridiculously expensive cat food Ginger had neglected to eat that was now stinking out the entire flat, her phone vibrated with a new message from Ross.

I hope you haven't spent the whole evening beating yourself up about not being good enough. Because you are good enough just as you are. X

Chapter Twenty-seven

Lottie wasn't sure her nerves could take much more. She was on permanent tenterhooks, and if her phone so much as lit up with a notification, she grabbed it protectively. She'd been refreshing her inbox at five-minute intervals for days. Even over the weekend when she knew no one from the charity would be emailing her, she couldn't stop herself checking her inbox just to make sure. She'd tried her hardest not to think about the job on Saturday, and helping Em with Alex's birthday party had certainly given her little time to fixate on it too much; she'd spent most of the day trying to stop fifteen five-year-olds from killing each other and themselves. And then Ross had called her on Sunday and kept her so entertained with stories about his great-aunt and great-uncle's ruby wedding anniversary party, where the guests seemed worse than the five-year-olds for getting themselves into mischief, that they'd barely talked about her interview. She wondered whether he was trying to keep her distracted on purpose.

But when work came round again on Monday morning, it

was almost impossible for Lottie to stop herself daydreaming about what could be. Rachel even had to nudge her hard in the ribs during their editorial meeting to bring her back to earth, and Lottie saw Reg frowning at her again. Her heart quaked in her chest and she resolved to really knuckle down. She couldn't afford to be turned down for the charity role only to lose her job at the dictionary. She'd contemplated telling Rachel and Guy about her interview, but the thought of seeing their disappointment if she didn't get the job had quickly dissuaded her.

The following day, she was midway through a conversation with Rachel about whether they should include *periodt* as an alternative spelling to the regular word without a 't' or whether Reg would think it was too 'down with the bloody Gen Z-ers', when her phone started ringing in her pocket. She'd turned silent mode off just in case, and now her mobile was telling the whole office that she was getting a call.

'I'd better get this, Rach, sorry. I've been waiting all week for this call from erm ...' She couldn't bring herself to lie directly to her friend, so she tailed off in embarrassment and jogged to the meeting room at the end of the office. She shut the door and, now a little breathless, swiped her phone.

'Hello, Lottie Brown speaking,' she said in her poshest phone voice.

'Oh, hi, Lottie, it's Lucy from Literacy For All. Thanks so much for coming in to see us last week and apologies it's taken a while for us to come back to you.' There was a pause and Lottie briefly imagined she was on *The X Factor* and Dermot was about to announce who had won the final.

Thankfully, Lucy quickly started speaking again. 'So, yes, I wanted to call you this morning to say that we would love to offer you the role!'

As glitter fell onto the stage and the audience cheered, Lottie shook herself. She'd actually done it; she'd actually got the job!

'Lottie? Are you still there?'

'Yes, sorry, I'm just a bit lost for words,' she gasped, only realising the irony of what she'd just said too late. 'But thank you. Thank you so much!'

'Well, thank *you*, we think you're going do a brilliant job. Your passion just shone through in your interviews. Obviously, you've got a steep learning curve ahead of you, but we think you're up to the challenge.'

'I am. I am *definitely* up to the challenge!' Lottie replied.

'Excellent! I'll whizz over an official offer and all the details on email shortly, but do just let me know if you have any questions at all. We're really looking forward to working with you, Lottie.'

They said goodbye and Lottie stared at the phone, her hand shaking. She couldn't quite believe that the charity had chosen her, above all the other candidates. So much of that was down to Ross, she knew, and she quickly tapped out a message to him.

The charity just called – they offered me the job!!! (If ever a situation called for multiple exclamation marks it's now!!!) Can you believe it! London, here I come, baby!! Xx

Immediately two blue ticks appeared and she could see he was typing.

I can definitely believe it – and you'd better believe it too!
Lottie, I'm so pleased for you, that's bloody brilliant news. I'm
in the middle of a meeting and furtively typing this under the
table, but I'll call you later. This job is made for you and you
deserve it. Rx

Lottie needed to tell someone in real life. She knew she should wait for the offer to be made official on email before she told Reg, and of course Guy and Rachel, who wouldn't be able to hide their happiness for her – the secret would be out before she could say, 'But don't tell anyone.' So Lottie dialled her little sister.

'Lots, that's amazing!' Em squealed down the phone as small children squealed even more loudly in the background. 'Oh, that has absolutely made my day – in fact, my year! I'm so happy for you. God, I actually feel a bit teary!'

'Me too!' Lottie laughed, swiping at her eyes. She was determined not to cry, even if they were happy tears for once.

'Call Annie this minute and let's do an impromptu pub club tonight? I know it's a day early but it's not every Tuesday your sister gets a fucking amazing new job!'

'Em! Did you just swear?' Lottie gasped in shock.

'I'm blaming you, and possibly the fact I'm in the middle of soft play hell. Right, let me order Luca home early and we'll synchronise watches later.'

Annie was just as pleased for Lottie in her own very different way.

'Yes! I so hoped that's what you were calling to tell me,' she cried. 'I'm so pleased for you. This is the perfect job for you – it really is.'

'That's what Ross said too.' Lottie smiled.

'Did he now? And, yes, I'm definitely up for pub club this evening. I'll get Charlie to come and pick me up afterwards. One of the joys of pregnancy is it's turned him into a "me man, me protect you" caveman, and, I have to say, I'm not complaining.'

'Call yourself a feminist!' Lottie laughed.

'I call myself a feminist who never looks a gift horse in the mouth, especially when my stomach seems to be expanding at a rate of knots. Although that could also be the amount of biscuits I'm eating. Anyway, I'll see you later. And, Lottie?'

'Yes?'

'You're going to smash this job, you really are.'

A few hours later, the three sisters were sitting at their usual table in the Rope and Anchor and Em had presented Lottie with a glass of the pub's finest prosecco, which Annie had proceeded to sneak a small sip of so she could feel she was 'celebrating properly, despite the small human I'm incubating'.

'What did everyone at work say when you told them?' Em asked.

'Well, Reg was surprisingly nice about it,' she replied. 'He said he was pleased for me and that he thought it was exactly the right time for me to leave the dictionary and that this was the challenge I clearly needed. I couldn't decide whether that meant he was glad I'd got an exciting new job, or just glad he didn't have to ask me to leave.'

'He'd never have done that, he knows how good you are,' Em said loyally. Lottie wasn't so sure, but it was fairly immaterial now, and she wasn't going to tell her sisters quite how close she'd actually been to losing her job.

'And how did Rachel react?' Annie prodded.

'Rachel was … very Rachel. I obviously waited to tell her until I'd been in to see Reg. And she did exactly what I told Ross she would: she did a massive whoop and shrieked "Lottie's that's a-mazing!" and started dancing round the office. Subtle she ain't, but I'll really miss her.'

'You'll still be able to see her whenever you want, though. It's not as if you're actually going anywhere, except on the train to work every day,' Annie pointed out.

'True, but you know what it's like when you're used to seeing someone every day of your working life. I'll just have to make the most of my last month there. It'll be weird having new work friends, though that's if they don't all immediately see through me and realize I have zero experience working for a charity.'

'You will be brilliant, Lots!' Em assured her, and Annie nodded vigorously.

'Of course you will. You're my sister, after all!' Annie joked. 'Ooh, I was going to ask if you both fancy coming shopping with me on Saturday afternoon? I can't fit into my clothes any more and I need to buy some maternity stuff, but I can't face the thought of doing it on my own. Could you both come and help me? We could grab an early dinner afterwards if you can swing it with Luca, Em?'

'Of course!' Em beamed. 'I gave most of my old maternity clothes to the fundraiser the boys' nursery ran last year, but I've probably got a few bits I can dig out. I'll bring those over too.'

'I very much doubt any of the gorgeous clothes you wore with your neat little bumps will fit me – I already feel huge! But thank you,' she replied with a grin. 'Lottie?'

'I don't suppose we could make it next Saturday instead, could we?' Lottie pulled an apologetic face.

'Why, do you have a hot date?' Annie joked.

'No, of course not! Ross just said he's going to try to fly down for the weekend and suggested we go out for dinner on Saturday to celebrate the job and everything,' she replied, aiming for nonchalant, which apparently didn't land; her sisters exchanged a look and both of them sat up a bit straighter.

'That sounds very much like a hot date to me, and I'm not even joking this time,' Annie said, fixing Lottie with a beady stare. 'I didn't realize you two were so close.'

Lottie shrugged. 'We're just good friends.' Her sisters exchanged another look she couldn't quite read. 'What?'

'We're your sisters,' Em said gently. 'This is a safe space. You can tell us how you really feel.'

Lottie looked at first Em's and then Annie's expectant faces. 'What? Seriously, you two!'

'Who was the first person you told that you'd got the job?' Annie said.

'Ross, but—'

'Who's top of your Recent call list?'

'I don't see what—'

'Who's your most recent WhatsApp from?'

'You, actually, Annie!' Lottie gave her sister a 'see, you're not as clever as you think' smile.

'Other than us, obviously.' Annie rolled her eyes and then looked smug when Lottie didn't answer. 'I rest my case. It seems to me that you are definitely more than just friends with Ross.'

Chapter Twenty-eight

Lottie clapped her hand over her mouth. Her heart rate felt like it was galloping and she could feel sweat beginning to pool in the small of her back.

'Do I?' she whispered. 'Do I *like* Ross?'

Her sisters grinned at her. 'Only you can answer that, Lots,' Em said. 'But it sounds very much to us like you do.'

'But ...' Her mind spun as she searched for all the reasons it couldn't be true, before landing resolutely on the obvious one. 'But what about Leo? I can't just ditch him for his cousin.'

'Leo's dead, Lottie,' Annie said quietly. 'You can't ditch someone who's dead.' Em opened her mouth and Annie held up her hand to her. 'I know, I know, Em, and you're right, maybe I shouldn't have said it quite like that, but it doesn't make it any less true. I know you're still working through everything that's happened over the last five months, Lottie, and no one's saying you *have* to act on your feelings, but have you thought about what it is you're so scared of?'

Lottie looked at both her sisters, her eyes wide. 'Oh, I don't know, just the fact that my boyfriend died a few days after I told him I loved him, and now I think I might have feelings for his cousin – who, let's not forget, was pretty horrible to me the first time I met him. His cousin who's still grieving the man he thought of as a brother. His cousin who very likely sees me just as a friend. His cousin who lives over three hundred miles away. Take your pick!' Lottie blew her cheeks out, then added more quietly, 'And, yes, of course I'm worried that I'd be betraying Leo. Does me liking Ross – and I'm not saying I do, but hypothetically – does that not somehow invalidate what me and Leo had? If Leo hadn't died, there's no way we'd ever be discussing my feelings for Ross, especially after how he behaved towards me. Yes, he explained why he acted the way he did, but if he can be like that with me once, he can be like that with me again.' She let out a steadying breath and looked at her sisters. 'If I'm truly honest, I'm not sure I could take any more betrayal or heartbreak. I'm just starting to put myself back together again, and this job is a chance for a fresh start and a way for me to find my way back to the person I want to be again. How do I know Ross wouldn't hurt me?'

Neither Em nor Annie said anything for a few seconds, and then Annie spoke. 'You don't,' she said simply. 'You don't know Ross won't hurt you. But then none of us ever know that about the partner we choose, do we? We have to put our trust in that person and hope what we have is strong enough to weather the storms that will inevitably blow in.'

The three of them sat in silence for another moment, before Annie stood up. 'I think there's a lot to unpick here, but I have to admit I'm busting for a wee – another joy of being pregnant! I'll be back in a sec with some more drinks. I think this conversation calls for drinks, even if I can't have the gin and tonic I'd like. Do you want another prosecco, Lottie?'

Suddenly fizz seemed inappropriate and Lottie shook her head. 'I'll have a glass of lemonade, please.'

They watched their older sister walk off and Em smiled. 'My overriding memory of being pregnant is having to make sure there was definitely a loo within a hundred metres. I remember the midwife telling me off during one of my appointments because apparently I was dehydrated. I was so miffed I nearly shouted, "I already go for a wee three times an hour, if I drink more water I might as well set up camp in the loo until I give birth!"'

Lottie laughed. 'I mostly just remember you looking utterly radiant and happy.'

'I think you have a very bad memory!' Em smiled at her then reached for her wrist and gave it a squeeze. 'I know you think there are lots of obstacles standing in the way of you and Ross, but if it's what you both want – and I totally get that is a very big *if* – then all those obstacles can be overcome. Especially the distance thing. It's perfectly possible to have a relationship with someone when you don't live in the same city, or even the same country. Luca and I managed it, after all, when I came back here for my final year at uni and he stayed in Italy. That's not to say it was easy – it was bloody hard, to be honest. But all those missed phone calls, awful goodbyes and arguments because the other person had misconstrued something the other wrote in a text – it was all worth it to have what we have now. I think we had to go through that time to realize we both wanted to get to this point. And I know I'm incredibly lucky and privileged to have the life I do, and of course not every long-distance relationship makes it, but love can span cities and countries, I promise.' She dabbed the corner of her eyes with her sleeve. 'God, sorry, I don't know why I'm so emotional! I guess I just don't want you to let something that could be good slip through your fingers because you're too scared to give it a go.'

Lottie grabbed her sister's hand. 'Thank you.' She tried to swallow the huge lump in her throat. 'I had no idea your relationship with Luca was so tough when he was in Italy. I just remember you going over there all the time and having these gorgeous, romantic-sounding weekends in Milan with the man of your dreams.'

Em smiled. 'Of course, there were some gorgeous, romantic weekends, when we wandered through the city hand in hand like love's young dream, but there were also weekends when Luca was pulled into the office and I was left to wander miserably around Zara and McDonald's on my own and barely saw him. Our relationship definitely wasn't perfect, and it's certainly not perfect now, but it's ours, and that's what matters.'

'It looks pretty perfect to me,' Lottie replied.

'How many times do we have to tell you that no relationship is perfect?' Annie butted in, plonking their drinks on the table and unceremoniously prodding Lottie's legs out of the way so she could get to her seat. 'Em and Luca's isn't, mine and Charlie's definitely isn't, and even yours and Leo's wasn't, was it, if you're truly honest with yourself?'

Lottie stared at her, her hackles automatically rising. 'You weren't there, Annie, you don't know what it was like. You can't say that.'

Annie's eyes flashed and she opened her mouth, but then shut it again and took a breath. 'I'm sorry, Lottie, you're right, I wasn't there. But I have been there these past few months when you've talked about Leo keeping secrets and not being open with you, and I know how important honestly is to you. You said yourself that even if Leo had still been alive, you weren't sure if you could have had a future together, once you knew that he dealt with his problems by running away and burying his head in the sand. And I'm not saying what you and Leo had wasn't special – of course it was. But sometimes the most important parts of a relationship are the bits in between the perfect moments. You and Leo were still in your honeymoon period when he died, and maybe all the time you spent together did feel perfect – only you can know that. But maybe if you think back now, there were some little moments where you thought, "That's a strange thing for him to say, there must be something behind that," or "I don't like how moody he was last night," or even something as stupid as "I really hate that awful wallpaper he has behind the fireplace – what on earth possessed him to buy that?"

'I suppose what I'm saying is there is no man in this world who matches up to our individual idea of perfection, but it's how we deal with these imperfections that is important. Someone's past can sabotage their present relationship, their politics and views can cause arguments, and their likes and dislikes can make you see them in a different light. And it takes time to see – or maybe *want* to see – these imperfections, the baggage they bring with them, their past that influences their future, for better or worse. But you can't have the perfect without the imperfect, because that's what makes that person who they are, and your relationship what it is.'

'So do you think I could never really have—' Lottie's voice shook, but she swallowed hard and forced herself to keep talking. 'Do you think I could never really have loved Leo because we were together such a short time?'

'No, that's not what I'm saying,' Annie replied fiercely. 'You loved the parts of Leo you knew in those three months, and that love was valid and true. What you had was special and can never be taken away from you. You're allowed to grieve for those amazing weeks you had together – and for the weeks, months and maybe years you didn't get to have together. The chance you never had to know him on an even deeper level, to find out the dark to his light, the imperfections to his perfections, whether he did always run away from problems instead of facing them. But when the time is right, when you feel strong enough, you're also allowed to move on and find new happiness, whoever that's with.'

Somewhere in the deepest recesses of Lottie's brain, a switch flicked. She might not have been quite ready to admit what she did or didn't feel for Ross, but hearing her sister's words made her realize that maybe it was okay for her to feel something, maybe even – one day – love, for another man. She smiled at her older sister. 'Annie Brown, you never cease to surprise me!'

For the first time in Lottie's memory, Annie blushed and looked embarrassed. 'Maybe it's pregnancy hormones, maybe it's finally realising that science and experiments can only prove so much, I don't know. And I don't profess to have all the answers, but I ... I care too much about your happiness, Lottie, to let you continue to punish yourself for wanting to be happy. You deserve all the happiness. And if you think Ross can help you find that, then you have to give it a go, surely?'

Lottie felt her eyes well up yet again. Both of her sisters grabbed her hands and each other's, and they grinned through glassy eyes. 'I'm not sure why we end up in tears every time we sit around this table,' Lottie said with a sniff. 'God knows what Alf thinks. "There's those three weirdos crying into their drinks again," I imagine.'

'But at least we keep him in profit and he doesn't have to clean the table once we've left – our tears will have done that for him!' Annie laughed. She dropped their hands, wiped her eyes and reset her shoulders. 'Right, come on, enough weeping and wailing, let's get down to practicalities. Say, hypothetically of course, that you do finally admit to yourself that you like Ross – what are you going to do about it?'

Lottie raised her eyebrows at her. 'I imagine you're about to tell me, hypothetically, of course.'

'If you insist. It's obvious, though, isn't it? You need to tell him how you feel.'

'And if he doesn't feel the same?' Lottie immediately shot back.

'Then at least you know. At least you can make decisions based on fact not hypothesis.'

'Glad to see the scientific Annie making a return.' Em giggled. 'But, actually, I think she's right, Lots,' she said more seriously. 'It comes down to the old *you never know unless you try* cliché, I guess. It's a cliché for a reason, after all.'

Lottie looked at her sisters, knowing they were probably right, but also knowing it wasn't as simple as it sounded. Because to try meant having enough courage to put herself out there, emotions and all. And after everything that had happened, she wasn't sure she had much courage left.

Chapter Twenty-nine

As the day of Ross's arrival grew closer, Lottie felt more and more confused. Once her sisters had helpfully pointed out her own feelings to her, it hadn't taken long for her to admit to herself that, yes, she did feel more than just friendship for Ross. He was one of the truest, most thoughtful people she had ever met, and despite their unfortunate first meeting, he seemed to totally 'get' her in a way not even Leo had.

Leo had been devastatingly handsome with his perfect mane of mussed-up hair, manicured stubble and piercing blue eyes to rival Daniel Craig's, and Lottie had constantly had to pinch herself that a man that model-gorgeous would be interested in her. In contrast, Ross's good looks were more understated and laid back – more on Lottie's level, if she was being honest. He had the rugged complexion of a Scottish man, while Leo had the smooth complexion of a man with a skincare regime and the hair of a man who spent hours applying products. They were chalk and cheese in many ways. And that was Lottie's problem. It wasn't that the two men were so different that worried her, it was the way she constantly compared them. When she'd met Leo she hadn't had a proper relationship in years, so she had little to compare him with and was able to just enjoy everything about him freely. But even if she was to tell Ross how she felt, and even if he did feel the same way and think they could have a future together, she was always going to feel the urge to compare what they had with what she'd shared with Leo. And she knew that wouldn't be fair.

But the other option was to never know what might have been between them, to stay just friends and hope the candle she held for him would eventually burn out and leave their friendship unsinged. It was the safe option, the steady option, the option Lottie would definitely have taken a year ago. But she wasn't the same person as she had been then.

Ross had told her he was landing at Heathrow at eleven o'clock on Saturday morning and then jumping on the coach to Oxford, so they'd agreed he should drop his bag at the hotel before meeting Lottie mid-afternoon. Determined not to spend her whole morning in exactly the same way she'd spent the evening before – sending herself crazy running her thoughts round in circles – Lottie decided to give the flat a good clean. She shooed Ginger out after realising the awful smell she thought was emanating from the kitchen was actually coming from him, put on her most embarrassing but favourite Spotify playlist, and mopped and wiped and vacuumed, only stopping to pretend to be Freddie, Elton and Mariah as she screeched along to their most diva-ish songs.

Two hours later as the last bars of 'I Want To Break Free' sounded and the playlist came to an end, she surveyed her efforts and felt rather pleased with her small but now sparkling home. Somewhere in the back of her mind, she wondered whether she had gone to all this trouble just in case Ross came back there later, but she shook the thought away immediately.

She clicked onto her 'Chill Out' playlist and threw herself onto the freshly plumped sofa, determined to give herself the luxury of ten minutes relaxation before she got up to get ready. But as the first song began, she sat bolt upright. The unmistakeably melodious piano chords and swooshy sea sounds of 'The One' sent a shiver through her body, and before Elton John had even sung his first line, tears were stinging her eyes.

By the time the notes swelled towards the final chorus, salty water poured down Lottie's cheeks, and she fought to swallow back a sob that would completely undo her. She gulped for air and forced herself to breathe more deeply as the pace of the song slowed and the final sweet notes rang out.

She paused the playlist and allowed the flat to be filled with the sound of silence. She hadn't listened to that song since Leo's death and it had immediately taken her straight back to that moment when he'd first played it to her, when she'd started to realize that he was her One. And here she was, about to meet his cousin and tell him that she thought *they* had a romantic connection. What was she thinking? Had she really loved Leo enough if she was feeling this way now – had he really been The One? Hadn't she thought at one point that Elliot was The One in fact? She could feel her thoughts starting to spiral into an unhealthy place again and she dug her fingernails into the fleshy part of her hand and forced herself to take some calming, deep breaths and remember what her sisters had said about being allowed to find happiness again. Leo would always be someone special in her life, despite him only being part of it for such a short time, but maybe there was also space for someone else? Someone like Ross.

Standing outside the entrance to Oxford's natural history museum a few hours later, Lottie smiled at the couples and families who passed her. She'd read somewhere that smiling was infectious, and even if you didn't feel like grinning from ear to ear, the more you smiled at people – and they smiled back – the happier you felt, because it released waves of endorphins. She hoped it hadn't just been pseudoscience; she could do with all the endorphins she could get to counteract the adrenalin that was coursing through her body and making her heart beat uncomfortably fast.

She'd chosen to stand close to the door so that she'd be

able to see Ross coming down the road from as far away as possible, giving her a chance to compose herself before she actually came face to face with him. She spotted him well before he saw her and she had time to take some deep breaths. She watched him look up and saw his face bloom into a smile when he noticed her, and she couldn't help but grin back.

'Hi, soon-to-be literacy champion. Fancy seeing you here!' he said, and enfolded her in a hug.

'Hi!' she replied, her brain seemingly unable to reach for any of the tens of thousands of words that normally resided in her vocabulary.

'You look nice,' he said, taking a step back to admire the peg-leg trousers, round-necked jumper and denim jacket; an outfit she'd agonised over but wanted him to think she'd just thrown together. 'Not an unbuttoned waitress shirt in sight!'

Lottie's cheeks coloured and she pushed him lightly on the arm. 'I thought we agreed not to mention that again.' She pulled her fingers through her hair and turned towards the entrance. 'Anyway, shall we go and see some dead animals?'

'Sounds like an offer I can't refuse.'

They wandered around the ground floor of the impressive building, stopping to read each other snippets of information from the plaques on each of the exhibits. Lottie noticed that Ross seemed lighter, less intense than he had any of the other times she'd seen him in the flesh.

He was more like the Ross of their text chats and her heart soared with hope and anticipation.

Although she had been to the museum more times than she could remember, she always found something new to look at. Even so, her favourite part was the dodo display.

'"The last confirmed sighting of a dodo was in 1662 and it is widely believed to be the first noted extinction of an animal caused at least in part by humans,"' she read out loud. '"The museum holds the dried head of a bird, now known as the Oxford Dodo, which is the only soft tissue of the dodo that remains anywhere in the world." It's incredible, isn't it? No matter how many times I read it, I can never get over the fact that, even in the seventeenth century, man was responsible for wiping out an entire species.'

'It's scary,' Ross agreed. 'For all the good humans can do, it's our power to hurt and frighten and damage others that is so often remembered and so often creates the biggest ripples.'

They were both silent for a second and Lottie felt a small ball of anxiety building in her stomach for reasons she couldn't quite put into words. 'Shall we grab a drink in the cafe before we see the other exhibits?' she said quickly.

Fuelled by hot chocolate, they spent the rest of the afternoon checking out the other displays and Lottie enjoyed the sensation of walking around with Ross by her side. Finally, though, they both agreed it was time they headed into the centre of town to find an alcoholic drink before dinner.

'Cheers!' Ross said, raising his pint of lager. 'Congrats on your amazing new job, Lottie.'

She clinked her glass against his and savoured the hit of Rioja. 'Thank you! But I couldn't have done it without your coaching.'

'Of course you could. But I was happy to help.' He smiled at her and butterflies fluttered in her chest. Then he handed her a paper bag with the unmistakeable crest of the museum on it. 'I got you this.'

He must have nipped into the shop when she'd gone to the loo before they left, she realized. She peered inside and lifted out a small soft whale toy.

'It's a blue whale,' he explained. 'Like the dodo, they were almost hunted to extinction by man, but they were saved by some of the most powerful people in the world coming together and agreeing new laws. I guess I wanted to remind you that there are good people in the world, who care enough to try to make a difference. Like you.' He smiled.

Lottie was completely wrong-footed. It was one of the sweetest gestures anyone had ever done for her and she searched her brain for the right thing to say. 'I shall put him on my bedside table, so that when I start my new job, and realize I haven't a clue what I'm doing, I can look at him and remember that at least I'm not trying to save the largest animal on the planet. Thank you, you are very sweet.' She leaned over to give him a kiss on the cheek, pausing for a second longer than she probably should have done, before pulling herself back upright and taking a gulp of her drink. She smiled as Ross began telling her a story about a small child he'd seen having a meltdown in the shop when her mum told her that she already had a grey seal toy at home, and no, it didn't need a friend.

Despite the to-ing and fro-ing going on in the secret safety of her head, Lottie felt like conversation flowed between them. Ross seemed genuinely interested in what she had to say, and although he sometimes grew serious, especially when he was talking about his work, he still had a lightness of tone that stopped things becoming too intense.

They finished their drinks and Lottie led the way to the restaurant Ross had booked for dinner, passing various people in worrying states of drunkenness, considering it was barely seven o'clock in the evening.

'I've been in that pub, I remember,' Ross said, pointing to a building on the opposite side. 'Leo must have taken me there a few times, I think.'

Lottie glanced up at him, trying to read his expression, but he just smiled back at her, clearly not noticing the significance of what he'd said.

'Yes,' she said, nodding. 'It's where the three of us went for lunch when he introduced us.'

'Oh. Yes. Not my finest hour,' he said with an awkward smile. They continued walking to the restaurant in uncomfortable silence that was only broken by the waiter showing them to their table.

Once they were seated, and had been handed menus and

told in excruciating detail about the specials, Ross immediately excused himself to go to the loo. As Lottie stared, unseeing, at the list of dishes in front of her, she wished she'd kept her mouth shut about the pub.

The waiter came to ask what they wanted to drink, and she realized she didn't even know Ross well enough to be sure he drank wine. She ordered a bottle anyway, needing a glass of something alcoholic in her hand as soon as possible.

'Does the menu look good?' Ross asked as he returned to his seat. 'When I checked online, it all looked delicious. I might need our waiter to run through the specials again, though – they all sounded very complicated!'

Relieved that Ross seemed to be back to his previous good-humoured self, Lottie nodded. The waiter brought the wine and asked Ross if he wanted to taste it, but Ross waved it over to Lottie and politely asked for a pint of lager instead. Once they'd been talked through the specials again and the waiter had left them to decide, Ross said, 'Sorry, I should have told you I don't really do wine. I've tried really hard to like it over the years, but I just can't! My dad loves the stuff and completely despairs of me.'

'It's fine, all the more for me!' Lottie said with a laugh. 'And I can always take the rest of the bottle home. What are you going to have?'

'I was thinking the lamb for main, but I already can't remember what he said it came with,' he replied ruefully.

'I think he essentially said potatoes and vegetables but all of them with a posh, chefy twist.'

'Do you think I could ask for chips instead?' He smiled.

She put on an affected voice, 'No, sorry, sir, we only do posh potatoes here. But maybe I could interest you in some pommes frites or straw potatoes instead?'

'Only if I can have ketchup too!'

They grinned at each other. Lottie found herself relaxing and reminded herself not to overthink everything – and even actually enjoy it. They polished off starters and mains and then agreed they'd share a cookie dough skillet between them. She sipped her wine; both Ross and their waiter had kept her glass so well topped up that she hadn't noticed how much she was drinking, and she was surprised to see the bottle was now almost empty.

When their dessert and two spoons arrived, they both dug in and made appreciative noises. As much as Lottie wanted to shovel the whole thing into her mouth, she put her spoon down and instead reached for her wine. She took a far-from-ladylike gulp, then began speaking.

'Thank you for coming all the way down this weekend, I've had such a fun day,' she said, and Ross nodded as he chewed his mouthful. His forehead crinkled, showing off all the lines etched into his features. Lottie couldn't help wanting to run her fingers along the lines and find out the story behind each and every one. She shook herself a little and tried to focus. 'I feel like laughs have been in short supply recently, for you too, probably, so it's nice to let off a bit of steam.'

'I've had a great day too.' He smiled. 'L—'

'Ross—' Their words clashed over each other.

'Sorry, you go,' he said.

She took a deep breath. 'I wondered if you wanted to do this again sometime. As more of a date thing, I mean.' He started to open his mouth, but she rushed on. 'I know it wouldn't necessarily be easy, but I think maybe the two of us have something. What I mean to say is, I like you, Ross. And I don't know for sure, but I think maybe you might feel the same?' She ran out of steam and grabbed the stem of her glass.

'Lottie,' Ross said, looking at her with a tenderness that gave her hope. 'I just think we'd be better off as friends, don't you?' His words may have been said gently but they ricocheted around her body like a pinball in a machine. 'You know I think you're brilliant and one of the loveliest people I've ever met, but it doesn't matter how I feel. Too much has happened. It wouldn't be fair on any of us.' Lottie didn't trust herself to speak, and when Ross grabbed her hand, it took all her of strength not to recoil and snatch it back. 'I'm sure you've remembered that tomorrow is Leo's six-month anniversary. It's one of the reasons I came down this weekend, so I could see Margaret and Eddie tomorrow. I know it'll be a tough day for them. It's just too soon, don't you think? And I couldn't bear to lose you as a friend if things didn't work out. This way we still get to be friends no matter what. That's got to be a good thing, hasn't it?'

Lottie found herself nodding and attempting a fake smile, trying to force out the endorphins she so desperately needed. The significance of tomorrow's date had completely passed her by – she'd been so wrapped up in herself and her feelings – and that only made her feel even more ashamed and embarrassed. 'Of course,' she managed. 'I understand. You're completely right.' Ross sank back into his chair, relief flooding his face.

Lottie had no idea how she got through the next fifteen minutes as they waited for the waiter to bring them the bill. Finally, they were back in the fresh air and she was able to turn to Ross and say she was tired, that she was going to order a taxi home and he should head off to his hotel. All she could focus on was being on her own and away from him, but he wouldn't hear of leaving her by herself. The two-minute wait for her car felt like two hours. Ross chatted away about the beauty of the city at night, and she nodded in what she hoped were the right places.

'Here it is!' she cried as a car drew up in front of them. 'Thanks so much for dinner, Ross,' she forced out, using every last bit of resolve she had left. 'Give Margaret and Eddie my love and tell them I'm thinking of them.'

'I will,' he said, drawing her into a strong hug that knocked any remaining emotional stuffing out of her. 'You are a beautiful, amazing person, Lottie, never forget that,' he said fiercely into her hair.

Lottie was incapable of answering and instead got in the car, grateful for once for the darkened windows. The driver confirmed the address and pulled away. She jabbed her phone and pressed the Call button, tears already running down her cheeks.

The One

'Annie? Yes, I'm OK. Actually I'm not, I'm really not. Can I come over? Thanks, I'll be there in ten minutes.' She ended the call and couldn't hold back her sobs any longer.

PART THREE

TWO MONTHS LATER

Chapter Thirty

Lottie sat on the train chugging away from the twinkling lights of the capital, her notebook on her lap and her headphones sitting snugly over her ears. The carriage was full of other commuters, some sipping daintily from Christmas-themed paper coffee cups as they read the latest celebrity autobiography, others desperately gulping from not-so-festive cans of lager as they stared at impenetrable spreadsheets on their laptops. Despite the darkness outside and the stifling heat of the aircon inside, Lottie felt somewhere close to content.

She'd started her job at Literacy For All a month ago, and while she'd spent the first few days feeling like the biggest fraud ever to walk the streets of London, she'd quickly realized the small team she was now a part of were not only some of the most passionate, driven people she'd ever met, but they were also some of the most welcoming. And if an hour passed where she hadn't asked a question, at least one of them would take it upon themselves to call her over and explain exactly how a process worked and ask her if she had any ideas how they could make it more efficient. They prompted, supported and advised, and celebrated all of her little achievements. So now, four weeks later, while she knew she still had a *lot* to learn, her confidence was growing and her excitement was building for the New Year, when she would be launching the first stage of the outreach programme the whole charity was so passionate about. Even during those first few days when she'd felt like a fish out of water and the commute had still been a thrilling novelty, she'd known somewhere deep in her belly that a fresh challenge was exactly what she needed after everything that had happened.

She allowed herself to cast her mind back to that Saturday night two months ago when she'd laid her heart not just on her sleeve, but on the line, for Ross. It was only in the past few weeks that she'd been able to even think about it at all, and that was only thanks to the counselling she'd been having.

That night, back at Annie's, she'd broken down completely, the feelings of shame, embarrassment and pain so great she'd have agreed to anything her sister suggested. But even waking up in the cold light of the following morning in Annie's spare room, eyes swollen and red and her heart battered and bruised for the second time, she'd seen the truth in her sister's advice. And although she'd felt distinctly uneasy about bypassing the free NHS services and their four-month waiting list, she'd given in to Annie's proposal to fudge things so she could use Charlie's 'family' private medical insurance. It meant pretending she lived with her sister, which was near enough the truth anyway. Both Annie and Em had confessed how guilty they felt for encouraging her feelings for Ross so forcefully, and Lottie had spent most of the next few weeks at her older sister's home and then every weekend in the Cotswolds with Em, as they held her in a metaphorical, as well as often physical, hug.

Another of the positives about being at Annie's house so much was that she'd got to know Charlie a bit better, and she'd finally started to understand what had made her sister fall in love with him. She'd never bothered to spend much time with him before, always preferring easy-going Luca of her two brothers-in-law, but now she saw Charlie in a new light. He was passionate about the financial world he worked in, and, yes, sometimes Lottie's eyes would glaze over when he started mentioning hedge funds and bonds, but he was subtly witty and impressively clever without ever being overbearing, and he loved to give Annie her chance to shine, whether it was in a conversation over dinner, or when he was telling Lottie how proud he was of his wife for sticking out cycle after cycle of IVF.

And once he'd heard Annie's idea of using his insurance to fund some counselling sessions for Lottie, he'd immediately made the necessary phone calls, so that within a month, Lottie had been waiting outside a non-descript building hidden down a side street in the heart of Oxford, daring herself to walk in for her first counselling appointment. She'd been hesitant to tell Lucy, her new manager, but practicalities had superseded any self-consciousness, and the charity couldn't have been more supportive. They'd readily agreed to her working from home whenever she needed to so she could attend her appointments. Lottie couldn't imagine what Reg's reaction to a similar request would have been, although he'd probably just have said yes as quickly as possible to avoid any kind of a conversation about her mental wellbeing. Lucy had been calm, supportive without prying, and open about the positive effects having therapy herself had brought. She'd told her it was definitely not something to be ashamed of. Lottie had even begun to feel embarrassed that everyone but her had seemingly been having counselling and getting their lives together while hers fell apart. But better late than never, she'd told herself, before taking a deep breath and walking into her appointment.

Counselling hadn't been exactly what she'd imagined. Until recently, she'd not known (or at least, thought she'd not known) anyone who'd been through it themselves, so all her preconceptions were from bad American films and offbeat British comedies. Yes, she'd expected to have to tell her story warts and all, but once she'd got it all out, she'd thought that the nice lady sitting opposite her would tell her exactly what she should do to make everything okay again. It had been immediately clear that wasn't the case. Yes, her counsellor Jane had seemed very nice when she'd introduced herself, but she'd quickly explained that this kind of talking therapy would help Lottie to find her own solutions to her problems and anxieties. It wasn't about anyone telling her what she should or shouldn't be doing or feeling; it was about talking, and being listened to, about her thoughts and emotions so she felt better equipped to take control.

Once she'd got her head around the idea, Lottie had decided to fully embrace her sessions. She had nothing to lose, after all, and she felt guilty enough about taking up another person's time when someone with 'real' problems could be having her slot. When she left at the end of each appointment, usually having made full use of the box of tissues Jane had helpfully left within arm's reach, she was completely wiped out. But she found it helped knowing that for one hour each week she had an outlet to admit to emotions she'd been carrying around not only since her conversation with Ross, or even since Leo's death, or even her broken engagement to Elliot, but maybe even since she was a child.

Her counsellor had suggested she set aside time during her week to process what they'd discussed in their sessions, but it had only been recently that Lottie had got to a point where she felt able to examine some of those feelings outside of the therapy room. She found listening to a podcast on the train home from work sometimes gave her the headspace to do that. Deep down, she still felt like it was too self-indulgent to sit there and do nothing but listen and let her brain work away in the background – she felt she should be working on the outreach programme, or even using her commute time to learn a new language or read one of the many books she'd been meaning to start for so many months. But she was trying, and for now that had to be enough.

She'd also surprised herself by making a kind of peace about her relationship with Ross. He'd messaged her the day after their trip to the museum, and she'd forced herself to politely reply. There'd been occasional texts, but despite Ross's insistence that he wanted them to stay friends, over the next few weeks their communication had almost fizzled out. Lottie had missed it. She'd missed his messages telling her there was an amazing programme on iPlayer he thought she'd really like; she'd missed the updates about the latest exploits of his eighty-five-year-old great-aunt and great-uncle; she'd missed *him*.

Annie had been typically forthright in her views the Wednesday after Lottie's first counselling session, when they'd met as usual in the pub, albeit half an hour later to give Lottie time to get there from the train station. 'It's for the best,' Annie had declared. 'You need to make a clean break. Or at least as clean as you can while still staying in contact with Leo's parents, if that's what you want.'

Em had eyeballed their older sister and then turned to Lottie and said more gently, 'You should do what feels right to you, Lots. We're not the ones with all the answers – that's pretty clear, I think. But nothing has to be for ever. I'm sure it all feels too raw right now to try to be friends, but who knows how you might feel in the future?'

The only feeling Lottie had been sure of at that point was the emptiness inside where her friendship with Ross had been, so whether it was a good idea or not, the next day she'd sent him a link to an article she'd read on the BBC website about blue whales being spotted in large numbers around a British Antarctic island for the first time in fifty years. She added the words, *It seems the good people really ARE making a difference.*

His reply had come back within a few minutes.

Come on, you blues! Love this article, thank you. How are you, Lottie? I was thinking about you the other day. You must start your new job very soon! How are you feeling about it?

Yes, I start on Monday, in fact! It's my last day at the dictionary tomorrow – I'm a bit scared of what Rach and Guy have got planned for my leaving do, to be honest. I *think* we're doing karaoke, but I wouldn't put it past Rachel to have hired a male stripper or something!

I can't even imagine your face if she did that!

I'm sure Rach would make sure she plastered a photo of my mortified face all over social media, don't you worry. How are things with you?

It hadn't been long before they'd fallen back into messaging most days and even FaceTiming each other at weekends. When she'd mentioned to her counsellor that they were back in regular contact, Jane had nodded and asked her what she wanted to get out of her relationship with Ross.

'What do you mean?' Lottie had replied, puzzled.

'What does a meaningful relationship with Ross look like for you? To always remain friends, continuing to message each other snippets of your lives? To become closer friends, maybe, so you're involved in each other's lives when it comes to family and other friends? Or in an ideal world do you still want what he said you can't have – to be together romantically?' Jane had sat back in her seat, her arms loose in her lap. Her face, while not smiling, had been open and calm, inviting Lottie to honestly express her feelings.

As Lottie had tried to put her jumbled thoughts into an order of sorts, silence had filled the room, but she'd learned over the weeks to quell her desire to speak immediately, instead giving herself the time to figure out what she really thought. 'I think that in an ideal world, yes, of course I still want to have a romantic relationship with Ross. I can't just turn off what I feel for him. But he has made his own feelings clear, which wasn't an easy thing for him to do, and I have to respect that. For me, being friends – close friends, hopefully – is far better than having nothing at all. And maybe the more time I spend with him as his friend, the more I'll be able to cement my friendship with him. He's too important to me to not be in my life at all, and if it can only be as friends, then that's how it will be.'

Despite baring her soul to her therapist, Lottie had played down her renewed friendship with Ross to her sisters, knowing they both felt it was too soon for her to be back in contact with him after getting so hurt. So she was more than happy for them to believe that the upturn in her general mood was purely down to her new job and the benefits the counselling was bringing. They had met up for dinner the previous Saturday evening to celebrate Em's birthday and both of them had remarked how well she looked.

It had been almost a fortnight since the three of them had all been together, as December had proved busier than ever for them all. Em had been juggling Luca's parents' imminent arrival for a month-long stay at their house, with running Dante's nursery Christmas fundraiser and organising the reception class's intricate-sounding nativity play; the teacher seemed to have washed her hands of it the minute Em came along.

'I literally don't know how you're doing it all,' Lottie had said to her sister. 'Especially trying to marshal all the little ones into something resembling a stable! Seriously, Em, it's impressive.'

Her sister had smiled. 'Thank you. But I've loved doing the nativity. The kids are so sweet and as soon as you tell them your name's Mrs Ricci, they decide you're a teacher and they have do what you tell them. Except Alex, of course. He doesn't take any more notice of me than he normally does, sadly!' She paused and then said shyly, 'I actually wanted to tell you both something tonight. I've been looking into doing a PGCE and training to be a primary school teacher. And, well, I've been accepted onto a course that starts next September.'

Lottie had promptly shrieked, dropped her fork onto her

plate with a clatter and leaped up to hug her little sister, followed a few seconds later by Annie and her growing bump.

'Next year is going to be a pretty big year all round it seems!' Annie had said. 'Well done, Em.'

'You'll make such a fantastic teacher,' Lottie had added. 'You're just brilliant with the kids, Em. I'm so proud of you.'

'And I'm so proud of *you*!' Em had replied immediately. 'You seem much more . . . Lottie-like, I guess. I'm so glad.'

'I *feel* a bit more Lottie-like. I think my new job and the counselling and getting excited for my new niece's arrival – and now your teacher training – have all helped me see what's important and how lucky I am to be surrounded by amazing, inspiring, beautiful people.'

'What about fat, heartburn-riddled, permanently knackered people?' Annie had said rubbing her bump with a theatrical grimace.

As her train trundled on past Reading, making its way further towards Oxford station, Lottie allowed herself to examine some of the things she'd talked about in her counselling session that week. They'd been discussing Annie's imminent arrival and how, while she couldn't be happier for Annie, it didn't stop her feeling a twinge of jealousy that she still didn't have everything her sisters did. And her counsellor had said something that had lodged itself inside her brain. 'You might not have a partner or children or a job that pays millions, but you have your sisters, your nephews, your new niece, as well as your friends – isn't that creating a family for yourself?' Lottie had just nodded and said, 'I suppose so,' at the time, but the more she thought about it, the more she could see her therapist was right.

She'd also finally felt able to tell her counsellor about her Leo daydreams. She could see now that they had been a coping mechanism for her grief, but she did still occasionally find herself imagining that she was curled into Leo's chest.

'What did Leo do during these daydreams that made you want to keep having them?' her counsellor had asked.

She'd thought for a while before replying, 'He said whatever I needed him to say at that moment. I still wanted to feel that happiness, that contentment he'd brought me during our relationship, and I was able to do it on my own terms. But as time went on, I found it harder and harder to conjure him up. I wanted to feel close to him, but I didn't have the right words to put in his mouth.'

'Do you think you know the right words to put in his mouth now?'

'No.' Lottie had shaken her head. 'I think that part – or rather, those parts – of Leo will always be closed off to me.'

Her counsellor had nodded. 'And what about the right words from your own mouth? Is there anything you'd still like to say to him, do you think?'

'I – I don't know.'

Usually when she said 'I don't know' to a question, her counsellor asked her to think about her answer between their sessions. This time, she'd set her some homework: to have one final conversation with Leo, telling him all the things she felt she wanted to but never had. Lottie had been putting it off for several days, but now glancing out of the window again, she clicked her pen and began to write.

Dear Leo

This is the last time I'll visit you in Dreamland or any-where else, so I wanted to say goodbye – and thank you. Thank you for the amazing three months we had together, you helped make me the happiest I'd ever been. What we had during that short time was so special and I will be for ever changed by it.

But although we thought we knew each other, we never really did, did we? I loved the Leo I knew, but he wasn't the same Leo other people knew. There were so many pieces of you that you chose to keep hidden from me, and maybe those pieces, in the end, would never quite have fitted with mine. Maybe, too, there were parts of me I didn't show you. You never got to meet my sisters, to see me as part of that trio, to understand how the three of us fit together, so you never knew that side of me, which I'll always feel sad about.

This year has taught me so much. I am starting to under-stand who I was, who I can be – but more importantly, who I am right now. Do you remember when you said you worried you lived so much in the past and in the future that you some-times forgot to live in the present? Well, now I am ready to live in my present.

Goodbye, Leo.

Lottie x

Lottie closed her notebook just as the train began to pull into the station. She gathered her things together and joined the throngs wearily making their way home for one of the last times before the Christmas break, but instead of rushing up the steps as she would usually, she felt a calmness wash over her. This feeling of peace stayed with her as she unlocked her bike from the station cycle rack and began her journey home. She stretched her legs out as she pedalled her way through the town centre and out towards her flat.

She'd just turned off her lights and was rooting around in her bag for her keys when she heard a car door slam behind her.

'Lottie?'

She spun around, dropping the keys and catching her shin sharply on the corner of her pedal, taking her breath away for a second. By the time she'd unscrunched her eyes from the pain, a man was standing in front of her.

'Ross? What on earth are you doing here?'

Chapter Thirty-one

'Sorry, did I scare you?' Ross bent down and retrieved her keys from under the wheel of her bike. 'Here you go.'

'Thanks.' She smiled at him but didn't say anything else to fill the silence and briefly wished her counsellor could see her new-found restraint in action.

'How are you? You're looking well,' he said.

Lottie glanced down at her embarrassingly bright yellow reflective jacket and laughed. 'Thanks! Do you want to come in and warm up?' As she asked the question she did a mental check of the state she'd left the flat in at seven-thirty that morning and hoped she'd actually remembered to put the dirty laundry into the washing machine rather than leaving it in a pile on the floor.

'No, I mean, I wondered whether we could go for a walk.' Her face must have betrayed her surprise, because he hurriedly added, 'I know you've had a long day at work and it's dark and bloody freezing, but we could walk to somewhere that sells hot chocolate maybe?'

Lottie had never seen Ross seem so unsure of himself. He looked what she could only describe as *scared*, and her heart contracted. 'OK, the hot chocolate seals it. But I need to get changed and find some extra layers first, so come inside while I get ready.' She opened the door, wrangled her bike inside, told him to make himself at home and fled to her bedroom. She refused to allow herself to think too much about anything as she pulled on a vest, long-sleeved thermal top and Fair Isle jumper, as well as the thickest, non-holey socks she could find. She located her boots, gloves, bobble hat and puffer jacket and reappeared in the living room. 'Right, I'm dressed for the Arctic, so I'm ready if you are?'

He grinned and took from his pocket the biggest, snuggliest-looking pair of gloves Lottie had ever seen, along with a scarf and hat. 'It was snowing in Scotland when I left so I came prepared,' he explained in response to her raised eyebrows.

'So you did. OK, we might as well walk into town – that's where the best hot chocolate is to be found. Lead on, McDuff!' Lottie cringed at herself and was glad when they got outside and the darkness swallowed the redness on her cheeks. They walked in silence for a while before she glanced up at him and said as casually as she could, 'So are you going to tell me why you were in Scotland this morning but are now walking the freezing cold streets of Oxford?'

'I wanted to check in on Margaret and Eddie.' She nodded, but he immediately began speaking again. 'That's not true. Well, it is true, but it's not the reason I drove for seven hours to get down here today.' She heard him swallow. 'I wanted to see you.'

Lottie could sense his eyes on her, even though her hat made it difficult to see unless she turned her whole body towards him. 'To see me? There is a little thing called FaceTime you know!' she joked.

'Sometimes only seeing someone in real life will do,' he said quietly. 'I owe you an apology, Lottie.'

'No, you don't,' she replied automatically, even though she knew her therapist would have something to say if she could hear her.

'I do.' He breathed out deeply and the air in front of them misted. 'After our trip to the museum, I told you it wouldn't be fair on anyone for us to try to have a relationship, and that I wanted us just to be friends. But I lied. I was scared and I didn't want to face up to how I felt. I let you put your feelings out there, but I was too scared to do the same, and I ended up hurting you. I haven't been able to stop thinking about that since it happened, especially as it was all for nothing. Because, Lottie, I do like you, I do want us to be together.'

In those first few days after Ross's rejection, when she'd had to start piecing her heart back together again, Lottie hadn't been able to stop herself dreaming what it would feel like for Ross to tell her he'd made a mistake, that he felt the same, that he liked her in the same way she liked him. But she'd forced herself to stop the 'what if's and 'if only's.

Now that it had happened, and he had actually told her that he felt the same way as her, she didn't jump into his arms or pull him in for a kiss as fireworks went off around them like she'd imagined. Instead, she didn't say anything. She just carried on walking, trying to straighten out her thoughts. Finally, her brain landed on the three most important words.

'What about Leo?'

Ross sighed. 'For the last few months, even before our museum trip, when I haven't been thinking about you and me, I've been thinking about Leo. I've been waiting for some kind of sign from him that he gives me his blessing to try to make things work with you. But although I waited and looked, and looked and waited, there weren't any shooting stars or rainbows or anything else that might honestly be described as a sign. So I convinced myself he didn't give his blessing and we shouldn't be together. But then something Margaret said to me on the phone two nights ago made me stop and think clearly for the first time in weeks. I'm pretty sure she doesn't know about us – I certainly haven't said anything to her, or anyone else – but we were talking about Leo, and she said it always made her sad to think that the past had held Leo back from living life to the full for so long. And she made me promise that I wouldn't let the same thing happen to me, that I would take a chance on happiness whenever I could. So, I guess that's what I'm doing: taking a chance on happiness with you. Will you take that chance with me, Lottie?'

Tears pricked Lottie's eyes. She could hear the emotion weaving through his words. But she blinked back her tears and tried to steady her breathing. She knew she needed to give Ross an answer, and while half of her wanted nothing more than to bury her head in his soft, warm scarf and stay there, the other part of her knew it meant there was no going back to just friends if it didn't work out – which meant he would disappear out of her life for ever. She wished Annie and Em were there to tell her what to do, even if she knew Em would be swept away by the romance of the twinkling Christmas lights, and Annie would be assessing the probability of it all going wrong. Lottie was in the middle; the choice was hers and only hers.

She smiled. 'Yes,' she said. 'I'll take a chance on happiness, too.'

They came to a stop, facing each other among the little wooden Christmas market huts lining the city's main street and grinned at each other.

'Thank you,' Ross whispered.

Then, before she could reply, he'd pressed his lips to hers in a way that made her forget anything she had been about to say.

A few minutes later, even the chemistry flooding between them was no match for the British weather in December. 'You're shaking!' Ross grinned. 'And while I'd like to take the credit, I think now's the time to get that hot chocolate. There's a hut over there selling hot drinks that miraculously doesn't look like it has a queue.'

Lottie nodded and Ross sprinted over to place their order before someone jumped in front of them, while she wandered over more slowly, stamping her feet to try to get some feeling back into them. She smiled as she heard him talking to the server about the weather back home in Scotland, where the man was obviously from too.

'Here you go, this should warm us both up,' Ross said, grinning at her as he handed her a cup. 'Richard here added a touch of brandy for us!'

Lottie cupped her hands around her drink and smiled at the cocoa heart stencilled on the top. As the hot liquid hit her stomach, she breathed a happy sigh. Taking Ross's hand, she gazed up at the fairy lights encircling the stall's name and saw the words 'Lion's Luxury Chocolate'.

Maybe Leo was sending them a sign, after all.

Acknowledgements

This book was written and edited during various lockdowns, and it would not have happened without the encouragement and support of my agent Tanera Simons, who always gives me a calm, reassuring and wise point of view, and makes me believe I can do it, even when I'm sitting at my dining room table in the middle of a half-built extension, surrounded by plaster dust and chaos. I'm also indebted to the whole dream team at Darley Anderson for their continued hard work on all my books.

There's not a day goes by that I don't pinch myself that I get to work with all the amazing people at Simon & Schuster. Sara-Jade Virtue is not only the biggest champion of books and authors I have ever met, but she is also a talented and perceptive editor who has helped make this book into something I am truly proud of. Alice Rodgers was also invaluable in shaping *The One*, with her knack of putting her finger on exactly why something doesn't work and how to make it better, while Bianca Gillam's input was also super-helpful, and fabulous Pip Watkins is responsible for the utterly gorgeous cover. Copyeditor Louise Davies's eagle eyes (and maths) were a lifesaver and Cassie Rigg's proofread was so helpful. There are a whole host of people who work behind the scenes at S&S, but without whom this book would never have found its way into readers' hands – so a massive whoop for Sabah Khan and Sarah Jeffcoate, as well as Maddie, Kat, Dom, Joe and Rachel.

I've been lucky enough to have the support of many book bloggers, blog tour members and Bookstagrammers, and I am hugely grateful for all their hard work, cheerleading and amazing photography skills! Thank you also to all my fellow authors, journalists and reviewers who have read my books and said nice things – it means so much.

Like so many people, I found the hardest part of the last few years was not being able to see my family. But whether we're hugging in real life or via a phone call, Zoom video or WhatsApp chat, I am so grateful to be surrounded by the best people. Annie and Em are purely fictional characters, but the bond Lottie feels with her sisters comes from my own experience. The upside of the lockdowns was that I was able to spend more time with Steve than ever before (he may disagree with the 'up' bit of that sentence!), and even after 23 years we have never run out of things to say to each other, which I think means we're doing something right.

Finally, I wanted to say, as always, a huge thank you to every person who has bought, borrowed and recommended my books. Hearing from readers is one of my favourite parts of this job, so if you've enjoyed *The One* or just fancy saying hi, do send me a message on Twitter or Instagram (and then tell me to get off my phone and get back to my laptop as I'm supposed to be working!).

Love, Claire x

Twitter: @FabFrosty
Instagram: @TheRealFabFrosty

If you loved *The One*, don't miss out on another Claire Frost novel . . .

married at first ~~swipe sight~~

In the modern tech-fuelled world of dating,
is it possible to find true love?

Hannah lives life on the edge. Never one to pass up on a new adventure, she has truly been living her best life. But once the adrenaline wears off, she wishes she had someone to spend the quieter moments with too. Learning that her best friend's online dating business has taken a hit, she comes up with an idea that just might solve both of their problems . . .

Jess has been with her husband for twenty years. They have a stable marriage, great kids and run their own businesses. But what looks like a perfect life from the outside has its own problems within, and with her business on the brink Jess can't help but wonder where the spark has gone in her life, and whether settling down is all it's cracked up to be.

When Hannah embarks upon her latest scheme: finding a man using Jess's dating app and meeting him for the first time at the altar, both women start to realize the grass isn't always greener. Can Hannah help her friend save her failing business or will Jess stop her from making what could be the biggest mistake of her life?

'This witty, fantastically warm laugh-out-loud read is the perfect antidote to lockdown blues' *Fabulous, The Sun on Sunday*

AVAILABLE NOW IN PAPERBACK AND EBOOK

SIMON &
SCHUSTER